BACK OFF

Mia took her coffee and headed for her car. She held on to the cup as she dug through her purse for her car keys. She finally found them, but they slipped from her hand and fell to the sidewalk. A passerby stooped to pick them up for her and she thanked him. He glanced at the Civic and did a double take. "If that's your ride, you're not gonna get far, keys or no keys."

"What do you mean?"

He pointed to the tire closest to the sidewalk. "Looks like someone took a knife to it."

"What?" Aghast, Mia saw the slash he was pointing to. A dire instinct took hold. She circled the car, examining each tire. Her blood pressure rose as the instinct was born out.

Someone had slashed all four of her tires.

Books by Maria DiRico

HERE COMES THE BODY

LONG ISLAND ICED TINA

IT'S BEGINNING TO LOOK A LOT
LIKE MURDER

FOUR PARTIES AND A FUNERAL

THE WITLESS PROTECTION PROGRAM

Published by Kensington Publishing Corp.

THE WITLESS
PROTECTION PROGRAM

Maria DiRico

Kensington Publishing Corp.
www.kensingtonbooks.com

KENSINGTON BOOKS are published by

Kensington Publishing Corp.
119 West 40th Street
New York, NY 10018

All Kensington titles, imprints, and distributed lines are available at special quantity discounts for bulk purchases for sales promotion, premiums, fund-raising, educational, or institutional use.

Special book excerpts or customized printings can also be created to fit specific needs. For details, write or phone the office of the Kensington Sales Manager: Attn.: Sales Department. Kensington Publishing Corp., 119 West 40th Street, New York, NY 10018. Phone: 1-800-221-2647.

First Printing: April 2024
ISBN: 978-1-4967-4462-3

ISBN: 978-1-4967-4463-0 (ebook)

10 9 8 7 6 5 4 3 2 1

Printed in the United States of America

CHAPTER 1

Tavern on the Green was as lush and elegant as Mia always dreamed it would be. Chandeliers decorated the stunning Crystal Room, complementing fairy lights twinkling in the trees visible through the glass walls that made the space feel like a Victorian conservatory. "I've always wanted to come here," she said to Shane, her ridiculously handsome date. "What's the occasion?" She crossed her fingers under the table, hoping the *occasion* was the romantic one she'd spent the last few months waiting for.

Shane reached for Mia's hand across the table. She uncrossed her fingers, then lifted her left hand from her lap and placed it in his. He laced his fingers through Mia's and stared at her soulfully. Mia's spirits lifted. *Could it be? Finally?*

"No occasion," he said.

Her spirits instantly dropped.

"My mother, God rest her soul, always told me you never knew when you could be hit by a bus," Shane continued. "Not that she was ever on one in

Florida. I swear, I half expected her to write 'Bury me in my Cadillac Escalade' in her will. But she loved to say we should live for now and not save special stuff for fancy 'occasions.'"

Like a marriage proposal, Mia thought glumly.

Around three months earlier, Shane had pledged his love for her in a speech so moving Mia wondered if he was actually proposing to her. After weeks of debating this with friends, she hesitantly broached the subject with her boyfriend. Shane understood Mia's confusion and set her straight. Yes, he loved her, but no, that spontaneous moment wasn't an official proposal. "When I ask for your hand in marriage before God and the universe for which He stands," Shane told her, somehow mashing up a declaration of love with the Pledge of Allegiance, "I'm gonna do it up right. In a *big* way."

Mia was the prototype of a strong, independent woman. Since her father Ravello's recent heart scare—doctors had inserted a stent to unclog an artery blocked by a steady diet of Fettuccine Alfredo—she'd basically been running Belle View Banquet Manor. The catering facility, located on the Flushing Marina, with a lovely view of Flushing Bay and a less lovely view of a LaGuardia Airport runway, was the family business, as well as a Family business, since it was one of the Boldano crime family's legitimate and completely legal enterprises. Under Mia's savvy tutelage, Belle View had blossomed into a premiere party site in the New York City borough of Queens.

Lauded by local business organizations as the kind of female entrepreneur Queens could be proud of, Mia never imagined she'd be someone anxious for a marriage proposal. Yet ever since coworker Shane's florid pronouncement, she'd been on tenterhooks waiting for the ring to drop.

Could it be hidden in the gorgeous bouquet of flowers Shane impulsively handed her one night? Would he pull a small jewelry box from the pocket of his chinos during their moonlight cruise of the Long Island Sound? A romantic weekend getaway to the Hamptons produced an impressive tan but no sparkler.

Mia's napkin, which her event planner instincts pegged at an impressive 400 count cotton, no polyester blend, slid off her lap. She bent down to retrieve it. When she sat back up, she saw Shane had refilled her champagne glass. He stared at it, frowned, then summoned a waiter. "There's something in my girlfriend's drink," he said, pointing to the glass.

OMG, this is it! Yaassss! Ring in the champagne glass. Classic proposal move.

Mia feigned innocence as she glanced into her champagne glass—where she saw a fly flat on its back, having expired amid the bubbles.

"Oh sir, I'm so sorry." The waiter whisked the glass away. "I'll bring you fresh glasses and a complimentary bottle of champagne."

"Thanks, man. I appreciate it. And if you could bring our dessert now, that'd be great." Shane turned away from the waiter and leaned in toward Mia. His peridot eyes bored into her crystalline-blue orbs. "I ordered a special dessert for you. Kind of a once-in-a-lifetime treat."

Mia dared to hope again—especially when Shane excused himself for a moment. *He's not really going to the bathroom. He's bringing the ring to the*

*waiter to make this a truly "once-in-a-lifetime treat".
Well, technically, twice in a lifetime for me.* She glowered, recalling the whirlwind relationship with Adam Grosso that led to their ill-fated nuptials. The conniving adulterer had been declared missing and presumed dead after a powerboat containing the body of his mistress but no Adam washed up on Paradise Island in the Bahamas. With memories of her disastrous first marriage relegated to the never-darken-my-door-again file of Mia's memory archive, she was ready for a lifetime with . . . dare she say it? . . . her soul mate.

The love of her life's return to the table coincided with the waiter's. Shane responded with satisfaction when Mia gasped at the sight of the exquisite small box made entirely of chocolate placed in front of her. "Oh, Shane . . ."

His smile grew wider. "Open it."

Heart hammering, Mia lifted the lid. She was greeted by the sight of . . . more chocolate. This time in the form of mousse.

"I know how much you love chocolate," Shane said, practically glowing with pride at his choice. "Especially mousse."

"Right. Yes. I sure do." Mia said this as she delicately poked around the dessert with her spoon, hoping for metal to hit metal. No such luck.

"Go on," Shane urged. "Dig in."

I'm guessing that means there's no chance I'll swallow an engagement ring, Mia thought with an internal sigh. But Shane seemed so pleased with himself, it touched her. She hid her disappointment and took a spoonful of mousse. Her eyes almost rolled back into her head at the taste of it. "OMG, this is incredible. It's the best mousse I've ever had."

Shane leaned back in his floral-upholstered chair and flashed a smile. "I take care of my girl."

"You do, sweetie," Mia said, completely sincere. "You do."

Mia polished off the mousse, sharing a few spoonfuls with her boyfriend. She debated saving the chocolate box, then inhaled that, too.

Dinner over, the couple left the Crystal Room and stepped outside the restaurant. The twin towers of the San Remo, a spectacular Art Deco confection on Central Park West, loomed in all their elegant glory above the park.

Suddenly, Shane dropped to one knee.

Mia sucked in a breath. She placed a hand on her heart. *Now? Of course! It all makes sense. The end of an amazing evening. This incredible view.* A horse-drawn carriage clip-clopped up to the front of the restaurant, adding to the ambience. *And that! Perfect timing! I want Anne Hathaway to play me in the rom-com version of this moment!*

Mia inhaled, then slowly exhaled, trying to calm herself. Shane held up something that glinted silver under the fairy lights. *Platinum!* she exulted. *He remembered I'm a Winter and look best in cool metal tones like platinum and silver, not gold! I love him so much!*

"Found a quarter," he said, triumphantly flashing it.

Mia deflated with the speed of a popped balloon. She stared at the piece of change. The carriage horse let out a loud whinny, then released a giant pile of horse dung. Mia wrinkled her nose as the pile's noxious scent wafted up from the street to mingle with the warm, late-summer air.

Also perfect timing.

* * *

Fellow Belle View event planner Cammie Dianopolis scanned Mia with a critical eye. "You gotta lose the frown, sweetie. We're selling weddings here, not funerals."

The two women stood behind a U-shape of tables at the display they'd set up at the massive wedding expo taking place at Manhattan's Javits Convention Center. In keeping with the bridal theme, they both wore white minidresses. While Mia's was a sleeveless sheath with swirls of beads decorating the sweetheart neckline, Cammie's dress sported the poofy sleeves popularized by Princess Di's wedding gown. Mia's coworker had found her style in the 1980s and stuck with it.

An array of Belle View food samples ranging from appetizers to mini cupcakes covered the center folding table Mia had coiffed in a peach underskirt with a pale peach lace overlay. Another table showcased a variety of stunning table settings available at the venue. A big-screen TV on the third leg of the "U" showed a compilation video of wedding celebrations interspersed with testimonials ranging from young newlyweds to seniors renewing their vows. Behind the women hung a giant poster showcasing the marina and bay vistas visible from Belle View's ballrooms, photographed in a way that expertly blocked out the LaGuardia runway.

"Sorry, Cammie. I'll try to get my happy on." Mia gave the expo a dispirited scan. Future brides, some with their grooms, some with their mothers or friends, some with their same-sex significant others, packed the cavernous space. Their excited chatter combined with multiple wedding bands blasting music samplings created a headache-inducing cacophony. Mia rubbed her forehead. "To be honest, it's kind of hard for me to be here. I've reached the point where I don't think I'm ever gonna need any of my own wedding services because Shane's never gonna propose. I need to face the fact I'm gonna die alone and be one of those old ladies they find partially eaten by her own pets."

Cammie winced. "Ugh, gross. Look, Shane's a good guy. I don't know why he's taking his sweet time popping the question, but he'll come around eventually."

"Maybe. I dunno."

"Listen to you. When did you get so insecure?" Cammie put her hands on Mia's shoulders and looked her in the eye. "Stop it. You hear me? *Stop*." Mia gave a resentful grunt. Cammie released her. "I blame that chunk of human chum, Adam Grosso. He left you with a bad case of PTRD: Post-Traumatic Relationship Disorder."

"It takes two to make a mistake like that," Mia said, sniffling. "And I'm one of them."

A young woman accompanied by an older woman started toward them. Cammie poked Mia in the ribs. "Mother of the bride alert. Girl looks to be in her late twenties, which means Mama's probably controlling the wedding purse strings, and mamas like to spend on their baby girls. Force a smile and suck up to them."

Mia swallowed her feelings and plastered on a smile. "Hello, and welcome to Belle View, where we handle every detail of our bridal 'belles'' incredibly special day."

She followed this with an exaggerated wink as Cammie navigated her way around the tables to

the women. She showed off two of the special pro-
motional items Mia had ordered for the event:
tiara headbands with a veil attached. Elegant printing on one veil read FUTURE BELLE VIEW BRIDAL
BELLE. Printing on the other veil read MOTHER OF A
FUTURE BELLE VIEW BRIDAL BELLE but in smaller
print, to fit in every word.

"May I?" Cammie asked.

The bride-to-be eagerly nodded. Cammie positioned the headband on her, then did the same
for the girl's mother. The two squealed and took a
flurry of selfies, then handed their phones to
Cammie, who took more pictures. The impromptu
photo session over, the bride-to-be's mother's focus
turned to the poster behind Mia. "Oooh. Lovely.
We're from Brooklyn, but it might be worth the
trip to Queens for a view like that."

Mia, used to this attitude, gave a vigorous nod.
While Brooklyn and Queens were basically on top
of each other, denizens of one borough tended to
approach a trip to the other with the same wari-
ness American settlers felt when heading west
across the prairies. "You won't find views like this
at the prices we offer anywhere in the city. We also
have a bank of windows facing west, so you can see
the Manhattan skyline. I always dreamed of my
own wedding happening in our very own Bay
Ballroom at twilight. You could watch the sunset
over the skyline in one direction and the boats
lighting up in the marina in the other." Mia's
lower lip quivered. "It would've been beautiful.
But it's not gonna happen. I gotta let go of the
dream. Ouch!"

The exclamation of pain was a response to Cammie giving Mia's foot a warning stomp. Cammie

handed the nonplussed potential customers each a mini cupcake. "Have a sample of our famous tiramisu cupcakes. We can talk about our From Wedding Soup to Jordan Almond Nuts Package while my partner here *takes a break*."

Mia got the not-so-subtle hint. "Thanks for stopping by our exhibit. And speaking of Jordan almonds . . ." She handed each woman a small gauze bag of the candy-coated wedding treat. "Our card is inside. I hope you give Belle View Catering Manor the opportunity to plan your special, special . . ." Tears Mia had been fighting to control bubbled over her lower eyelids. "Day." She sobbed out the word and escaped before embarrassing herself further by dissolving into a flood of tears.

She made a pit stop in the ladies' room, where she splashed cold water on her face. "Get it together, Carina," Mia muttered to her image in the mirror. She left the ladies' room and wandered around the exhibition hall, forcing herself to focus. She picked up cards from a couple of DJs and rental companies and listened to a pitch from the operator of a hot-air balloon who swore he could launch it from the Belle View parking lot, begging off the question of where guests would park.

On the way back to the Belle View exhibit, Mia passed Marjan's Cakes and Desserts, a bakery she'd used in the past to glowing reviews from customers. She and Marjan, a lovely émigré from London, exchanged greetings. "Anything new and exciting in the wedding cake world?" Mia asked.

"We're doing a lot of displays instead of cakes lately," Marjan said. "You know, like tiers of different-flavored macarons. For cakes with multiple layers, a lot of couples want a different flavor with each layer. And since carrot cake feels dated, I've created a ginger spice alternative. Try it." The baker pointed to small, frosted squares in paper cups.

"You don't have to tell me twice." Mia picked up a sample and took a bite. "OMG, Marjan, this is fabulous. So much better than boring old carrot cake." She polished off the sample and took another. "I love how the frosting is a blend of spices. Yum." She spoke with her mouth full as she inhaled a second sample. "I'd hire you for my own wedding, but it looks like it'll take some kind of divine intervention for Shane to put a ring on it."

"I'm sorry to hear that." Mia reached for a third sample. "But if you don't mind leaving some samples for potentially paying customers . . ."

Mia retracted her hand. "Right. Got it."

She continued her wander back to the Belle View display, casting a disconsolate glance at the bridal gowns on parade as part of a runway show. An ear-splitting screech of joy distracted her. She craned her neck to see who released it. A tall blonde she pegged to be around twenty-five jumped up and down as she pointed to a particularly elaborate sequined, beaded, and rhinestoned bridal gown. She let out another screech. "Ahh! That's it! That's the gown I told you about, baby! The one I wanna get married in! It's so bee-you-tee-ful! I'm *dying*!"

The *baby* in question, a man about the same height as the bride-to-be, turned to see the dress. He locked eyes with Mia. A wave of nausea coursed through her. For a moment, she thought she'd pass out.

The Miami police presumed her husband was lost at sea. Mia took great comfort from knowing her cheating spouse literally slept with the fishes. But in an instant, what she'd long feared had come true.

Adam Grosso didn't sleep with the fishes. He wasn't dead. He was there. At the bridal expo.

And Mia was looking right at him.

CHAPTER 2

Mia stood frozen in place, locked in a staring contest with the man who'd come close to destroying her life. She'd spent months after his disappearance in Miami PD's crosshairs as their primary person of interest. Given her father's position as a lieutenant who ran illegal gambling games for the Boldano Family and the occasional incarcerations of her dad and brother Posi Carina—who was currently finishing a stint at the Triborough Correctional Facility for indulging in his habit of stealing luxury sports cars—Mia found herself enduring the kind of notoriety usually trained on celebrities. Public interest in her eventually faded but left her battle-scarred, to say nothing of the emotional toll her relationship with Adam had taken on her. But finally, almost two years later, Mia's life was on track. A great job. A nice home in Astoria she shared with her grandmother Elisabetta. And a boyfriend who would hopefully propose to her before senile dementia set in for one or both of them.

But now, this. *This!*

A cluster of attendees sauntered by, blocking her view of Adam. They passed, revealing an empty spot where he'd been standing. Mia shook off her temporary paralysis and ran through the crowd searching for him. Given her petite height of five foot four, she ran on her toes for the extra height that might help her catch a glimpse of his familiar head. It didn't help.

She raced back to the table, where she found Belle View executive chef Guadalupe and sous-chef-slash-dessert chef Evans replenishing the samples table. "Oh, thank God, tall people!"

"Huh?" Evans, who leaned toward taciturn, only needed the one word to express his confusion.

"I saw Adam Grosso."

Cammie gasped. "What?! *No.* Adam?! *The* Adam?"

"Yes. Adam Grosso. My husband. He's here. With a fiancée."

"Fiancée?" Evans sounded even more confused.

"No time to drill down on this. I need you to help me find him. You remember what he looks like? Average height and weight, bald spot shaped kind of like a starfish?"

Guadalupe nodded. "Your dad turned a picture of him from the newspaper into a dartboard. My image of him has a lot of holes in it, but it's still pretty good."

"Good. Go. Hurry!"

Guadalupe, who'd spent years as an army cook in Iraq, gave Mia a salute. "Yes, ma'am."

She, Evans, and Mia took off in separate directions, leaving Cammie to man the exhibit. Mia scoured her section. Her heart raced when she was sure she spotted him from the back, but when the man turned around, he proved to be a bride's father and a good twenty years older than Adam.

After wasting an hour searching the expo for the phoenix that was Adam Grosso, Mia called it quits. The crew reconvened at the Belle View exhibit. "Any luck?" Cammie asked.

"Nope," Evans said.

"'Fraid not." A dark look crossed Guadalupe's face. "Better for him I didn't find the S.O.B. If he wasn't dead then, he would be now."

"Same here if I found him," Evans said.

Cammie raised her hand. "Dibs on taking him out first."

"You guys, stop." A darker look than Guadalupe's colored Mia's face. "Taking him out is *my* job." She swiped one of the napkins from the table-setting display and used it to mop perspiration from her brow. A dollop of strawberry frosting sat glued to where it landed on her dress when she collided with Marjan, who had stepped out from behind her exhibit to hand out cake samples. "But he's gone. I swear, that moron does a better job of disappearing than a magician."

"Or . . ." Cammie paused. She exchanged a look with Guadalupe and Evans.

Mia crossed her arms in front of her chest. She pursed her lips. "I saw that look, you guys. Or what?"

"Maybe you *thought* you saw Adam," Cammie said.

Mia bristled. "Uh, *hello*. I think I know the man I shared a bed with for five long, miserable years."

"Still doesn't mean it was him," Guadalupe, always matter-of-fact bordering on blunt, declared.

"I'm telling you, it was Adam," Mia insisted.

"If you say so," Evans said in a tone indicating he, too, didn't believe it.

"You know what, just forget it."

Mia stomped behind the table. She bent down to retrieve a sparkling water from a cooler stashed under it and wet the napkin. Fueled by annoyance with her doubting friends, she scrubbed at the strawberry stain, which sat front and center on the lacy white cocktail dress she wore to emulate a wedding gown.

"I've got a Tide stick." Cammie removed one from her purse and set to work on the stain. "All I'm saying—"

"All *we're* saying," Guadalupe corrected.

"Is that you and I were just talking about Adam before you took a break. You're all tense about this whole proposal thing with Shane, which has to make you think about your first marriage, and I know there's part of you that's worried about making sure you get it right the second time. With all that going on, there is a chance you might have seen someone who looked a lot like Adam and thought it was him."

"Argh, we're never gonna get this stain out. I might as well dye the dress pink." Frustrated, Mia tossed the napkin into the trash. She collapsed onto one of the folding chairs the crew had brought from Belle View. "I hate when you might be right." She sighed. "Why would he be in New York anyway? I always thought he disappeared because he got involved in some sketchy business. Besides dying, the only thing I thought might have happened to him was ratting out whoever he was grifting with and going into the witness protection program. And they wouldn't send him here to New York."

"Wrong," Guadalupe declared. "Hide in plain sight. Big city's the best place for that. Standard operating procedure for the WPP."

Evans stopped snacking on the cake sample he'd scored from Marjan. He eyed Guadalupe. "Why do I get the feeling there's something you're not telling us?"

The chef barked a laugh. "Ha. If I outed a criminal, you'd best believe I'd be in his face and not hiding out in some program. Or her. Don't wanna be sexist here."

A few rings of a bell sounded over the intercom system, followed by the announcement that the expo was a half hour from closing. "Walk the crowd with sample trays and give out a business card with each sample," Mia instructed Evans and Guadalupe. "Cammie and I will start packing up."

The chefs hefted trays and disappeared into the crowd. Cammie checked the swag bag. "We only have a few headbands left." She took one and placed it atop her frosted hair, whose poufiness duked it out with the pouf of her dress sleeves. She then took another headband and positioned it on Mia's dark brown/almost black long, thick head of hair. "You're gonna get to wear a real one of these. Promise."

She hugged Mia, who eked out a smile. But her thoughts were on the heart-stopping sighting of the man who might be Adam. She said a prayer her friends were right and she was caught in a case of mistaken identity. But the more she thought about it, the more convinced she was that she'd locked eyes with her living, breathing, still-married-to husband.

CHAPTER 3

Mia parked in the garage behind the two-family house in Astoria she shared with her grandmother. She grabbed a container of leftover cake samples from the passenger seat of her pre-owned Honda Civic, then strode through the postage-stamp backyard. She climbed the few steps that led to the cement deck behind her grandmother Elisabetta's first-floor home and entered into the kitchen through the back door.

Elisabetta's terrier mutt, Hero, lifted his head from his food bowl to bark a peremptory greeting, then resumed eating his dog food flavored with bits of his human's homemade lasagna. Elisabetta stood by the stove, warily eyeing whatever was in a large pot Lin Yeung, her elegant future daughter-in-law and Mia's future stepmother, was stirring. Unlike Shane, Mia's father, Ravello, had proposed to his girlfriend, a federal prosecutor turned Lower East Side florist. She and Elisabetta were taking turns teaching each other their respective cuisines—Vietnamese on Lin's part, Italian—of course—on

Elisabetta's. The look of distaste on Elisabetta's face confirmed Mia's instinct that poor Lin had her work cut out for her.

The women exchanged greetings. Mia planted a kiss on each cheek of her grandmother and gave Lin a quick hug. She glanced into the pot. "Pho? Yum. You'll love this, Nonna. It's loaded with noodles."

"Made with rice," Elisabetta said, sounding unconvinced. "Who makes pasta from rice?"

"Many Asian cultures, Nonna," Mia said with a warning note in her voice. She loved Lin and didn't want to offend her.

"Whatevs." Elisabetta's TV diet mainly consisted of youthful, dystopian dramas, so she'd picked up some of the lingo.

Lin put a spoon to her broth and gave it a taste. She added a dash of fish sauce and stirred it in. "How was the expo?"

"Good. I think we connected with some potential new clients. I brought home cake samples for dessert." Mia placed the container on Elisabetta's vintage dinette table. She debated sharing the news about the possible Adam sighting and decided to go for it. "I thought I saw Adam."

Nonna gave the fish sauce bottle a suspicious sniff. "Huh. *Interessante.*"

"Yes," Mia said, a little insulted by the casual reaction. "Very interesting. Considering he's supposed to be *dead.*"

"We have some interesting news here, too," Lin said, unfazed by Mia's acerbic tone. She called into the living room. "Ravello, love, bring in our surprise guest."

Mia's large oak tree of a father appeared in the

doorway. Remarkably, Ravello's coal-black hair had maintained its natural color until his recent bout with heart trouble. Whether from stress or some mysterious physical quirk, it was now snow-white, which stood in stark but handsome contrast to his olive skin. "Ciao, bambina." He blew a kiss to his daughter. "What a joy it is to have both my children home at last."

"Both?" Mia responded, mystified.

Ravello stepped aside to reveal Posi Carina, Mia's scofflaw of a brother.

Mia let out a surprised scream, then threw herself into Posi's arms. "OMG! This is incredible." She embraced him in a tight hug. "Are you out? You got early release?"

"Not quite." Posi broke from the hug. "I got transferred to a halfway house for the last six months of my sentence. I have to get permission to leave the house and be back by curfew, seven o'clock. And I have to wear this when I'm out." He lifted a pant leg to show an ankle encased in a monitor.

"Still, we can see you without a guard yelling, 'Visiting hour's over!'" Mia hugged him again.

"We thought you'd like this surprise." Ravello shared a smile with the others.

"Time to celebrate." Lin turned off the heat under her pot of pho. "*Mangiamo.*"

"Let's eat," Elisabetta translated with approval.

"It's *Chúng ta hãy n* in Vietnamese."

Elisabetta shook her head. "I got no idea how to say it like you did."

The five took seats around the folding table Ravello had set up in Elisabetta's living room, their faces reflected in the giant mirror attached to the wall behind a couch covered with an afghan crocheted by Elisabetta in bilious colors she got for cheap at the local yarn shop. Lin ladled soup into pasta bowls. Posi picked up a goblet of red wine for a toast. "To me!" he declared with the dimpled smile that had made way more than one woman weak-kneed and led him to try and go viral as a #hotconvict.

"To you!" his family chorused.

They drank to Posi and began chattering excitedly about his future post-halfway house. The unexpected and wonderful development pushed all thoughts of Adam Grosso from Mia's mind.

"Seconds?" Lin asked Mia, noticing she'd cleaned her pho bowl.

"Absolutely. It's fantastic."

Mia held out her empty bowl for a refill. As Lin ladled, her engagement ring reflected light from the ceiling fixture above. "You got your ring sized."

"Yes." Lin placed the pho pot on a trivet in the center of the table.

"Dad did good by you." Mia tried and failed to keep a hint of wistfulness from her tone.

"Still nothing from Shane?" Lin shook her head. Like pretty much everyone else in the world, she knew about Mia's frustration. "It's obvious to anyone who spends a minute in your presence that the two of you are deeply in love. Why does the fact he's taking his time to propose upset you so much?"

No one had asked this of her. The event planner found herself briefly stymied. Then she said, "Because it's the logical next step in our relationship." She winced at the answer, which managed to be simultaneously cold and lame.

"So?" Lin took a delicate sip of her soup. "You

have a strong relationship already, don't you? Think of cake."

"I often do," Mia, who had a sweet tooth, joked. She wondered where Lin was going with this.

"A solid relationship is the cake. Engagement and marriage is the icing. You're much better off having cake without icing than icing without cake."

Mia pondered the statement. "Is this some kind of Vietnamese parable?"

"Good lord no," Lin said, chortling. "I thought it up when I was eating a slice of cake one day."

"It makes sense," Mia said. "Kind of. I'm generally team icing. But thank you."

Lin rejoined the conversation. Mia took a peek at her grandmother's bowl of pho and noticed it was full. She took a closer look at Elisabetta and saw her grandmother sneak a bite out of a container in her lap. "You're sneaking gnocchi?" she whispered. "You're terrible."

"*Sono fame,*" Elisabetta whispered back. She gestured to the soup bowl with her head. "And this ain't doin' it for me." She stood up. "I'm done. You need me, I'll be in my office."

Elisabetta marched off. "She has an office now?" Posi asked, amused.

"Ever since we got her a laptop for her birthday," Mia said. "It's the second bedroom, formerly known as the junk room. We brought over my old school desk from Dad's basement and bought her an office chair. She's in there for hours now."

Posi let out an amused chortle. "Any idea what she's doing when she's on the computer? I'm guessing she's not a gamer. Although with Nonna, you never know."

"I can tell you what she's not doing." Mia held up a decorative pillow crocheted in a riot of clashing colors. "Making more of these."

Much as she loved icing, Mia found it hard to argue with Lin's relationship analogy when she gave it more thought the next night as she dressed for a Mets game. Cake was the sturdy underpinning of any frosted dessert. In all her years as an event attendee and planner, she'd never seen icing served without cake. But she had seen—and served—cake without icing. From that perspective, a strong relationship was far more important than the symbolic gesture of marriage. *And now I want cake,* Mia thought.

She dispelled the craving and stepped over her Abyssinian ginger cat Doorstop, who was splayed out across the bedroom carpet, to pull a jersey from her closet. A lifelong Mets fan, she built her fall schedule around the team's games against their mortal enemies, the Atlanta Braves. After a brief moment of indecision, she went with heavy hitting first baseman Pete Alonso's jersey rather than the one paying homage to shortstop Francisco Lindor.

Pet parakeet Pizzazz, on a break from her cage, amused herself dive-bombing Doorstop, who responded with annoyed paw swats. "Behave, you two," Mia scolded. "Mommy's got a man waiting for her downstairs. A good man. A man who gave up his allegiance to the Cardinals for me. A total piece of cake."

She added a baseball cap featuring Mr. Met to top off her outfit. After giving Doorstop a kiss good night on his furry head and guiding Pizzazz back to her homey cage, she hurried downstairs and outside to where Shane waited for her in the purple Tesla she'd received as a gift and passed on to him because driving the all-electric car with its weird computer instead of a dashboard freaked her out.

"Hello you." Mia hopped in the car, and the couple locked lips. After a steamy moment, they reluctantly parted. Mia took in his jersey. "You went with Pete, too. You da best."

Shane lifted the corner of his mouth in a half grin. "Like they say, great minds."

Mia returned the grin. "Indeed."

Traffic was light midafternoon and they made it to Citi Field in record time. But the time they made up on the road they lost waiting in line at the Shake Shack behind center field. Armed with flat-top hot dogs, crinkle cut fries, and two chocolate shakes, they climbed the steps to their seats in the upper deck behind home plate, pausing to sing the National Anthem with the crowd.

Mia screamed her support for the Mets and loudly booed the Braves for three innings. In the break before the fourth, it occurred to her Shane wasn't participating in the lusty chorus of catcalls. "You okay?" she asked, a little worried. "You've only taken a couple of bits of your hot dog and your fries are lukewarm by now. I know you hate cold fries."

"I'm fine. Fine."

He twisted in his seat to look up the aisle. A ray of sunshine illuminated his naturally blond hair and Mia squelched a sudden and highly inappropriate urge to have her way with him right there in the stands. *I don't care if we ever get married. I'm the luckiest woman on earth to be with this guy.*

"I want some peanuts. You want some peanuts? Where's the peanut guy?" Shane anxiously searched the upper deck. "There he is!" He jumped up and frantically waved to the vendor.

"I'm full," Mia said. "I don't need peanuts."

"I do. I have to have them. And you should, too. We both need peanuts, and we need them *now*."

Mia shot him a look. "That's a little intense for a bag of nuts that aren't even really nuts. They're legumes."

"YO!"

Shane finally got the vendor's attention. The man made his way over to their section and tossed a bag to Shane, who passed cash up to him. Mia gaped at the bill. "A fifty? That's some pricey bag of nuts. You better get change."

Shane thrust the bag into her hands. "Open it."

"I told you, I don't want peanuts."

"Open it!" Shane practically yelled this at Mia.

"Fine!" she yelled back, angry. "I'll open the stupid bag of not-even nuts!"

She tore open the bag. A middle-aged man wearing a Tom Seaver memorial T-shirt pointed to one of the stadium's Jumbotron screens. "Hey, look! Youz two are on kiss cam."

Mia's heart skipped a beat. She looked inside the bag. Instead of peanuts, it contained a small jewelry box. She looked up to find Shane on one knee. The stadium grew silent. "Mia, I didn't know what love was until I met you." Shane's voice was thick with emotion. "Every minute I'm not with

you is a minute too long. Every minute we're together feels like it could go on forever. I want *us* to
go on forever. As one."

"Oooh . . ." Tears streamed down Mia's face.
She opened the box to reveal a stunning diamond
ring.

Shane reached for Mia's hand. "Mia Carina, will
you do me the honor of becoming my wife?"

Mia bit her lower lip to contain her emotions,
then released it. "Yes. Yes!!!!"

Shane rose to his feet and the couple embraced.
The stadium roared, then began chanting, "Kiss!
Kiss! Kiss! Kiss!" Shane and Mia eagerly complied.
Shane slipped the diamond on the ring finger of
her left hand and she admired it. "Is . . . is it
shaped like a peanut?"

Shane gave a proud nod. "So you'll always remember this moment."

"Oh, Shane." Mia burst into tears and wrapped
her arms around her future husband's neck. They
kissed again, to more roars from the crowd. The
couple broke apart and waved to the kiss cam.
Fans in their section showered them with congratulations. "May you have a lifetime of happiness
and bring luck to the Mets because they're down
by three," a woman called from a few rows down.

"Thank you, and from your lips to God's ears on
both counts," Mia called back to her with a wave.

Mia's hand froze in midair. Her stomach churned.
"No," she muttered. "*Noooo.*" She turned to the fan
sitting on the left of her and Shane, who'd resumed watching the game through a pair of binoculars. "Can I borrow those, thanks."

She grabbed the binoculars from him, eliciting

a yelp of outrage, and trained them on a bald spot several rows below as the person possessing it moved down the aisle. A bald spot shaped in the unusual pattern of a starfish. As if feeling her eyes on him, the owner of the bald spot slowly turned.

And Mia once again found herself locking eyes with Adam Grosso.

CHAPTER 4

Mia tossed the binoculars back to their owner. Shane gestured to the kiss cam. "They want us to kiss again." He put his arms around Mia but found himself kissing air when she slipped through them.

She climbed over rows below theirs, apologizing to some fans, accepting congratulations from others. She reached Adam's row too late. He was gone. "Sonuva—"

She let loose a stream of profanity that made the older woman in the seat next to Adam's empty one wince. "The guy you're marrying know you got a mouth like that?" the woman asked with a frown.

"Excuse me, sorry, excuse me, thank you, I'm sure we'll be very happy, I think." This all came from Shane as he climbed over rows to join her. "Mia . . ." Perplexed and upset, he raised his hands in a questioning gesture, then dropped them. "What the eff?"

"You see?" The judgy woman fan gave an approving nod. "You can get your point across without a mouth like a drunk sailor."

Mia took Shane's arm and pulled him into the aisle. "I saw Adam again."

"Again?" Mia's now-fiancé looked at her like she'd lost her mind.

"Yes. I saw him at the expo yesterday, but Cammie and the others made me think maybe I was wrong and it was just someone who reminded me of Adam. But I wasn't wrong then and I'm not wrong now. His bald spot is bigger, but it's the same shape. Like a starfish."

"So? What if you did see him? Who cares? It doesn't mean anything. Unless . . ." Shane sounded hurt. "You still have feelings for him."

Mia stared at Shane in disbelief. "Are you out of your mind?! Of course I don't have feelings for him. But if he's alive, it means I'm still married to him, which means we can't get married. We're in big fu—effing trouble, Shane."

"Argh! You're right." Shane slapped his forehead. "Sorry, I didn't think of that. Well . . . Petra gave me a divorce eventually. We just need to make that happen here."

Months earlier, a supermodel Shane married during a drunken binge in his early twenties had reappeared in his life, determined to punish him for rejecting her in favor of Mia by refusing to grant a divorce. It took some doing, especially on Mia's part, but Petra finally came around to granting the divorce and, if rumors could be trusted, was swanning around the Mediterranean on a besotted billionaire's yacht.

"Of course, but just one problem." Mia illus-
trated this by holding up a finger—the middle
one. "We knew how to find Petra. But we have no
idea how to find Adam. It's like we're dealing with
a living ghost because every time I get close to
him, he's gone." She flashed the finger at his
empty seat, which was next to another empty seat.
Having caught a glimpse of blond hair when she
spotted Adam through the binoculars, she assumed the second seat had housed the girl she'd
seen with him at the wedding expo.

Mia pulled her cell phone from the back pocket
of her jeans. She began furiously typing a text.
"I'm putting out a call to the Family. We need all
hands on deck for this." She finished typing. A
spotlight caught her diamond, which sent out a
prism of rainbows. "And speaking of hands, mine
has never looked better." She held it up for Shane
to admire, then kissed him. "I love you so much."

"I love—"

Mia's phone chimed. She checked it, then
grabbed Shane's hand. "No time to finish the sentence; Donny Senior got right back to me," she
said, referring to the head of the Family. "He's
called an emergency meeting. Come on."

She grabbed Shane's hand and they ran up the
stairs. A roar reverberated in the stadium. "What
happened?" Mia yelled to a fan.

"Alonso hit a grand slam homer," the fan yelled
back. "The Mets are up by two now."

"And I missed it?" Mia shook a fist at the heavens. "Curse you, Adam Grosso!"

* * *

The drive from Citi Field to the emergency meeting took twenty minutes. By the time Shane and Mia got to Donny and Aurora Boldano's white-clapboard, Colonial mansion in Long Island's Stony Harbor, the couple's beautifully appointed living room was already filled with members of the Boldano crew. Mia took in what was a sea of men ranging in age from early twenties to late fifties attired in everything from tight black T-shirts and gold chains to high-end polo shirts, also accessorized with gold chains. "Wow, is this group a ways from reaching gender parity," Mia commented in an aside to Shane. "Not that I'd encourage a woman to go into the Family business, but still . . ."

The front door opened in the front hallway. Mia craned her neck and saw a guard stepping aside to allow Ravello access to the house and the meeting. Mia went to her father and Shane followed.

The three exchanged hugs and dual cheek kisses. "Posi wanted to come," Ravello shared, "but we figured it would be hard to get the halfway house to sign off on extending his curfew so he could attend a meeting at Donny Boldano's."

"No kidding."

Ravello noticed the engagement ring decorating Mia's finger. "You did it," he said to Shane.

Shane gave a nod. "Yes, sir. At the stadium, as promised. I asked your father for permission to propose," he explained to Mia.

"A little 1950s for my taste, but I respect that," Mia said.

Ravello kissed Shane on both cheeks and gave his hand a vigorous shake. "Welcome to the family, son—the Carinas, not the Boldanos; I'd prefer you keep your nose clean. And congratulations, bella bambina." He called out to the group, "Everyone, my baby girl is engaged! I'm one proud papa." Choked up, Ravello rained more hugs and cheek kisses on the couple.

"This is a good segue to why we're all here tonight," Mia said, separating from her father.

She marched toward the front of the living room and claimed a spot next to where Donny Boldano Senior, the aging *capo di tutti capi* of the Family, stood. He greeted her with additional hugs, cheek kisses, and congratulations on her engagement. "Aurora and I are so happy for you," the patriarch said. "She'll have a card and a check for you before you leave tonight. A couple of the guys, the younger ones, asked if they can send their engagement present to one of your money apps."

"That's very generous of them, but let's put a pin in the engagement presents for now. We've got a situation." Mia placed two fingers in her mouth and emitted an earsplitting whistle, silencing the chatter. Shane wended his way around the other men and the room's tasteful décor to take his place beside her. "First off, Shane and I thank you for the congratulations on our engagement," Mia said. "Unfortunately, there's a roadblock to our future and his name is Adam Grosso." This instigated a chorus of angry reactions. Mia gave another whistle. "I cannot be Mrs. Gambrazzo if I'm still Mrs. Grosso, although I don't mean that literally because I plan on retaining my birth name as half of our combined married last names."

"And I totally support her on this," Shane piped up.

"Bottom line, we need to find Adam. The problem is, I'm sure he's living under an assumed name, and I have no idea what it is. We're all gonna have to dig deep here. Very, very deep."

"No worries, babe. We'll take care of him for you." A youthful tough Mia didn't know said this with a heavy dose of arrogance. He was part of the black T-shirt crowd, his shirt straining to cover overly developed biceps and abs. He had the meticulously shaved head and facial stubble of a hipster, but the tattoo of a high-powered assault rifle on his cheek marked him as someone far more dangerous. Mia, who knew pretty much everyone associated with the Boldanos, took an instant dislike to the newcomer.

"Thank you . . ."

"Orlando. Orlando Maladugotti." He accompanied this with a smirk and a slight bow of the head. There was something so stereotypical goombah about him that Mia wondered if he was working undercover for law enforcement.

"But no 'taking care of,' if it means what I think it means." Mia fixed the men with a look telegraphing she meant business. "I don't want anything illegal here. Repeat, *do not do anything drastic or illegal.*"

"What if we have to?" asked family stalwart Bobby Poppaccino, sounding a little too eager about the possibility.

"*No.* My goal is to be a divorcée, not a widow. Ya got it?" She glared at the assemblage. There was some grumbling, but they acquiesced. "That's better."

Shane stepped forward. "We're gonna break you up into teams and assign each team a section of either Queens, Brooklyn, or Manhattan. We figure those are the boroughs where we're most likely to find him."

"I got one of those rolling cork boards like you see on TV," Boldano said. A couple of underlings rolled it front and center from the side of the room. A map of the New York City boroughs had already been pinned to it. The head of the Family got everyone's attention with one clap of his hands. "Okay, people. Let's do this."

Mia retreated to the back of the room to let Shane and Donny Senior organize the men. She noticed Donny Junior, Boldano's firstborn, had slipped into the meeting at some point and went to him.

"Hey." She gave him a hug he returned.

"Hey yourself. Sorry I was late. I couldn't get away from the restaurant. They needed me to take care of a few Maydays."

Mia excused the note of braggadocio in his voice. For years, Donny Junior had managed to somehow be both obnoxious and a lost soul, crippled by the knowledge that he didn't have what it took to inherit his father's mantle as head of the Boldano Family. But recently he'd put his skill set as a party animal to use running events at an Astoria hangout called Singles, which had changed its names from Mingles after deciding the former name was too subtle for the crowd it wanted to attract.

Mia was happy Donny Junior seemed to have found himself, and sympathetic to his struggles, which were made worse by comparison to his younger brother Jamie—or half brother, as it had turned out, much to the surprise of everyone, surprise, especially Jamie.*

Jamie, the golden boy of the family, eschewed a mobster's life altogether, opting for a master's degree in marriage and family therapy. He and wife Madison were expecting their first child, and nothing upped an Italian offspring's profile like a grandbaby.

"No worries, DJ," Mia said. "I appreciate you getting here at all."

"And if you need me to do anything, say the word, Meems."

This came from a disembodied voice. Bewildered, Mia searched to see who spoke. Donny Junior held up his cell phone, revealing brother Jamie on the screen, who waved to her. "Hey, sister by another mister. And mother. Wow, that doesn't work at all, does it?"

"The mash-up is 'frister,'" Mia said, laughing. "Friend-sister."

"Frister. Love it. Anyway, I'm there for you if you need me. Sorry I can't be at the meeting in person. Madison had a late-afternoon ob-gyn appointment."

"Thanks for being here at all," Mia said, deeply touched by his offer. "By the way, nice job hiding the pregnancy for as long as you did. Taking notes for the future. Rachets down the operatic hysteria and endless showers from the future *nonnas*."

*For the details of this story, see *It's Beginning to Look a Lot Like Murder*.

Jamie guffawed. "You know it."

She and Jamie said their goodbyes and Donny Junior ended the call. An argument broke out in one of the clusters Shane had organized, drawing Mia and Donny Junior's attention. They saw Orlando Maladugotti had obviously appointed himself head of a subgroup, none of whom looked too happy about it. "Yo, nobody gets all the strip clubs in Ridgewood, okay? We split the list up fairly like. Capisce?" The others mumbled sullen agreement.

Mia wrinkled her brow. "Who exactly is this Orlando guy?" She put this to Donny Junior sotto voce. "He's new to me. I don't get a great feeling from him, although I give him props for wrangling his group when it comes to the Ridgewood strip clubs."

Donny Junior twisted around to see who Mia was talking about. "Oh, Orlando. Remember Fatsy Milanese? Died of a heart attack while doing time at Clinton Correctional upstate? Orlando's his great-nephew. His sister's daughter's kid. Grew up in Buffalo, only came down to Queens and our family a coupla months ago. I hear he's got 'great potential.'"

Donny Junior slung air quotes around the last two words. Mia felt for him. She knew the realization that his father and the Family never saw him as a leader still hurt. She gave her friend a pat on the shoulder. "Eff him. You're doing so much better than any of these mooks. I bet you end up owning Singles someday."

Donny J brightened. "Thanks, Meems. I appreciate that."

Mia checked out the room. "Speaking of mooks, I don't see Tulio Longella." A thought occurred to her. "You know what . . . he was at Singles the night I met Adam. More than that, the two of them came over to our table. Tulio introduced him to us, and Adam said he wanted to buy me and my table a bottle of champagne because I made his heart 'bubbly with love.'"

Donny Junior made a face. "Even I wouldn't go with a line that lame."

"It was cute at the time," Mia said, a little defensive. "Oh, who am I kidding? I was an idiot. And I'm paying for it now. Anyway, I never knew if Tulio was already friends with him or if they met that night. Either way, they hit it off as bros. If there's anyone who might be in touch with Adam, it's him. Yo!" Mia called to the room. The focus turned to her. "Anyone know where Tulio Longella is?"

"He called in sick," Boldano responded. "Summer cold."

"Oh. Thanks."

Donny Junior stood up. "I better join up with a group before all the strip clubs in the city are gone."

Mia shot him a look. "Seriously? I swear, the sexism in this crowd is off the charts."

Unfazed, the Boldano offspring strode off to score what he considered a plum assignment in the hunt for Adam Grosso. Mia's stomach growled, reminding her that in the excitement of her engagement, she'd never finished her flat-top hot dog. She wandered over to a table groaning under the weight of what Aurora Boldano would classify as "a few snacks" and piled a china plate with anti-pasto, Italian cold cuts, and a few mini cannoli.

As she ate, she pondered Tulio's absence. When Donny Boldano Senior called an emergency meeting, Family members showed up, no matter what the circumstances. Mia recalled her father relaying a story about how one lieutenant recovering from a gall bladder operation had himself wheeled in on a gurney, IV attached and nurse in tow.

Chomping on a cannoli, Mia narrowed her brow. A lifetime of secrets, lies, and prison stints for her father and brother had ingrained in her a deeply suspicious nature. She knew in her heart there was way more to Tulio's absence than a "summer cold."

The meeting wrapped up shortly after Mia's second round of desserts. Shane came to her. She handed him a full plate. He kissed her forehead. "You're a lifesaver. I'm starving."

"How'd it go? Are people gonna check out any location besides strip clubs?"

Shane stifled a laugh, narrowly avoiding the chunk of provolone he'd placed in his mouth going down the wrong pipe. "It took some doing, but yeah. I think we're in good shape. We're gonna find Adam."

"We better, and soon. He may be willing to be a bigamist, but I'm not."

Shane speared another chunk of provolone so hard the plastic fork broke. "Trust me on my life when I say this, Messina Carina. Nothing this SOB Adam Grosso can do will ever stop me from making you my partner for the rest of my life."

The force of her fiancé's emotions worried Mia. "When you say it like that you scare me, *cara mia*. Please, please, don't do anything that could get you in trouble."

"Don't worry, amore. I'll be cool."

But to Mia, the blazing anger in Shane's spectacularly beautiful green eyes said otherwise.

CHAPTER 5

Mia showed up early to work the next morning—but not nearly early enough to beat her coworkers. The minute she entered the lobby, a banner unfurled from the top of the stairs leading to the second-floor Bay Ballroom. Cammie, Guadalupe, Evans, and a number of part-time waiters, waitresses, and kitchen workers popped up from where they were hiding on the staircase landing. "Congratulations!" everyone yelled. They followed this with whoops and applause as they ran down the stairs to envelope Mia with hugs and more good wishes.

"Thank you all so much," Mia said, overwhelmed to the point of tears. "I have the best staff in the world. I love you all so much."

"But not as much as Shane." Kristi, a nineteen-year-old who worked as a waitress when she wasn't attending Queens College, said this in a singsongy voice, opening the door to an old-timey round of "Shane and Mia sitting in a tree, k-i-s-s-i-n-g . . ."

Mia, laughing, waved her hands to stop them.

"Okay, okay. Enough. We've parties to plan and run."

"Including your own wedding." Cammie gleefully rubbed her hands together at the thought of the big event.

"Right," Mia said, her good mood slightly dulled. "That." She forced a smile for her staff. "Well, let's get to it, gang, and show Queens we've got the best staff at the best venue in the borough!"

The group cheered. "When's Shane showing up?" Guadalupe called from the landing. She hadn't joined the others below. "We're gonna roll up the banner and release it again when he gets here."

Mia hesitated. "Shane may not be in today. He's out on other Belle View business." Cammie gave her a quizzical look she ignored.

"No worries," Guadalupe said, "we'll do it tomorrow."

Evans helped the chef reroll the banner while the others went off to their respective jobs. Mia retreated to her office. There was a rap on her door moments later, and then Cammie entered without waiting for a "come in." She took a seat on the folding chair across from Mia's desk. "What's going on? And don't tell me you broke up with the world's most handsome man because I'll have to do one of those things where you hospitalize someone against their will for mental illness treatment."

"Of course we didn't break up. Here. Look."

Mia extended her hand to show Cammie the engagement ring. Cammie covered her mouth with her hand in a show of emotion. She dropped the hand and checked out the ring with a discerning eye. "Not bad."

"You want to get your jeweler's loupe?" Mia said dryly.

"Don't need it. Excellent quality. Looks flawless. Is it me or is it kind of shaped like a peanut?"

"It is. So I'll always remember when and where Shane proposed."

"Sentimental. I like it." Cammie released Mia's hand and sat back. "But what's the problem? Because I know there is one."

Mia paused, then said, "I saw Adam again."

Cammie's jaw dropped. "No."

"Oh, yes. And don't tell me I imagined it because I ID'd him from his bald spot."

"The one shaped like a starfish? I remember from the photos of Adam your dad liked to alternate on the dartboard."

"Yes. Anyway, he disappeared again when I tried to hunt him down, so Mr. Boldano called an emergency meeting for me last night and now everyone is out trying to find him. Including Shane."

Cammie sucked in a breath. "Wow. It won't be pretty for Adam when someone from the Family finds him."

"They're under strict orders not to resort to violence. Like I told them, I want to be a divorcée, not a widow."

Cammie snorted. "Good luck to you."

"There was some grumbling for sure, but they got it. Donny Senior's been cracking down on them lately, trying to pivot them away from their sketchier instincts. Jamie told me his dad is so happy with how Belle View is doing, he's trading more and more illegal enterprises for legal ones, and dragging the crew along with him."

"They'll find Adam. What happens to him once they do, don't know, don't care. Moving on to . . ." Cammie took the laptop she'd tucked under an arm and opened it on her lap. "Your wedding." She opened a file and perused it. "Let's see, weekend openings a year from now. Might be tricky. We're already pretty booked. If you're okay with pushing back six months . . . eight months . . ."

"I've got a date. October 19. This year."

Cammie gaped at her. "That's only five weeks away. And a Monday."

"Exactly. We've got an opening on the schedule. No one gets married on a Monday, so we'll get breaks from all the vendors. But it's still a three-day weekend for anyone who needs to travel and wants to take the day off from work. And it gives us Saturday and Sunday if Shane and I decide to do any weekend events, which we probably won't because I wanna keep this whole thing simple. I want a great dress, pretty flowers, good food, a nice favor for the guests. I don't want a huge guest list or a ridiculous number of activities or extra events, like a day-after brunch or night-before cocktail party, or a reception after-party. Kind of like a mini version of a big wedding."

Cammie looked doubtful. "Okay, but you're dreaming about the not-a-huge-guest-list part. The Boldano Family alone will tip us over the fire code limit for either ballroom. And even thinking simple, it's a lot to pull off in five weeks."

"We've done it in less time. Like the pregnant bride who decided she wanted to get married before the baby came and showed up here in her eighth month. We put together a dream wedding for her in three weeks and her water broke as she was waving goodbye to the last guest."

"True," Cammie acknowledged. She tapped an index finger topped with a pink-frosted fingernail against her lip.

Mia eyed her friend. "What?"

Cammie stopped tapping. "Just wondering why the rush." She gave Mia a look. "Anything you want to tell me? Should we be taking a page from the pregnant bride wedding folder?"

"What?" It was Mia's turn to gape. "No. No, no, no. It's just . . . I'm not a kid. I'm thirty-two. I want a real wedding because I never got that with Adam. But I don't need all the other stuff. The engagement party, the yearlong buildup to the big event. I love the idea of a fall wedding and don't want to wait a year. And from the conversations Shane and I have had where we kind of touched on the subject, I'm sure he doesn't either. But I'll confirm with him, of course." She shot off a text on her phone. Seconds later, a chime indicated a response. Mia checked and smiled. "He wrote back, 'Five weeks? We have to wait that long?' "

"Then October 19 it is. And you're right. If we can't pull off your dream wedding in five weeks, we should turn in our event planner business cards." Cammie tapped on her laptop keyboard. "Okay, so no engagement party. And based on previous experience, I'm assuming no bachelorette party."

Mia shuddered. "God no." A recent bachelorette party had taken her to New Orleans, where the event devolved into chaos, ending with an attempted murder.* She'd sworn off them ever since.

Cammie wagged a finger at her. "But you're getting a shower. As your maid of honor, it's my duty to throw you one. And I'm gonna go big on it—all on Pete's dime, of course."

The Pete in question was NYPD Detective Pete Dianopolis, Cammie's ex-husband. Pete wrote a self-published mystery series featuring a detective named Steve Stianopolis. Prior to publishing the first tome, Pete divorced Cammie to make way for the hordes of groupie fans he expected to bang on his door. Unfortunately, sales for the series were in the tens of books and not a single groupie materialized. Pete had been desperately trying to woo Cammie back ever since, and she wasn't making it easy or cheap for him.

"Maid of honor, huh?" Mia crooked her lips in a half smile. "Maybe the fog of love has clouded my brain, but I don't remember asking you."

"You know you were gonna, but you've got a lot going on, so I thought I'd save you the trouble. You're welcome." Cammie stood up. "Now, I've got a shower to plan. But first, a call to Pete's credit card company to request an increase in his spending limit by at least a few thou."

Despite the confidence Mia expressed to Cammie about their ability to pull off her wedding in five weeks, she was assailed by an attack of nerves on the drive home from Belle View. The

*For the story of this bachelorette party, see *Four Parties and a Funeral*.

timeline was predicated on finding Adam and getting a quick divorce. Given the circumstances—his philandering and subsequent disappearance—she was less worried about the latter than the former. Even with the full force of the Boldano Family behind her, Mia feared her slimy husband would slip their grasp.

She spotted a rare empty parking spot in front of her house. To her surprise, she noticed Shane's car was parked in front of hers. She exited her car and saw her fiancé standing on top of the stoop in front of the door. "Hey, sweetie." She bounded up the stairs into his arms and they shared the kind of kiss usually reserved for a couple reuniting after one of them had spent a year at sea. "I didn't expect to see you here." Her pulse quickened. "Did you find Adam? Please, oh please, tell me that's why you're here."

"I wish," Shane said. "Your grandmother called and said to meet you both here."

Mia wrinkled her brow. "That's weird. I hope everything's okay."

"It's more than okay!" Elisabetta sang out, throwing the door open and startling the couple. "I wanna give you your wedding present. First, let me set the alarm." She punched a series of numbers into a security system she'd recently had installed. "*Bene.* Now come. Andiamo."

Elisabetta stepped outside, pulling the door shut behind her. She was clad in a velour track suit, her go-to outfit even during the lingering heat of mid-September. This outfit was a cheery turquoise. As Mia and Shane followed her down the front steps, Mia noticed a large appliqué on the back of her grandmother's hoodie. "'Grandmother of the Bride'? How fast did you order that? I haven't been engaged a full twenty-four hours."

"I've had it in a drawer for years," Elisabetta said. "All I had to do was blow the dust off and it was good to go."

She crossed the street, beckoning for the others to do the same. "Do you know what's going on?" Shane whispered to Mia.

Mia shook her head. "Not a clue."

Elisabetta stopped in front of the house directly across the street from the one she and Mia shared. Lived in for years by an elderly recluse who'd recently died, the house hovered on the edge of barely maintained. Unlike every other house on the block, this one wasn't attached to a twin, two-family home. The reclusive owner had torn down the second home at some point. Neighborhood gossip said it was to give him more privacy, which was borne out by the fact that the empty parcel where the second two-family once stood now sprouted nothing but weeds. The only healthy vegetation on the lot was a dividing wall of high hedges that provided a barrier between the recluse and the next set of homes.

Elisabetta pushed open the gate of the chain-link fence surrounding the property. She gestured for Mia and Shane to join her in the home's barely tended front yard. Elisabetta threw her hands in the air triumphantly. "*Mia bellissima e mio bello*—welcome to your new home!"

Stunned, the couple stared at Elisabetta. After a moment, Mia found her voice but could only stammer out, "Wha . . . wha . . . How? I . . . I . . ."

"Thank the computer you got me for my birthday," Elisabetta said, beaming. "I got to poking around on it and started watching some videos. I took the money I saved in the bank and learned—what they call it?—the day-trading."

"You've been trading stocks?" Mia rubbed her forehead, trying to make sense of the unexpected development. "That's what you've been doing all those hours you disappear into your 'office'? I thought you were playing online solitaire or something."

"Feh." Elisabetta waved her hand dismissively. "That's for old ladies."

"No offense, but—" Shane wisely didn't finish the sentence.

"I made enough money to buy this place when the old guy who lived here died," Elisabetta said. She gave her hair, shaped in a stylish pixie cut, a pat. "And had money left over for a new wig."

Mia was still having trouble wrapping her mind around the whole thing, "Nonna, you must have made a lot of money. Home prices around here are out of control."

"Why do you think I had an alarm put in at our house? So nobody would steal my computer and see how I do it. What do the kids say?" She scratched her head, knocking her wig slightly askew. "*Fatto banca.* Make bank. So nobody'd steal it and know how I made bank." She repositioned her wig. "But I got a good deal on this place because the catch to buying it was you couldn't go inside to look at it."

Mia blinked. The situation was growing more bizarre by the minute. "You bought the house without ever seeing what it looked like inside? Nonna . . ."

"What? The land alone's worth what I paid for

it." Elisabetta walked up the steps to the front door. She reached into her tracksuit pants pocket and produced a key. "I ain't been inside yet. I wanted the first time to be *con voi*. The happy, beautiful couple." She put both hands on her heart, then dropped them and inserted the key in the front door lock. "*Vieni*. Come see your new home."

She disappeared into the home. Mia and Shane trailed her. "I'm terrified," Mia whispered to her fiancé.

"Don't be," Shane whispered back. "She's right about the land being worth plenty if this place is a teardown." They stepped into the first-floor foyer, pitched dark due to the fact that it was painted black. "Which I'm guessing it is."

"*Marone a mia. Marone.*"

"Nonna," Mia called, panicked. "Are you okay?"

She ran into the living room and froze in shock at the sight that greeted her.

A life-size, colorful comic strip featuring circus scenes decorated every wall in the room. A handsome character clad in a superhero version of what a trapeze artist would wear swung on a trapeze from one wall to the next, where he was shot out of a cannon onto the next wall, where he walked on a tightrope. The chest of his costume was emblazoned with the letter *C* over a big top tent. A red cape bellowed behind the character as he traveled.

"Circusman!" Shane cried out. He turned in a circle, taking in each wall. "Wow." He spoke in a reverential tone. "This is awesome."

"Who's Circusman?" Mia asked, overwhelmed by the bright cartoon images.

"A cult superhero character who uses circus

skills to battle crime. He was created by a man named Dan Fee. I don't think anyone else ever drew him."

Elisabetta gave a vigorous nod. "Si. That's the name the lawyer said. I got the house from—what was it?—the estate of Dan Fee."

Shane squinted his eyes at the character. "Oh, that's interesting. It's Circusman's body but not his face." He removed his phone from his back pocket and tapped the keyboard, then held up the phone to the others. "He painted his own face on Circusman. How cool is that?"

Mia tore her attention away from the murals. She took in the room, which appeared to be packed floor to ceiling with a collection of detritus. "I'd be more impressed if the drawings came to life and pitched in to go through all the junk in here. It's gonna take the power of ten Circusmen to clean the place up. And if this Dan Fee was famous, we can't exactly call 1-800-GOT-JUNK. There may be stuff of value here."

"Philip's the only person I told about this," Elisabetta said, referring to the newest neighbor on the block, a lawyer turned interior designer now focused on being an at-home dad to the toddlers he shared with husband Finn. Despite a forty-year age difference, he and Elisabetta had become neighbor besties. "His wedding present is gonna be helping you design the place."

A large dust ball rolled by Mia. "He doesn't know what he's in for."

Her cell alerted her to a video call. She checked and saw the caller was Teri Fuoco, ace reporter with the *Triborough Tribune*, a local publication.

Teri had inserted herself into Mia's life in an array of annoying ways, the latest being as Chef Evans's kind-of girlfriend. Given the relationship, Mia had reluctantly moved Teri from the category of enemy to frenemy.

Knowing Teri would hound her until she responded, Mia reluctantly took the call. The reporter's freckled face filled the screen. She skipped salutations and went straight to the headline. "Word's out you're engaged, but your husband who was presumed dead is in town and no one can find him."

"I can't talk right now," Mia said, annoyed. "I'm in the middle of something."

"I'll take that as a yes. I have a little engagement present for you." Teri pulled a copy of the *Tri Trib* out of her ever-present backpack. A banner headline read, HAVE YOU SEEN THIS MAN? Underneath was Adam's headshot from his days managing a Miami branch of the Tutta Pasta restaurant chain. "This publishes tonight. With multiple contact info."

Mia thawed. "This *is* a great present, Ter. Thank you."

"It's the least I can do as one of your bridesmaids."

"Excuse me? I never asked you—"

"So, what are you up to?" Teri interrupted. She leaned into the frame. "What's that image behind you? Whoa. Is that Circusman?"

"Apparently it is." Mia quickly filled her in on the day's other big story, Elisabetta's home purchase. "I gotta go. Thanks for the Adam cover story. We'll deal with the rest later." She ended the call. "Teri made hunting down Adam the *Tri Trib*'s front-page story. Say a prayer it works."

Shane and Elisabetta each clasped their hands together to pray.

Unfortunately, the prayers went unanswered. Days went by with no one reporting a sighting of Adam. However, the front-page story Teri posted did garner a lot of attention, much to Mia's aggravation.

Once word got out that comic strip legend Dan Fee was the late homeowner of Elisabetta's wedding present, fans began making pilgrimages to the hallowed site. A trickle of them turned into a stream and then a flood. "'Circusman, Circusman, does way more than a circus can,'" they sang in sepulchral tones. Luckily, complaints from neighbors on the block evaporated when they realized there was money to be made off the mourners. Food stands popped up, turning 46th Place into an international food fair, with scents of calzone, spanakopita, falafel, and more mingling in the air.

But Mia had bigger problems.

Ever since word of her engagement got out, her in-box had exploded with congratulations and expectations of a wedding invitation. Given her family—and the Family's—must-invites, paring down the wedding guest list was proving a daunting challenge. "This is turning into the goombah event of the year," she muttered one night, deleting a name, then, after a brief hesitation, reinstating it.

She soldiered on, but after another fruitless hour, she gave up. Stiff from too much time hunched over her keyboard, she stood up and stretched. Mia checked the ornate wall clock she'd inherited from a neighbor who'd moved to a senior facility, along with all the elderly woman's gold-gilded-and-red-velvet-upholstered furniture, which would look more at home in a bordello than Mia's unassuming apartment. "Bedtime for dollies and kitty cats," she said to Doorstop, in what was their evening good-night ritual. Having fallen asleep long ago, he didn't respond.

Mia started for the bathroom to get ready for bed. Then, from outside, came the squeak of the back gate slowly being opened. She froze. Despite her grandmother's security additions to their home's exterior, Mia had opted not to grease the gate. She considered its squeak a cheap and effective alert to an intruder . . . which seemed to be happening at that very moment.

She stood in silence for a moment, waiting for confirmation. The gate squeaked again and then shut. Mia grabbed the souvenir Pete Alonso bat that Shane had given her as a birthday present and snuck onto the back staircase landing. A shadow moved in the yard below. "Yo," she called down. "I know you're there. And I called the police."

"Ah, sonuva—"

A familiar voice let loose a stream of profanity. Mia gave herself a shake to make sure she wasn't having a nightmare. Then she leaned over the back stairs railing. "Oh no. No, no, *no*. You are *not* standing in my backyard."

The intruder stepped closer to the house, triggering the security camera. The flash of light was brief but long enough for Mia to see his hair had thinned and his face was more lined. He was barely thirty, but Mia saw flecks of gray in his trendy facial hair stubble.

Adam Grosso mimed tipping a hat to her. Then he flashed the cocky smirk that haunted her like a recovered memory and said, "Hey, babe. Your hubby's home."

CHAPTER 6

Mia emitted a furious growl. She then ran down the back stairs, brandishing the bat. "What are you doing here?" she hissed at her nemesis.

Adam took a step back. "Whoa. Easy with that thing, babe."

It took Mia's last ounce of willpower not to bring the bat down on his dumb, empty head. "Don't you dare '*babe*' me, you cheating, scummy lowlife."

"Sorry about the whole cheating thing. My bad."

Mia shook her head, dumbfounded by his utter cluelessness. "You sleep with another woman—other *women* because I'm sure there were multiples of them—a boat washes ashore in the Bahamas with a body, but you disappear, then suddenly reappear with another girlfriend who I'm guessing is also your fiancée; . . . and all you can say is '*my bad*'?"

"I probably should have led with '*Sorry*,'" Adam

said, somehow managing to phrase it like a punch-line.

"Argh! You are *the worst*. You know what, I don't care why you're here. Go. Now!" She held up the bat in a threatening manner. "Before I take this thing to you."

Adam took another step back, putting him under the glow of a nearby streetlamp. Mia started at the close-up of his face. The bruising on it made her wonder if someone had beaten her to a physical altercation with him. An ugly black-and-blue mark covered his whole left cheek. Dried blood adorned his split lower lip. "Meemster—"

"No nicknames!"

"Fine. Okay. Messina—"

Mia gave her head a shake so vigorous she sent her ponytail holder flying, releasing her thick head of dark hair. "No full names either. In fact, no names at all. You've lost the right to call me anything but your ex-wife."

"That's what I wanna talk to you about." Adam took a step toward Mia, who took a threatening step right at him, bat in hand. He backed away, but as he spoke, he stepped toward her again, triggering her angry reaction. This turned into an a bizarre dance between them. "You wondered why I'm here. I can't go into specifics because it would put people in danger—"

"By *people* you mean *you*," Mia said, knowing Adam all too well.

He didn't correct her. "Circumstances led me to assume a new identity. Thanks to the Witness Protection Program, I'm Gerald Katzenberger, with a cool new career as a web designer. And yes, I have a girlfriend I'm kind of engaged to."

"*Kind of engaged*? Please. That's like being '*a little pregnant.*'"

"Annarita and I were living in Los Angeles, but we couldn't deal with the traffic. I'm telling you, it's exactly like they show in the movies. The Long Island Expressway is an empty country road compared to those freeways."

"Get to the point."

"I love you, Mia," Adam blurted. "That's the point. I didn't wanna go to that wedding expo, but I did it for Annarita. When I saw you, it was fate. I knew God sent me to that expo to see you again. Then, when I saw you at the Mets game, it was the sign from Him that confirmed everything. I tried to fight it, believe me. I tried sticking it out with Annarita. But I gave up. The heart wants what it wants, and what it wants is for us to get back together."

Mia stared at him for a second, then released an infuriated howl. She brought down the bat, but Adam ducked and began running in circles as Mia screamed curses at him. "You're insane! I will never, ever get back together with you! If it was between that and death, I would happily, *happily*, choose death and disco dance all the way there!"

Mr. Righetti, Mia's senior-citizen, next-door neighbor, threw open his first-floor bedroom window. "Eh, shut up out there! I'm trying to sleep. *State zitti!*"

Adam and Mia stopped running. She lowered her bat. "*Mi dispiace*, Mr. Righetti."

The old man slammed his window shut. Mia spoke in a low but urgent voice. "Here's the deal, you low-rent piece of dog feces. You were the worst mistake of my life. I have a man I'm incredibly in love with. We're engaged. He's my coworker and he also happens to be a former male model." Mia couldn't resist throwing that in.

Adam tsk-tsked. "A male model? I'm very disappointed in you, Mia. I had no idea you were so shallow." Mia released another infuriated, guttural growl and resumed chasing him. "I gotta get that bat away from you."

"I want a divorce and I want it now." Mindful of her neighbor, Mia delivered this in a low voice. "Then I never, ever want to see you again."

"I'm afraid I can't do that." Adam, growing tired from running, panted this. "I can't give you a divorce."

"Oh, I think you can. And you better. If you don't, I swear to you, Adam Grosso, you're gonna wish you were the body the Miami Police found on your flipping boat."

"I know you're upset. I get it. When you calm down, you'll see all of this emotion is coming from all the love you still feel for me."

"Argh!"

Unable to control herself any longer, Mia took a swing at Adam with the bat. He jumped out of the way and grabbed a scooter she hadn't noticed leaning up against the backyard chain-link fence. Scooter in hand, he jumped the fence and hopped on the scooter. "I'm gonna win you back, Mia Carina," he called over his shoulder. "And no one, repeat *no one*, will stop us from moving into the circus house and making it our forever home."

"That will never happen!" she screamed back, throwing open the gate and chasing him down the alley, ignoring Mr. Righetti, who'd thrown open his window to yell at them again.

Unable to keep up with Adam, who proved surprisingly skilled at riding the scooter, Mia ran back to her house. A sleepy Elisabetta, clad in a housecoat over her nightgown, stood on the cement deck. "*Ma che successe?* Mr. Righetti called to say you were yelling at someone in the backyard. I told him he should sleep in the front bedroom like me. You okay?"

"Don't worry about me. Go back to bed. I'll explain everything in the morning. Right now, I need my car keys."

Mia raced up the back stairs into her apartment. She grabbed her purse and raced back downstairs to the garage. She jumped into her car and screeched out of the garage into the alley. There was no sign of Adam. Mia cursed as she continued to drive. She quickly tapped on the car's small screen and put in a call to Shane. "Adam came to my house," she said before he could get a word out."

"Wha—"

Mia filled him in on the confrontation.

"Motherf—" Shane raged. "I'll kill that SOB."

"No, you won't. I can tell from the music in the background that you're at Singles. Only Donny Junior still has 'Sexy and I Know It' still on a playlist. Put him on."

"Fine," Shane grumbled.

There was a brief pause, then Donny Junior came on the line. "It's still a great song. A classic. It's too bad LMFAO broke up. They had a lotta great songs left—"

"No time!" Mia barked at him. She brought him up to speed on the Adam situation. "Shane wants to hunt him down, which I get and support, but I don't want him doing anything that could land him in jail. I need you to go with him and make sure he doesn't do something drastic."

"Mia, I can't tell you how much it means that you're honoring me with this important task," the reformed hothead said, touched.

"You're welcome, just do it." She squinted her eyes as she continued the search for Adam on the dark local streets. "God knows where that idiot is by now. He was on a scooter, though, so he can't have gotten too far."

"A scooter?"

"Yeah. I'm guessing he lost his license to one of his chronic DUIs. Only Adam could score those under two different identities. Now, go. Hurry!"

Mia ended the call. Her eyes grew accustomed to the dark as she slowly drove up and down the blocks and alleys of her neighborhood, perusing front yards, backyards, and the spaces in between. But after a couple of frustrating hours, she had to accept the fact that Adam had eluded her grasp.

By the time she returned home, it was one a.m. She shot off an e-mail to her father, brother, fiancé, grandmother, and assorted Family members alerting them to the development and called for an emergency meeting at nine a.m.

Mia took a shower to calm herself, then fell into bed—only to be bolted out of sleep by someone pounding on her door. "*Svegliati*," Elisabetta ordered. "Wake up. Everyone's here."

Mia rubbed her sleep-incrusted eyes and checked her clock. "It's seven a.m. I called the meeting for nine."

"Everyone hates Adam so much they got here

early. I been feeding them breakfast for a half hour already. *Vai*. Let's go."

Mia threw on clothes and followed her grandmother downstairs into Elisabetta's living room. The small space was packed tight with family and Family. Shane and Donny Junior were absent. Mia assumed they were still on the hunt for Adam. Posi was also missing due to the fact that the meeting didn't jive with his halfway house curfew hours.

Most of the men were scarfing down plates of Elisabetta's famous and extremely delicious Pasta alla Nonna, but Mia's anxiety about Adam's refusal to grant her a divorce left her with no appetite. The only women present were Cammie and Teri Fuoco. Mia hadn't invited the reporter, but she'd come to accept that if there was a way to insinuate herself into a Carina or Boldano event, Teri would find it.

Mia clapped her hands together. "Yo! Everyone listen up." The room quieted. "As you know from my e-mail, my sightings of Adam Grosso were confirmed when he showed up in my backyard last night. I have new information. He's going under the name of Gerald Katzenberger and calling himself a web designer. I told him I want a divorce and he refused to give me one."

"I'll kill him!" her father roared, jumping up from the couch.

"Dad, no." Mia pushed him back down. "No violence, you guys. Remember what I said. To repeat for the millionth time, I wanna be a divorcée, not a widow. Capisce?"

The men muttered their usual unhappy agreement about being forced to play by the rules. The doorbell rang. Elisabetta went to answer it. "I've looked everywhere in Astoria for Adam," Mia continued. "So have Shane and Donny. But we have a name and we have a business. The fact he doesn't have a car is also a plus. We can assume he's sticking to mass transit or the scooter I saw him on."

"We got a surprise visitor," Elisabetta called out from the hallway in a singsongy voice. She appeared in the arch separating it from the living room, then stepped aside to reveal Mia's mother, Gia.

Mia let out a joyful exclamation. She beamed with happiness. "Mom. Wow. Hi."

Mia went to hug her mother, who responded in kind. The relationship between the two had been fraught in the past, but they'd resolved their differences over the previous Christmas holidays. Gia, who'd been in dire financial straits, now managed the Boldano family vineyard in Italy.

Gia's ex-husband, Ravello, and Donny Boldano Senior both rose to their feet and greeted her with affection. "Your mama is doing one helluva job for us in Italy," Boldano said. "Vineyard sales have tripled since she's been running the place. We gave her a month off as a reward so she could come to Astoria and help her one and only daughter plan her wedding."

"That's incredibly generous of you, Mr. B.," Mia said. "But if there's no divorce, there's no wedding."

"Divorce?" Gia gave her daughter a questioning look. "What's going on?"

Mia sighed. "Short answer: Adam is alive, in New York, and refuses to give me a divorce."

"I'll kill him!" Gia roared. She did an about-face in the doorway.

"Not if I get to him first!" Ravello tried to pass her.

A Boldano underling turned to another and said, "If killing the guy is on the table . . ."

Suddenly, practically everyone in the room was up and making a run for the door, creating a log-jam of Italian mobsters. "Break it up!" Mia yelled to no avail.

"Yo! Enough! *Fermati ora!*" Orlando Maladugotti gave the order with such a commanding presence that the room instantly quieted. "You heard Miss Carina. No violence. Mr. Boldano, if you will?"

Orlando deftly handed off control to the head of the Family and retreated. He gave Mia a slight nod, which she returned. She had to admit, however grudgingly, he was a leader.

"Everyone, *si siedono.* Sit." Boldano turned to Elisabetta. "If you don't mind us being here a little longer, we're gonna map out a new plan for finding this *stronzo.*"

"I'll put up more coffee." Elisabetta headed for the kitchen.

Mia took a seat on the couch between her parents. She let Donny Senior continue wrangling the troops. As she glanced around the room, it occurred to her that once again, Tulio Longella was missing.

And once again, Mia wondered why.

CHAPTER 7

After the meeting ended and the attendees dispersed to their assigned tasks, Mia felt a need for comfort pastries. This entailed a trip to the family *pasticceria*, La Guli Pastry Shop.

The minute she stepped inside La Guli, the delectable aroma of baked goods calmed her. Every inch of the shop showcased an array of delicious sweets, but Mia eschewed the packaged goods on the wooden shelves for the fresh pastries tempting her from the glass display cases.

"Mia, ciao. And congratulations." Julie Monteleone, the bakery manager, left her post behind the cash register to deliver a hug and kisses on each cheek to Mia. Julie, who'd worked at the bakery for decades, wore her girth as a proud endorsement of La Guli's goods.

"*Grazie.* How are you?" Mia said this with her eyes on a tray of millefoglie, the Italian version of a Napoleon. Julie knew not to take it personally. In fact, she was more concerned if a customer ignored the treats.

"Good. Except this one's gotta go." She pointed to her right hip. "Left one already went. All that metal in me, I'm gonna be the bionic pastry woman."

"As long as you're healthy." Mia frowned. "Darn, I can't decide."

"I'll make a box for you. On the house. An engagement present."

Mia made a pro forma weak protest, knowing it was futile. Ten minutes later, she struggled out the door, weighed down by a large box of pastries under a tray of assorted cookies.

She drove to Belle View, carefully extricated the goodies, and made her way into the lobby, hip checking the glass double doors to open them. "Incoming from La Guli," she called. Her coworkers instantly appeared.

"Let me help you with those." Evans took the cookie tray.

"I'll get the pastries." Guadalupe relieved Mia of them. "We'll lay 'em out in the big kitchen. I already got coffee going."

"Does someone mind bringing me a hazelnut biscotti and a cup of coffee?" Mia asked. "I need to get to work on my own wedding plans before I dive into everyone else's events."

Cammie offered to make the delivery and Mia went to her office. When Cammie showed up a few minutes later, she found her boss typing like mad on her computer. "Thanks," Mia said without stopping as Cammie placed the coffee and biscotto on her desk. "I think I finally got my guest list under control, factoring in a ten to fifteen percent regrets rate. Given the time crunch, I'm going with paperless invitations. I've picked out the one I want to send and am making sure I have everyone's e-mail addresses. Now I just have to settle on my colors, a florist, a favor, the outside caterer, a DJ, bridesmaids' gifts, a registry list . . ." Mia's tone grew increasingly frenetic with each task. "And get it all done by the end of the business day. That's doable, right? I'm sure it's doable, it has to be, tell me it is, I can't—"

"Hey." Cammie grabbed Mia by the shoulders and looked her in the eye. "Calm. The eff. *Down.* I know your wedding's tight schedule, but you don't have to get all of this done today."

"I do," Mia, on the edge of hysteria, insisted. "Because, because, because—"

"Don't make me slap you like in the movies," Cammie warned. "You know I'll do it if I have to. Take a deep breath. A bunch of 'em." She grabbed one of the water bottles Mia kept in her office to offer clients. Cammie opened the bottle and handed it to Mia. "Here. Sips, not gulps."

Mia took a few deep breaths, following them with sips of water. "Thank you."

"Of course."

She closed her eyes and leaned back in her office chair. "I'm terrified I'll never get a divorce from Adam and never get to marry Shane."

"I know you are. You will and you will."

Mia opened her eyes. Overwhelmed with emotion, she took Cammie's hand and squeezed it. "You're such a good friend."

"You have no idea how good." Cammie pointed to the computer. "You take care of the guest list. I'll handle everything else."

"Really?" Mia couldn't help sounding skeptical. "What happened to coasting?"

When Mia moved home from Florida to help her dad run Belle View, fellow event planner Cammie had agreed to stick around under one condition: she be allowed to come and go whenever she pleased. This usually led to workdays of under a couple of hours, freeing Cammie to concentrate on her personal goal of making ex-husband Pete literally pay for divorcing her and then trying to worm his way back into her affections. Cammie was so skilled at her job, she was able to accomplish in a short amount of time what would take others days to do, so Mia never begrudged her coasting mantra. In fact, it eventually turned into a running joke between them.

"For you, no coasting. At least until after the wedding. Then it's full coast ahead." Cammie delivered this with an affectionate grin. "Send me any notes and ideas you have. I'll put together options for everything and run them by you. And no paperless invitations. We can do better than that. Well, *I* can."

Shane stuck his head inside the office. "Hey. I just got here. I hear we got La Guli in the kitchen."

"Give your fiancée a little love first," Cammie said. "She's having a moment."

She exited and Shane came into the office. Mia stood up and went to him. He reached for her, and she saw his left hand was covered with a heavy bandage. "Honey, your hand. What happened?"

Shane reddened under his gorgeous tawny skin. He looked down at the floor. "I'm an idiot. I was so angry about Adam and not being able to find him, I wasn't looking where I was going and slipped on an oil spill from my car."

Mia narrowed her eyes. She didn't believe him

for a minute. "That Tesla's pretty much brand-new. It shouldn't be leaking oil."

Shane shrugged. "Well, you know . . . stuff happens. Even to Teslas."

Mia crossed her arms in front of her chest and fixed a look on him. "I don't think Teslas use oil."

"Wow, look how much my fiancée knows about cars. Girl power, right?" Shane, caught, faked a laugh. "Yeah, they don't use motor oil, but they use lubricant. . . ."

"And how exactly does the lubricant leak? And how would you slip in it if leaked *under* the car?"

"I—I—I—" Shane stammered. Mia's cell rang and he almost collapsed with relief. "You better get that."

Mia picked up her phone. She made a face when she saw the caller was Teri and pressed Ignore. The phone rang again and she repeated the routine. The third time, she cursed and took the call. "What?"

"You might wanna go home."

Mia heard glee in the reporter's voice, which concerned her. "What did you do?"

"My job. Which is sharing breaking news. Like the fact that murals by legendary comic-strip artist Dan Fee decorate the walls of his living room."

"How did you find out about that?" Mia asked, steaming mad. "And why would you announce it to the world?"

"A—your grandmother showed me photos she took of the murals this morning after the meeting of the goombah brain trust at her place, and B—as a journalist, it's my job to share breaking developments with our readers, not hide them." Teri lost the pompous tone and giggled. "I got a bazillion likes on the post. I bet it goes viral."

"It better not. And forget about being my bridesmaid. You're fired." Mia ended the call. "Ugh. I hate that you can't slam down a cell phone."

She grabbed her purse and pushed past Shane. "I gotta go home for a while. Run things here while I'm gone. And don't think we're done with this whole oil story thing because I know you're lying."

Mia gritted her teeth as she sat stuck in a traffic jam a block from her own house—a jam caused by Teri's post. A group of twentysomethings crossed in front of her, heading toward Dan Fee's house. They were dressed as characters she recognized from the murals in her future new home. Mia cursed and hit her horn. They ignored her, and it didn't help move traffic along, but it felt good.

A traffic officer appeared from in front of her car. Mia recognized him as Jorge Avelar, who happened to live a few blocks away with his wife and kids. "Honking ain't gonna break up this clog, lady."

Mia stuck her head out the window. "Jorge, it's me. Mia Carina. From Forty-Sixth Place."

His expression lightened. "Mia. Hey. I heard your grandma bought the house the cartoon guy lived in. Who knew he was some kind of star? What a mess. But my wife's making nice pocket money selling containers of her homemade guac to the fans, so there's that."

"Is there any chance you can move me out of this line so I can get to my grandmother? I'm worried about her with all this craziness happening."

"Sure. I'll stop traffic coming the other way so you can zip out and around your lane."

Jorge held up a hand to pause cars heading in the opposite direction from Mia. He pointed to her and motioned for her to drive. She steered out of what had become a parking lot instead of a road and sped away, earning a few outraged honks from the drivers she passed. She called out thanks to Jorge as she drove by him into the alley behind her house.

Mia parked and checked Find My Friend on her phone to locate her grandmother. The app showed Elisabetta was across the street at the Circusman house. Worried as much for the recipients of Elisabetta's anger at the fan rubbernecking as for her grandmother, Mia ran around the side of the house and across the street.

She found Elisabetta manning a bake stand on the sidewalk in front of the comic artist's house, along with half a dozen neighbors selling their wares, including Jorge Avelar's wife. Elisabetta's stand featured an array of cookies that Mia knew from experience rivaled La Guli's in deliciousness. "I got all the pay apps," her grandmother was telling a young guy dressed like a ringmaster.

"Nonna—"

"Lemme finish this sale." The ringmaster typed information into Elisabetta's cell phone and handed it back to her in exchange for a paper plate piled high with ricotta cookies coated with frosting and rainbow sprinkles. He left and Elisabetta turned her attention to Mia. "*Bene.* I took a break from the computer for a little fresh air and cookie selling. The market's down on Wall Street but it's up on

Forty-Sixth Place." Elisabetta chuckled at her own witticism. "Like the kids say, whassup?"

"Okay, no one's said whassup in twenty years, but whassup is . . . *this*?"

Mia waved her hands to indicate the crowd, which continued to grow. A fan of about nineteen wearing a Strongman costume and driving erratically on a banged-up scooter stopped next to her. He carried a bouquet that had seen better days. Some of the bouquet's flowers were broken, others were wilted. A few lacked petals altogether.

The Strongman tossed aside the scooter. "This thing's useless. No wonder the guy using it just left it in the alley."

He started for the front yard's chain-link gate. Mia blocked his path. "Sorry. Off-limits."

"But I want to put this on the front steps. You know, like a memorial."

The fan held up the bedraggled bouquet, comprised of lilacs, purple irises, and tiger lilies—all of which were Mia's favorite flowers. She got a sick feeling in the pit of her stomach. "You said you found the scooter in an alley. Which alley?"

"The one behind those houses." He pointed across the street to Mia's home. "Found the flowers there, too. I was gonna buy some, but the ones the old lady down the street is selling are crazy expensive." A guilty expression crossed the fan's face. "Maybe I should bring the flowers and scooter back to the alley. The guy'll wonder what happened to them when he wakes up."

Mia inhaled, then exhaled slowly. She kept her voice even. "Can you describe this guy? In the alley?"

"Sure. I mean, from what I could see. He was passed out. He looked about my height. You know, five eight or nine. Stubbly beard. Pretty much looked like a lotta guys except for this weird bald spot."

"Shaped like a starfish."

"Yeah! Exactly. He did not look good. Dude's gonna have a serious overhang when he comes to."

Mia, trying to rachet down her emotions, made a little squeaking sound. "Excuse me. I need to . . . do . . . a thing. And um, I wouldn't worry about the flowers or the scooter. I have a really bad feeling the guy won't be in a position to miss them."

She left the fan scratching his head at her comment.

Mia anxiously searched the crowd for a police officer. She spotted one moving fans away from the house and hurried to him. "Sorry, miss." He motioned to her to back up. "You need to go. We're declaring this an unlawful assembly."

"Thank you for that," Mia said to the officer's surprise. "You're from our precinct, so you know Detective Pete Dianopolis, right?"

"Right," the officer said, his tone wary.

Mia placed a hand on her heart, hoping it might quell its rapid beating. The gesture didn't work. "Please call him and say he has to meet Mia Carina at the far end of the alley behind her house. Tell him . . . I think we're gonna find a body there."

CHAPTER 8

Mia and Pete Dianopolis stared at the lifeless body lying in front of Iris Villanova's dilapidated garage, which housed a 1978 Gold Ford Torino the nonagenarian hadn't driven in forty years. "You can confirm it's him?" Pete asked.

Mia gave a grim nod. "Yup. That's Adam Grosso, also known as Gerald Katzenberger. My husband." She corrected herself. "My late husband."

Pete stepped away to confirm with crime scene technicians working the site. Mia continued to stare at Adam. She couldn't keep up with the tsunami of emotions whirling inside her. Anger, grief, confusion—but if she was honest with herself, the dominant emotion was relief. She'd insisted ad nauseum she wanted to be a divorcée, not a widow. Yet in one day, all obstacles to her future with Shane had been wiped away.

Or had they?

Mia desperately wanted to believe Adam died a natural death. Otherwise, the consequences would be dire. If he'd been murdered, the list of suspects would be as long as her wedding guest list—and include a lot of the same names. People Mia loved would spend months or years under suspicion. One might go to jail for the deadly act.

Mia gulped. A new emotion shoved all the others aside—fear.

Pete ambled back to her side. "Theory is he was hit by a car, then dragged to this location."

Mia's spirits rose, however inappropriately. "So, it could have been an accident. I mean, still a crime but a hit-and-run."

Pete shot her a look. "Sure. Keep dreaming. What can you tell me about why he was here? On your turf? With flowers?"

Mia flashed on the image of the battered bouquet the Circusman fan had found. She scrunched up her face in an effort to keep from bursting into tears. "I'm guessing he was gonna try and woo me back."

He lifted his head and scanned the alley. "We're gonna be checking all the security cameras in the area. One of them must've picked up something."

"Good luck to you," Mia said. "This block is mostly full of seniors whose idea of security is a heavy lamp they can conk over the head of a burglar." She realized there was one home that did have a newly installed security system. "We've got cameras at our house. I'll make sure the security firm releases footage to you. But," she added, "you should start in Miami and whatever went on there that led to Adam entering the Witness Protection Program."

"Thanks for the tip on how to do my job," Pete said with an eye roll. He shook his head. "Man, are you a magnet for murder." His eyes lit up. "*Magnet for Murder.* Great title for my next Steve Stianopolis book."

The detective left for Dan Fee's house to check on the progress his underlings were making on finding possible witnesses to Adam's demise. Mia retreated to her apartment, where she was greeted by delighted meows and tweets from pets who assumed her unexpected midmorning visit meant a bonus meal. She gave Doorstop and Pizzazz enough treats to satisfy them, then forced herself to face the unenviable task of alerting her family and friends to Adam's death.

She sat down on her plastic-encased couch and dug out her cell phone from the depths of her overflowing purse. Mia noticed it had been accidentally switched to silent mode. She clicked it back on and the phone rang with one text alert after another, along with multiple calls from Shane. Someone had beaten her to the reveal of Adam's death and she knew who. She placed a call to Teri Fuoco. "How did you find out?"

"Oh, you saw my breaking news alert." Mia heard someone singing the Circusman theme song in the background of the call. She got up and walked to her bedroom, which fronted the street. She opened her window and stuck her head out to scan the crowd across the street. She saw Teri with her cell phone in one hand and a mini digital recorder in the other. Teri must have sensed her glare because she looked up from the sidewalk and gave Mia a cheery wave. "I've said it before and I'll say it again. When it comes to big stories, you're the gift that keeps on giving."

"I hate that, and you're still fired as my bridesmaid."

Mia shot Teri the bird, then ended the call and slammed the window shut. She sat on the edge of her bed and returned Shane's multiple calls. "Are you okay?" was the first thing he asked, the question filled with worry.

"I'm fine. Adam is not."

"Yeah. I saw Teri's news flash. She didn't have many details."

"Neither do I." She relayed what she could about the scooter, the flowers, and discovering Adam's body with Pete.

"I'm coming over," Shane instantly responded.

"No, don't. Between the Circusman house and Adam, it's a zoo here. I'll come to Belle View. I need to get out of the house."

"Okay. But be careful. I love you."

"I love you, too."

The call over, Mia placed the phone back in her purse. For a change, it wasn't Shane's *I love you* that lingered in her mind. It was his *Be careful.* The two words sent the message that he, like she and the NYPD, assumed Adam's death was no accident. At least she prayed it was an assumption on the part of her furious fiancé.

Mia left the house by the front door. She wanted to let her grandmother know she was heading back to Belle View. She met Elisabetta, a folding table under her arm, on the home's front steps. "I sold all my cookies." Elisabetta shared this news with unabashed braggadocio. "The news about Adam brought out a bunch of hungry lookie-loos."

"You heard about him."

"Si," she said, somber. "We all did."

Mia took the folding table from her grandmother and placed it in the vestibule. Elisabetta pulled a ricotta cookie out of the pocket of the apron she wore over the day's peach tracksuit. She offered it to Mia, who declined. Elisabetta munched on the cookie. "That Teri was acting like she won the lottery."

"For a reporter, I guess she did," Mia said with a wry expression.

"People are calling me. They don't know what to say or do." Elisabetta paused. She gazed at her granddaughter with compassion. "You are his widow."

Mia bit her lower lip. "I know."

"He didn't have family, did he?"

"No. Well, no one he was talking to. Everyone assumed he died at sea. No way we would have known he was in the Witness Protection Program."

"He was a *stronzo*. A cheat, a liar, a piece of *merda* I'd scrape off my shoe into a drain." Elisabetta launched an angry spit at the ground. "Still, we should honor his memory."

"I'll summon the troops for a memorial. Tonight. At Belle View. We're not booked for anything." The sooner she achieved closure regarding Adam's death, the better, Mia thought. Especially given the worry of what might come if Adam's death was classified as a homicide.

She walked Elisabetta to the first-floor kitchen. The octogenarian checked her investments on her cell phone—another gift from Mia and Ravello— then embarked on making more ridiculously overpriced cookies to foist on the Circusman fans.

Mia scurried upstairs and changed into a black

skirt and silky black top that could transition from work to the memorial service. On the drive to Belle View, she couldn't help reliving memories of her brief marriage. She managed to summon a few positive ones, but even in wistful retrospect, the bad outweighed the good. Still, Adam's unexpected death upset her. Mia hoped he didn't suffer and, when the end came, it came quickly.

Coworkers surrounded Mia the minute she walked into the catering manor. They peppered her with questions. "What happened to Adam?" "Why was he near your house?" "Do the police think he was murdered?" "Your grandmother called and said there's a memorial here tonight. Should I bake a cake, or is that not appropriate?"

Shane broke through the cluster of employees. He put a hand around Mia's waist. "No more questions. I'm gonna run the memorial. Cammie, you're in charge of letting everyone know it's happening. Make it for seven o'clock. Guadalupe, you do the meal, but make it easy on yourself. You can just order Italian deli if you want."

"Excuse me," the chef barked, insulted. "You want deli, get it yourself. I'm gonna put up a *real* meal."

"Yes, ma'am." Mia could tell her fiancé was suppressing a grin. "And Evans, I think a cake is fine. Just don't make it look like a coffin or a tombstone or anything."

"Okay," Evans said, clearly disappointed. He prided himself on creating cake sculptures that perfectly replicated common objects.

Shane checked his watch. "We've got five hours. Time to make the magic happen." The staff hurried off.

"Thanks so much for taking charge, honey," Mia said. "But you didn't give me an assignment."

"I've got one for you." Shane wrapped his arms around his fiancée, and she rested her head on his firm chest. "Your job is to think about anything *but* the memorial."

Mia gave her fiancé a grateful smile. "Yes, sir."

She followed Shane's order for the rest of the workday, returning e-mails from prospective clients, adding photos to the gallery on Belle View's website, and negotiating down prices with a few greedy vendors. Her last work task was hosting a tour for a young family scoping out the site for a party celebrating their daughter's first communion. "Mommy, look! Boats!"

The seven-year-old in question ran to the Marina Ballroom's wide expanse of windows and pressed her nose against the glass.

"It's a beautiful view," the mother agreed. "The whole room is lovely."

"We recently updated this ballroom," Mia said. She gestured to brand-new, gleaming silver chairs surrounding a round table covered with a crisp white tablecloth, then to the plush yet sturdy carpet featuring a swirly dark beige on light beige pattern. Mia gave herself, along with her staff, credit for creating the quality, once-in-a-lifetime events that had turned Belle View into a popular venue for Queens residents. She gave herself a mental pat on the back. *Who knows?* she thought. *Maybe Shane and I can spread our talents to other struggling sites. A husband-and-wife team turning no-goes to go-tos. Oooh, it could be a TV show!*

And then it hit her. She was free to fantasize about her future because Adam was dead. Who benefitted the most from his exiting the land of the living? She and Shane. If he was murdered, this made them the prime suspects.

"Are you all right?" the little girl's mother asked. "You went pale."

"Yes, sorry." Mia shook off her panic attack. "I haven't eaten much today." She forced a wide smile. "But that's about to change because we're heading to the kitchen for a tasting."

Mia wrapped up the workday by booking the family's party. Watching the young communicant bounce up and down with excitement as she paged through a website to pick out a party favor, Mia reflected on her own first communion, twenty-five years prior. The dress and veil were lovingly packed away and stored in her basement, to perhaps be brought out someday for her own daughter. This reminded Mia how long it had been since she attended Mass. *I should stop by St. Francis sometime,* she thought, feeling guilty. *A few prayers would come in handy these days.*

She heard voices in the hallway and checked the wall clock, a cute item she'd found on the Internet featuring different wedding cakes instead of numbers. The time told her people were drifting in for the memorial. Mia rose from behind her desk. She slipped on the pumps she'd shed and smoothed her skirt, then checked her reflection in the full-length mirror attached to the back of the office door. Satisfied she looked like a dignified mourner, she left the office for the first-floor Bay Ballroom.

The memorial proved to be a respectful, muted affair, odd in the fact that the only person in the room who knew Adam well, if at all, was Mia. Cammie had alerted Pete to the event, asking him to pass on the details to Adam's fiancée, if they'd tracked her down. If they had, she was a no-show. And once again, Tulio Longella made himself absent. Mia wondered if an incident had happened within the Family that accounted for his disappearance, but when she gently broached the subject with Donny Senior, he insisted that wasn't the case, and she had to take his word for it.

Mia was helping herself to a slice of Evans's devil's food cake when Cammie sidled up to her. "Evans restrained himself," Mia said. "He went with a plain old sheet cake. Although I appreciate him throwing a little shade by making sure we all know it's *devil's* food and not just chocolate cake. For the devil that was Adam."

"I think you should say a few words about Adam," Cammie said sotto voce. "But maybe don't lead with the devil thing."

Mia handed off her cake to Cammie and claimed a spot at one end of the room. Shane stood nearby for moral support. She picked up a glass of water from a table and tapped a spoon against it. Others picked up the cue and began tapping. More and more guests joined in, and a chant began. "Kiss, kiss, kiss, kiss!"

"It's a memorial, you idiots," Donny Junior yelled at them. "No kissing!"

The room quieted. Mia cleared her throat, then began to speak. "Adam Reagan Grosso was . . . a man. Sometimes a good man. Sometimes not. Frankly, a lot not."

"*E vero*," Elisabetta editorialized. "Truth."

"Amen to that," Ravello said, while his ex-wife, Gia, vigorously nodded. "He was a rat bas—"

"*But*," Mia interrupted, shooting a warning

glance, "he deserved to live a long and happy life. Well, happyish. The guy needed to make some serious amends. To a lot of people, not just me. Don't get me started on some of the stunts he pulled." Out of the corner of her eye, Mia saw Pete Dianopolis make a discreet entrance, his partner, Ryan Hinkle, in tow. Pete pointed to her and then to the lobby. She quickly wrapped up her eulogy. "But that's all in the past. May Adam find peace in the afterlife, amen. Shane, why don't you lead everyone in an Our Father?"

Mia turned the event over to her nonplussed fiancé and slipped out the ballroom double doors into the lobby with Pete and Ryan. "What's up? You've got your serious cop face on."

"You bet I do. We've discovered something very interesting."

Mia's heart hammered. It occurred to her the security footage she'd blithely offered up might not present her in the best light if it captured her chasing Adam around her yard with a bat. "Like what?" she said, trying to sound nonchalant.

"Adam Grosso was never in the Witness Protection Program."

Mia's jaw dropped. "What?" she said, stunned. "But . . . but . . . he said he was. He had a fake name and new career and everything."

"All of which he created on his own. The question is . . . why?"

CHAPTER 9

Pete instructed Ryan to cover the ballroom and make sure no one left. Then he stared down Mia.

"You're looking at me like I know the answer," she said, feeling defensive. "I'm as shocked as you are."

"Really?"

"Ugh, don't. I hate when people say *really* that way. Like, when they mean, *I don't believe it for a minute, but I'm gonna use the word* really *so it sounds like I'm thinking about what you're saying when I'm totally judging you.*"

"Apologies." Pete gave her the same look. "So?"

Mia glared back at him. "You're doing it again, only using a different word. Look, as you've heard me say so many times that people wanna scream, '*We get it,*' my marriage to Adam was a total disaster. I should have bailed days after we married, but I was embarrassed. So I kept trying to make it work, which was a joke and a giant waste of time because you can't make a relationship with a serial grifter and cheater work, no matter what you try. And believe me, I tried everything."

"Still . . ."

Mia scowled at the detective. "Don't *still* me either. You're oh for three, Pete. One of Adam's best-developed tools in his skill set was keeping secrets. Especially from me. Why do you think I didn't hear about his boat suddenly appearing with his girlfriend's body in it until Miami PD came knocking on my door?"

Memories of that horrible night came flooding back to Mia. Feeling nauseated, she found her way to the lobby's seating area and fell into a wingback chair. She noticed a small stain on the arm and made a mental note to have the chair steam cleaned. Focusing on the mundane task somehow calmed her, and her nausea improved.

"Oh, good." Pete took the seat opposite her, dropping his stocky body into it with a grunt. "I was on my feet all day and my dogs are barking." He stretched his legs, then planted both feet on the ground. "Miami PD'll be taking another look at all of Grosso's activity in the region prior to his disappearance and presumed death. And they'll be getting an assist from the FBI, because MPD has already determined he was no web designer. He was on the web all right. The dark web, where he was selling illegally imported cigarettes and stolen vape equipment. Which means he engaged in a federal crime."

"Really."

Pete gave her a reproving look. "You're gonna throw a *really* back at me? Miss Prime Suspect if the coroner report shows your late hubby was murdered?"

Mia grimaced. "You got the security footage from my house."

"What's that now?"

"Nothing," Mia said, covering, then deflecting. "You were saying about the FBI, federal crime, et cetera . . ."

Pete sat back in his chair. "I'm gonna make the not-so-bold assumption that someone offed Grosso. Him making like he was in the WP program when he wasn't widens the field of suspects to anyone who had a grudge against the guy." He pointed to the Bay Ballroom. "And considering the fact that he didn't want to give you a divorce, which includes pretty much everyone in the ballroom. Especially since we already got security video from the wedding expo showing all the Belle View employees who were there duking it out for the opportunity to kill the guy."

"Including your own ex-wife," Mia felt compelled to point out.

Pete bristled at Mia's touching the most tender of nerves. "Cammie would never. It was just words from her."

"Then why wouldn't it be from the rest of us?"

The detective didn't respond. He stood up with a groan. "Damn. I don't know which I should replace first, my knee or my hip." He did a halfhearted stretch.

"Talk to Julie at La Guli. She has a surgeon. At least for the hips."

"Thanks. Back to your late hubby. Even though we don't have an official cause or time of death, as long as you've got this mafioso meetup going, I'm gonna get a head start on suspect interviews."

"Is it legal, seeing as we don't know how Adam died?"

"I'm only asking some questions to see if any of them knows anything useful. It's not a reach to think he might have been in cahoots with a criminal enterprise like the Boldano Family, or at least reached out to see if they'd be interested in working with him. If anyone's got a problem with what I ask, they're welcome to call one of the fancy lawyers Boldano Senior's got on retainer. Oh, and nice try, trying to get me off the subject of your own security video. We should have it by tomorrow."

Mia watched as Pete headed into the ballroom, his gait stiff. Two things occurred to her: The detective was in serious need of an exercise regimen. And she should never make the mistake of underestimating the law enforcement officer's ability to do his job.

With only about twenty attendees at the memorial, including the Belle View staff, Pete and Ryan's interviews took a mere few hours. Still, the detectives didn't depart until almost midnight. Mia made sure they left with hefty to-go bags, which helped thaw the stony, just-the-facts-ma'am personas they adopted for the inquiries. Especially Pete, who Mia knew was laying it on thick to impress Cammie. Judging by her flirting with him, the tactic seemed to work.

Mia and her Belle View friends convened in the main kitchen to compare notes on their interviews. All except Shane, who begged off, saying the injuries from his fall necessitated a hot bath and lots of rest. Too tired to push back, Mia pretended to accept his excuse.

"Who wants espresso?" Guadalupe asked to a show of hands. She put up a pot.

"First off, is everyone okay?" Mia asked. Given the unexpected interrogations were prompted by her personal life, she felt responsible for her staff's well-being.

"We're fine." Guadalupe poured espresso into demitasse cups and distributed them. "With the number of bodies dropping around here, I think we all got our interview skills on lock."

The others murmured agreement. "Is it my imagination or does Pete look a whole lot hotter when he's grilling suspects?" Cammie said this with a dreamy look in her eyes. "Like he's the star on a TV cop show."

Evans dropped a sugar cube into his espresso. "It's you."

"Did anything come up that made you nervous?" Mia asked.

"Not for me," Evans said. He opened his mouth to add something, then snapped it shut.

From her years growing up around her father and brother's sketchy doings, Mia's ear was attuned to any hint of anything being off. Evans's response triggered an alarm. "You stopped yourself from saying *but*. Nothing came up that made *you* nervous, *but* it did for someone else. Who?"

Evans, uncomfortable, stirred his espresso. "Man, it takes forever for these cubes to dissolve. Worth it, though. Nothing like pure cane sugar."

"Evans, stop stalling."

"Fine." He put down his cup and faced Mia. "I went to my car to put away a slice of cake for Teri."

"Aww, such a good boyfriend," Cammie cooed. Mia shot her a look. "Well, he is."

"The detectives were by their car talking about their interviews," Evans continued, ignoring Cammie. "Pete said something about Shane."

He hesitated.

"Which was . . . ?" Mia prompted.

"He told the other guy he didn't buy Shane's story of slipping on motor oil. Not when Shane owns an all-electric vehicle."

The room fell silent. Mia knew the others were waiting for her response. "Yeah. Honestly, I don't buy Shane's story either."

The room seemed to breathe a collective sigh of relief. Cammie picked up a bottle of Strega, the Italian liqueur, and added a shot to her demitasse cup. "I think I speak for everyone when I say none of us did. What do you think he's covering up?"

The room fell into another awkward silence. "I know you're all thinking he might have killed Adam, but he didn't do it," Mia blurted out. "I'm a bazillion percent sure of that. Did Pete or Ryan mention to any of you that Adam was never in the Witness Protection Program?" The others shook their heads. "They wouldn't because they wanted to see if you knew this on your own."

Guadalupe furrowed her massive brow. "He faked it? I heard plenty in my life but never someone pretending to be in the WPP."

"Well, Adam did." Mia took the bottle of Strega from Cammie and heavily doctored her own coffee. "Which means he did something stupid that put him in so much danger he had to fake his own death. Whoever he messed with is a whole lot more likely to be his killer than anyone in our little circle."

CHAPTER 10

"Espresso at midnight is never a good idea," Mia said to the cat sound asleep next to her. "Especially when you add way too much Strega."

Mia had fallen asleep as soon as she got home. Unfortunately, it didn't stick. After barely four hours, she found herself wide awake and staring at the ceiling. She closed her eyes and tried to clear her mind, but that proved impossible. She'd quell the image of Adam's lifeless body only to have it replaced by a vision of Shane awkwardly lying to her about his injuries.

After a round of hot milk followed by deep breathing relaxation exercises that proved futile, Mia shed the sleep mask she'd donned and got out of bed. She picked up her cell phone from the rococo nightstand next to the bed and tapped out a text. A moment later her phone rang. "Hey."

"Hey," Cammie whispered.

"I thought you might be awake, too. I blame the espresso and Strega."

"That and . . . other things."

The innuendo in Cammie's voice telegraphed exactly what those *other things* were. "Pete's there?"

"I can't help it. Watching him grill suspects is a turn-on. Don't judge."

"I have a dead husband who was a criminal and was probably murdered and a fiancé who's lying to me. You never have to worry about me judging."

"Thank you."

Doorstop stirred. He meowed and stretched, kicking Mia with a paw, then went back to sleep. She adjusted her position. "After my super unpleasant experience with the Miami PD, I don't trust them to figure out what happened with Adam. I'm thinking the person who might know is his fiancée, Annarita. Can you manipulate contact information for her out of Pete? I'm sure the police have it."

"If they do, you know I can get it," Cammie said in her sexiest voice.

Mia made a face. "No details. But thanks."

Cammie signed off. Mia put her sleep mask back on and snuggled next to Doorstop. She stroked his golden orange fur and he purred. Comforted by the glimmer of a plan, Mia fell back asleep.

She woke up a few hours later to a text from Cammie containing an address and cell number for Adam's fiancée and way too many winking emojis. Mia showered and dressed for work. After a breakfast of leftover ricotta cookies, she decided it was a respectable time to contact Annarita. She typed out a text expressing her condolences: **This is Mia Carina. I'm so sorry about Adam. I'm sure you're going through a rough time. I'd like to get to-**

gether and talk. While she waited for a response, she ate another cookie. Midcookie, her phone pinged a response: **I told the police I don't know anyone named Adam. Go away.**

Uh-oh. Mia typed back another plea to meet with Annarita. It didn't go through. Adam's fiancée had blocked her.

Mia checked the address Cammie had shared and recognized it as a garden apartment in a complex not far from the airport. She knew it from visits to other people who lived there. Taking a chance Annarita might be home, Mia fed her pets, then made the short drive from her house to the Bay Manor Garden Apartments.

She parked in front of a Tudor-style, two-story building. The small collection of buildings clustered around the lawns and greenery that earned it the appellation garden dated back to the early 1940s. Mia quickly found Adam and Annarita's first-floor unit and rapped on the door. She heard the interior cover of the peephole slide open. "I know who you are. Go away or I'll call the police."

"Feel free to. I'm friends with a lot of them. Look, I really do know what you're going through. It's awful to find out someone wasn't who you thought they were. I've been there. With the same guy as you."

The pause that followed went long enough for Mia to fear she hadn't gotten through to Annarita. Then the door opened. A tall, unnatural blonde in her midtwenties stood in front of her. She was pretty, although her features were slightly off-kilter. Her mouth was small, her face long, and her long nose crooked at the tip.

She glared at Mia but stepped aside to let her into the apartment, which appeared to be a studio. Mia took in the space. Aside from a lot of boxes and a couple of suitcases, there was an inflatable mattress and the kind of folding chair kept on hand to bring to the beach. "Whatever you have to say, make it fast. My parents are gonna be here any minute. They're taking me back home to New Jersey now that my fiancé is dead." She fixed an ugly glare on Mia. "Or should I say *ex-fiancé* since he broke up with me after seeing you at the Mets game."

Mia felt for the girl. She'd been hit with multiple revelations and probably still didn't know the whole story. "What did Adam—"

Annarita stamped her foot like a child. "I keep telling everyone, *I don't know an Adam.*"

"Gerald. Where did you two meet? In Los Angeles?"

"No. Florida. I was a cocktail waitress."

Another cocktail waitress. Boy, did he have a type. "What did Gerald tell you about me?"

"That you were an old girlfriend he thought he was over, but when he saw you on the kiss cam with another guy, he realized he wasn't and had to break it off with me."

Annarita put her hands on her hips. She stared at Mia with so much venom it was unnerving. Mia debated wishing her luck and cutting out right there, then summoned the courage to deliver the truth. "The man you knew as Gerald Katzenberger was really Adam Grosso. He was a scam artist who got in trouble with the wrong people and faked a new identity to escape. And I wasn't his girlfriend. I was his wife."

Annarita mouth dropped open. Rage colored her face and she released a scream. "You ruined my life!"

She lunged for Mia, who managed to duck out of the way and grab the doorknob. She flung open the door. "I'm sorry! But blame Adam, not me."

She ran out of the apartment, slamming the door behind her. Fearing Annarita would give chase, Mia ran faster than she'd ever run in her life. She jumped in her car and screeched away from the apartment, panting from fear and exertion.

Mia drove a circuitous route out of the neighborhood in case Adam's raging, jilted fiancée might be following her. After a few miles, she saw a coffee shop on a corner and pulled over. A latte later, she felt marginally better. Given her suspicious nature, as she sipped her drink, Mia couldn't help wondering if at least part of Annarita exaggerated her reaction to the news her fiancé had a living, breathing wife. A jilted fiancée had as good a reason to kill Adam as anyone. What if Annarita blew up to cover up? Mia wondered the extent of what Annarita might or might not know about Adam's illegal activities. *Maybe she was in on them. But if she was, he was worth more to her alive.*

Faced with more questions than answers, Mia decided she needed to call Posi. He could always be counted on to provide comfort, along with criminal common sense. "Hey," he said, answering on the first ring. "I'm on laundry duty here at the house. Thanks for the break. What's going on?"

"A lot, and none of it good."

Mia shared the details of her run-in with Adam's

fiancée, along with her suspicions. "She could be covering," he said. "A lotta unknowns."

"Tell me about it. Literally. What are your thoughts on this?"

"Hmmm . . ."

Posi paused to contemplate the situation. Still shaky from the confrontation, Mia used the downtime to do a sweep of her environs to make sure Annarita wasn't lying in wait for her beyond a bush or the giant model of a coffee cup fronting the shop. Posi finally spoke. "The night you met Adam at Singles. Who were you with?"

"A few gal pals," Mia said, recalling the evening. "Rose Nunzio and Ruth Behling, and Ruth's boyfriend Mark Giuseppe. I lost touch with them all after I moved to Miami and haven't had time to jump-start the friendships since I moved back. The last time I saw any of them was when Ruth and Mark visited Adam and me in Miami. Tulio Longella was the only person who seemed to know him, which is why I find it very convenient he's suddenly MIA."

"Back up. If Ruth and Mark visited you in Florida, they might have picked up on a sketchy activity Adam was involved with and not want to tell you. You know, protecting a friend."

"It's possible." Mia pondered Posi's implications. She came to a decision. "You know what? I think it's time to reconnect with some old friends."

CHAPTER 11

On her way to Belle View, Shane texted that he was taking a sick day; his injuries were still bothering him. Mia tried phoning him, but he didn't respond, forcing her to text him: **I call BS on your *sick day*.** His response—**We'll talk**—didn't make her feel better.

Aside from that, the day proved uneventful, which Mia considered a blessing. She'd had enough drama to hold her for a while. With the holiday season only a few months away, bookings were brisk, depriving Mia of the time she needed to get in touch with old friends Rose and Ruth.

Unfortunately, after work, Mia arrived home to another dose of drama. The minute she stepped into the vestibule, Elisabetta yelled to her, "Mia! *Vieni.*" She followed her grandmother's voice into the living room. The scent of anise and vanilla wafted into the room from the kitchen, where yet another batch of cookies was in the oven. The octogenarian paced as friend and neighbor Philip studied a document. While Philip's first love was interior design, he'd kept his law license active and now handled some of the Carina and Boldano legal affairs. He didn't look happy about whatever document he was reading.

"We got a problem," Elisabetta announced as she wore a path in the room's decades-old carpet. "With the circus house."

"How? There are less and less people out there. It feels like interest is fading."

"That's not the problem." Philip took off his reading glasses and placed them in the pocket of his crisp, short-sleeve, button-down shirt. "There's a well-established fan club called the Circus Feeks. Their executive board has sued to have Mr. Fee's house declared an historical and cultural landmark. If they win, we can't touch the place."

Mia stared at Philip, slack jawed. "You have got to be kidding."

He shook his head. "I wish."

"Argh!" Mia slapped her forehead in frustration. "Can't we just put up a sign? You know, DAN FEE SLEPT HERE. Like they do with George Washington."

"I pitched that and got a no."

Mia began pacing with her grandmother. She stopped, causing Elisabetta to collide with her. "Sorry, Nonna. Philip, I want to meet with these people. The freaks or feeks or whatever they call themselves."

"I'm glad you said that because members of the board are on their way over."

"And we're gonna feed 'em a lotta cookies," Elisabetta said with a knowing wink.

* * *

Mia and Elisabetta worked as a team to make coffee and lay out a tempting array of homemade sweets. Shortly after they completed setting up the spread, Philip led the Circus Feek executive board into the living room. All ranged in age from mid to late twenties and sported the pasty skin of people who considered any outdoor activity anathema.

Opting for a charm offensive, Mia flashed her warmest smile at them. "Hello. Please make yourself comfortable. Help yourself to some of my nonna's fantastic cookies."

"'Kay." A skinny guy whose hair could use more than one wash, piled a plate with cookies. He'd introduced himself as Thomas, the club's treasurer. Rounding out the group were Raina, the club president, a petite Gen Zer whose dyed, bright red hair hung to her waist; vice president Eddie, who gave off a bombastic vibe and didn't walk so much as lumber; Hannah, the club secretary, a willowy, delicately boned girl who blinked behind tortoiseshell eyeglasses; and lastly, the membership director, a gangly tattoo of a twentysomething who'd legally changed his name to Circus Mann.

"Coffee?" Elisabetta, who had changed into her fanciest tracksuit—a golden velour number trimmed with fake pearls—brandished a carafe to a chorus of yesses. Mia got the impression this was a crowd that lived on caffeine with an occasional side of pot joints.

"Our friend and renowned lawyer"—hoping to make a daunting impression, Mia laid it on thick— "Philip Barnes-Webster has informed us of your lawsuit. It's been very upsetting for my grandmother, who's eighty-four and in delicate health."

Elisabetta, who the Carinas were convinced would outlive them all, clutched her heart. "*Non sto bene.*" She added an operatic moan for more effect.

Mia patted her grandmother's knee. "It's okay, Nonna. If anything happens, I have your nitroglycerin tablets." She gave her head a doleful shake, then addressed the visitors. "We invited you over to see if we could work out some kind of compromise with the landmark thing."

"Yeah, that would be a no." Eddie declared this through a mouthful of cookie.

"Excuse me. Club president here." Raina gave him a baleful look and held her hand up in the air in a sarcastic gesture. She turned to Mia. "Dan Fee always said he was going to set up a museum in Vermont. He put it in his will. But his lawyer said he never got a will from Mr. Fee, so we don't have any choice. We have to establish a museum in Dan's house here in Astoria."

Mia gritted her teeth. "You really don't."

"We really do," Raina said, polite but steely.

"Dan Fee is—was—a legend. An icon." Club secretary Thomas spoke with emotion on the cusp of a cultish passion. He had a deep voice that didn't jive with his slight, wispy appearance. "We can't trust his legacy to people like you."

"What do you mean, *people like us*?" Mia didn't bother to contain her anger at being judged by a fanboy who clearly considered bathing optional.

"Civilians," he said in a tone that couldn't have been more dismissive.

"Thomas, be nice. Please." Club secretary Hannah wrung her hands as she put this to him with a plaintive edge. Mia wondered why she was so nervous.

He looked at her with dismay. "You want to turn over what's basically a Dan Fee treasure chest of memorabilia to outsiders? Seriously? What is *wrong* with you? Everything in that house needs to be protected. And immortalized. The murals alone are priceless."

Hannah opened her mouth to respond, then changed her mind and retreated.

Circus Mann weighed in magnanimously. "Bottom line, we're not dropping the landmark application, but we will consider letting you help us catalog the inventory of our hero's home."

"A generous offer on our part, pretty lady." The crumbs encircling Eddie's mouth and cascading down the front of his too-tight T-shirt canceled out his attempt to flirt.

Mia pressed her lips together. She sucked in a breath through her nose, then released it through her mouth. "Philip, who owns the title to Mr. Fee's house right now?"

The lawyer gestured to Elisabetta. "Your grandmother."

Mia leaned back in her chair. She crossed one leg over the other. "Then I think that as long as we hold title to the house, our answer to letting you get anywhere near it is, oh *hell* no."

The interlopers gave up trying to present a professional front. They dissolved into alternating between yelling at Mia and arguing with one another. Elisabetta stood up. She thrust an arm in the air and pointed to the door. "Get out!" she bellowed. "*Adesso!* Now!" She grabbed the plate of cookies from Thomas's lap. "And no cookies for you! *Va!* Go!"

The board members hurried out the door. Mia slammed it behind them. She strode back to the living room. "No way are those twerps gonna turn my future home into some fanboy's wet dream. If Dan Fee said he wrote a will, he wrote a will. It has to be somewhere in that house. When Shane stops lying to me about why he's too injured to function, we're gonna search the place from attic to basement until we find it."

"While you're doing that, I'll stall them on the legal end," Philip said.

Mia raised a fist in the air. "All right! Teamwork."

"How ya wanna be paid?" Elisabetta held up a platter of assorted sweets. "Cash or cookies?"

"Oh, cookies, always," Philip said, swiping a hazelnut cookie from the platter.

Mia's cell rang. She picked up her phone from a side table and answered the call, carrying on a brief conversation while Elisabetta and Philip packed up a to-go box for him to take home to Finn and their kids. Mia ended the call and rubbed her eyes. "Oh boy."

Her grandmother stopped what she was doing. "Uh-oh."

Philip eyed them both. "An *oh boy* and an *uh-oh.* Yikes. What's going on?"

"That was Pete Dianopolis," Mia said. "He needs me to come down to the station. They established a time of death for Adam. And bad news for me—they watched the security footage from our backyard."

* * *

Philip accompanied Mia to the precinct, where he sat in on her interview with Pete, held in one of the building's drab interrogation rooms. "Thanks," the detective said, taking the box of cookies she offered him. "I'll share them with the other guys so they're not classified as a bribe."

"I would never," Mia said, feigning horror.

"Sure you would." Pete checked his notepad. "To bring you up to speed, we've officially classified Adam Grosso's passing as a homicide. The vic's time of death lines up with the two hours between when your security camera shows you exiting your garage and returning to it. The footage also shows you chasing the vic around your backyard with a baseball bat. We confirmed the incident with the next-door neighbor, who can be heard on the footage yelling at you to shut up."

"Does the footage also show Adam scooting away on a scooter?"

"It does. But what I'd like to know is where you were during those missing two hours after he scooted away."

Mia glanced at Philip. He gave a slight nod. She turned back to Pete. "I was driving around looking for Adam."

"Got any proof of that?"

Mia bit her lip. She knew if she told Pete about calling Shane, the police could verify her location through tracking the call to a cell tower. But she feared the real story behind his injured hand involved a dustup with Adam. Revealing the phone call risked raising his rank on the list of suspects. "Nope. Sorry." She could tell from Pete's expression he didn't believe her. "Are you gonna arrest me?"

Philip tensed. "Mia—"

"I'm not gonna do anything right now." Pete stroked his jowls. He looked miserable. "Cammie told me if I so much as thought about arresting you, she would never speak to me again but continue to spend my money at an alarming rate. Which she's already doing, but the thought of the spigot getting turned up . . ." He shuddered. "But I got a job to do. So I need a detailed itinerary of exactly where you were during those two hours. A map would be helpful. We'll check security cameras along the route to verify. CSI will also impound your car for a thorough examination, but they'll get it back to you fast as possible. If you did hit your hubby, there will be evidence on the vehicle, even if it's microscopic."

Pete rose.

"That's it?" Mia asked. "We're done?"

He gave a nod, and she released a sigh of relief. "Don't get too comfortable," he warned. "I got plenty more questions coming your way."

They left the interrogation room for the equally drab lobby. Philip addressed Pete in his most lawyerly voice. "If you need to speak to Ms. Carina again, please go through me."

Pete gave a mock salute. "Yessir, Lawyer, sir." He dropped his hand.

"Thanks, Pete, for going easy on me," Mia said, trying for a hint of a humorous attitude to break the tension. "If I remember anything else, I'll—" She didn't get to finish the sentence. Suddenly

Shane burst into the lobby. "Shane? What are you doing here?"

Shane thrust out his wrists to a bewildered Pete. "My name is Shane Pacino Gambrazzo. I want to turn myself in as a suspect in Adam Grosso's murder."

CHAPTER 12

"**P**ut your hands down, bud." Pete motioned to Shane. "But let's take this convo private."

He motioned for Shane to follow him. "I'm coming," Mia said. Thrown by Shane's dramatic entrance, she vowed to prevent him from doing anything stupid that might incriminate him in a murder he didn't commit.

Philip also insisted on being present for the interview, so they all trooped back to the room where Pete had interviewed Mia, pulling in an extra chair from the lobby.

Pete positioned himself behind the room's utilitarian metal table. "So," he said to Shane. "Give me the 411 on what's going on here. It's not every day—in fact, it's not at all—that someone volunteers themselves as a suspect."

Shane faced Mia. He looked stricken, which did nothing to affect his almost otherworldly handsomeness. "Mia, I lied to you about how I got injured."

"File that under *duh,*" she said, glaring at him.

"The night Adam confronted you, when you called and told me to go look for him, I did find the *stronzo*. I told him to get out of our lives, he refused, and we got into an argument. I grabbed him, but he got free. He hopped on his scooter and scooted off. There was another scooter someone left on the road, so I got it to work and tried following him, but those things are way harder to ride than they look. I fell and banged myself up."

"That explains your hand and I guess some of Adam's bruising. Wait a minute," Mia said. "Where was Donny Junior? He was supposed to be with you."

"A hot girl came into Singles and he got distracted."

Mia, ticked off at the junior Boldano, let a few invectives fly. Trying to get the conversation back on track, Pete said, "So instead of scooting, you ran after him, caught up, and killed him." He sounded hopeful.

"Don't answer that!" Philip was so eager to participate in the conversation, he yelled this, almost leaping out of his seat.

"I'm happy to answer the question, because the answer is no," Shane said, dashing Pete's dream of eliciting a confession and a quick conclusion to the case. Shane graced Mia with a soulful glance, melting her resolve to be angry at him for lying. "I would never risk the amazing life I plan on building with this spectacular woman. But if I'm a suspect, she can't be."

Pete's partner, Ryan, opened the door and stuck in his head. "Hey, Pete—"

Pete waved a dismissive hand at him. "Not now, Hinkle." He burned a look at Mia and Shane. "You two grew up around criminals. You know how this works. It's possible to have more than one suspect. A lot more. A million of 'em."

Ryan cleared his throat. "About that . . ."

He gestured to the lobby with his head. Irked, Pete gave the table a pound but got up and headed out of the room, the others in lockstep behind him. Their collective jaws dropped at the sight that greeted them.

Mia's friends and family packed the space. Elisabetta, Ravello, Guadalupe, Evans . . . even Lin, Ravello's former prosecutor fiancée. There was a hubbub as all present declared to overwhelmed officers that each and every one of them was a suspect in Adam's murder since they didn't have alibis for the time of death.

"The ETD isn't public knowledge," Pete said, taking in the chaotic scene. "How do they know?"

Cammie stepped out of the crowd and wiggled her fingers at her ex in a coy wave, her frosted pink nail polish catching the light. "Hi, sweetie. That info wasn't supposed to be shared? Oops."

"I gotta stop letting you seduce me into opening my fat trap," Pete muttered.

Everyone began talking again. Mia put two fingers in her mouth and released one of her signature earsplitting whistles. The space quieted. "I love you all and I'm so touched. But you don't have to do this."

"I disagree," Lin said. "All of us wanted Adam out of your life. None of us have alibis for the time of his murder. By making ourselves available for interviews, we're saving the detectives the time it would take to track us down."

"Si. Well put." Elisabetta gave Lin an approving

pat on the arm. "I don't like her soup, but I like her."

"You two take off," Ravello said, indicating Mia and Shane. "But the rest of us ain't goin' nowhere until we get interviewed."

Mia took a step toward her father, then stopped. "Can I hug them?" she asked Pete.

The detective shrugged. "Sure. Nobody's under arrest." He narrowed his eyes. "Yet."

"Make it a double," Mia told the Singles bartender. Badly in need of a drink, she and Shane had traded the police station for the local hangout. Mia also chose the location in the hopes Donny Junior was working and she could light into him about shirking her request to keep an eye on Shane during the late-night hunt for Adam.

The bartender delivered Mia's scotch and she thanked him. She took a sip, welcoming the burn as it went down. She closed her eyes and let the drink take the edge off her catastrophe of a day.

"Thanks." Shane accepted his own drink from the bartender, a bourbon on the rocks. "So. We got two definite suspects. The missing Tulio and the jilted fiancée, Annarita."

Mia, who had filled him in on her frightening encounter with Annarita, nodded. She put an elbow on the bar and examined the restaurant. It hadn't changed since the night she met Adam. The same dark wood tables, chairs, and paneling; the same dim lighting; the same strong drinks. Mia suspected all of this was done in a concerted effort to mask the flaws of potential hookups.

Her eyes landed on an empty table in a far-back

corner. She tapped Shane's leg and pointed to the table. "That's where I was sitting the night Adam hit on me. I wanted to track down my friends who I was here with that night, but I didn't have time today. I was too busy trying to save our future home and not get arrested."

Mia couldn't help feeling a tinge of satisfaction at the guilty expression on Shane's face. "I'm really sorry I wasn't there to help you handle those Circus Feek freaks. That won't happen again." Shane studied the table in the corner. "I got a thought. Before you talk to your friends, you should go over the night you met Grosso and see if you remember anything about it that might help ID his killer, if it's someone from around here."

He took Mia's hand and walked her to the table. "I'll tell you one thing," she said. "This floor's as sticky now as it was then. I don't wanna know what I'm stepping in." They sat down and Mia closed her eyes. "I was sitting here, facing the bar. I was with my friends Ruth and Rose, Ruth's boyfriend, Mark, and both Boldanos—Jamie and Donny. We were talking and laughing, and then our waitress delivered a magnum of Dom Pérignon to me."

"Good choice to make an impression." Shane's duties at Belle View included beverage management, so he knew what he was talking about.

"She pointed Adam out and I gave him a nod. He was cute—no you, of course, but who is?—but I didn't want to come across as too available. He took it as a sign I was interested, though, and walked over with Tulio. They took seats and made themselves comfortable." Mia scrunched her eyes in an effort to concentrate. "I remember that Rose flirted with Adam and Ruth gave Mark a hard time about never doing grand gestures like the Dom Pérignon delivery, which ticked off Mark. Adam tried to support Mark. He said he'd never done anything like that before." Mia opened her eyes. "Which I learned way too late was a lie. Dom delivery was his go-to move, according to a couple of friends of mine in Miami, who he hit on when we were married. Anyway, Adam trying to help only ticked off Mark more, and he left. Ruth went after him, so they were gone."

"I can see how that—and pretty much everything that SOB did—would make you want to take a fist to him, but it doesn't seem to qualify as a motive for murder six or seven years later. Do you remember anything else from that night?"

Mia closed her eyes again. "I was drinking mojitos and didn't want to mix the grain and the grape, so I passed on champagne. Rose didn't. I remember she joked she'd drink all of my champagne on top of hers. She flirted with him like crazy, but he didn't bite. She got ticked off, too, so she left. I think Tulio thought he might get lucky if he gave her some sympathy, so he went with her." Mia's eyes popped open. "After that, it was just me and Adam. And an epic disaster in the making."

Shane darkened. "Whoever took that guy out saved a lotta people the trouble." He glanced at the bar and saw the bartender trying to get his attention. "I forgot my credit card. Be right back."

He left for the bar, missing Donny Junior's entrance from outside. Mia crooked an index finger to beckon him over. "Uh-oh," he said. "I don't like that look. It's the one my mother gets when I done something wrong."

Mia glared at him. "I'm mad at you. You were

supposed to keep an eye on Shane, but you ran off with some girl instead, and now he's probably the number one suspect in Adam's murder."

"I had a good reason," Donny Junior said, defending himself.

Mia released a dismissive snort. "Good luck getting me to think a date with a Singles chick is a good reason."

Donny shared a conspiratorial grin. "Believe me, you're gonna be glad I did what I did."

A strawberry blonde clad in skinny jeans and a snug black tank top came out of the ladies' room. She headed for Donny, then came to a dead stop. "Mia? Mia Carina, is that you?"

Stunned, Mia rose from the chair. "Ruth?"

Ruth Behling responded with a shriek. She threw her arms around Mia.

"Told ya," Donny Junior said, unable to contain a self-satisfied smirk.

CHAPTER 13

Mia returned Ruth's hug. "I've been wanting to get back in touch with you," she said. "Things have been seriously busy."

Ruth released her. "I know. I heard all about the murders at Belle View."

"I was thinking more about the workload there, but yeah, that, too."

Donny put an arm around each woman. "Long time no see for all of us, huh? Maybe since the night Mia met Adam, may he rest in peace. I saw Ruth leaving the other night and I had to chase her down so we could all reconnect."

Mia got the message Donny was sending: He'd traded babysitting Shane for making sure Ruth didn't slip away. She mouthed a thank-you to him. He preened. "I was broken up when I heard this beauty was taken," he said with a nod to Ruth. "But in the spirit of old friends, I comped her and the future Mr. Ruth to dinner."

Mia raised a brow, impressed at Donny's machinations.

Ruth glanced around. She appeared uncomfortable. "Um, are you free for a bit?" She spoke sotto voce. "I'd kind of like to talk to you in private."

"Sure." Behind Ruth's back, Mia waved off Shane, who was coming her way with another round of drinks. He did a one-eighty and returned to the bar. "Donny, thanks so much for this. Ruth and I are gonna catch up a bit. I owe you. *Big-time.*"

"No problem. I'll make myself scarce." He winked at Mia and went to join Shane at the bar.

"This table's empty." Mia took a seat, as did Ruth. "It's where we were all sitting the night I met Adam." She released a theatrical sigh. "Brings back memories."

"Yeah." Ruth's discomfit increased. She tucked a loose strand of curly hair behind her ear. Like Mia and her other friends in their early thirties, Ruth had matured into her looks. She'd always had a delicate build, but now all baby fat was gone, freckles had faded, and there were hints of fine lines on her translucent skin. "I owe you such a huge, huge apology." She stared down at the table.

Oh, this is gonna be interesting. She can't even make eye contact with me. Mia didn't respond. Through the murder investigations she'd been thrust into, she'd learned silence prompted people to fill the void.

As if on cue, Ruth took a deep breath, then began talking. "Do you remember when Mark and I visited you and Adam in Florida? Adam insisted we go to that medieval restaurant, Joust for Fun, and you and Mark got food poisoning from undercooked turkey legs?"

"Yeah," Mia said, queasy at the mere memory. "I

don't think I've ever been sicker. I almost ended up at the hospital."

"Right. Well . . . Because you guys were sick, it was just Adam and me. And . . . we had a fling."

"Did you, now?" Mia responded with asperity, more annoyed than angry. The one thing she wasn't was surprised. Adam sleeping with another woman while his wife lay on what could be her deathbed seemed par for the course with him.

Ruth gave an unhappy nod. "It's what broke up my relationship with Mark. It made me realize that if I was attracted to someone else, I wasn't ready to settle down."

"How did Mark take that?"

"Not well," Ruth said with a grimace.

"No surprise there." Mia kept her tone casual but inwardly sparked at the possibility of a new suspect. Her memory of Mark pegged him as a guy with a chauvinistic streak who would not take well to his girlfriend cheating on him, especially if it led to her ending the relationship.

Ruth finally looked up. She brightened. "But Mark and I reconnected on social media about a year ago. It took a while but started dating again and we're engaged."

Mia raised an eyebrow at the revelation the once-spurned boyfriend was now the *Mr. Ruth* Donny referred to.

Ruth held out her hand to show off a perfectly acceptable engagement ring. Mia made the requisite admiring and congratulatory comments. "Mark will be here soon. He's coming from work."

"It'll be nice to see him again," Mia said, quickly figuring out a way to inject the topic of Adam's murder into the reunion.

Ruth looked at Mia with pleading eyes. "Are we okay?"

Mia didn't rush to respond. After all, her supposed friend had slept with her husband—and while Mia lay prostrate with food poisoning. Mia planned on milking Ruth for more details about Mark's reaction to Adam's moving in on his woman. Still, for a bit of vindication, she waited long enough to make Ruth worry about the answer to the loaded question, then said, "Sure. We're fine."

Ruth relaxed. "Phew. That's such a relief." She glanced at the restaurant's front door. "I want to check my makeup before Mark gets here. Be right back."

Mia affected a casual attitude until Ruth disappeared into the ladies' room. Then she jumped up and raced over to Shane and Donny, who had turned rock paper scissors into a drinking game. "We have a new suspect," she announced, gaining their full attention. She hopped onto a barstool. Shane and Donny leaned in to listen as she shared Ruth's confession.

"Whoa," was Donny Junior's single reaction.

Shane glowered. "I didn't think it was possible to hate Grosso more than I already do. I was wrong."

"Mark's gonna be here any minute. When we all say our hellos, we need to be sure we find a way to bring up Adam. I want to see his reaction."

Shane jumped off his barstool. "Got it."

The front door opened. A tall, good-looking guy in his mid-thirties came into the restaurant. His taut torso and biceps strained to break out of his white polo shirt, which indicated a dedication to the weight equipment at a gym. He wore his black hair slicked back and his skin was the deep brown of someone who either worked outdoors or favored a tanning bed. He scanned the room for Ruth, his glance passing over Mia without a flicker of recognition.

Determined to take advantage of a moment with him before he and Ruth went off for dinner, Mia feigned delight. "Mark? OMG, hiiii . . ." He responded with a befuddled stare. She hopped off her barstool. "It's me. Mia Carina. Ruth's friend."

A hint of recognition flickered across Mark's face. "Mia. Right. From Florida. How are you?"

"Good. Good. Well . . . except for what happened to Adam."

She affected a morose look. Shane came up behind her and put his hands on her shoulders. "It's okay, babe." He took one hand off her shoulder and extended it to Mark. Ruth's fiancé seemed slightly befuddled, but he took Shane's hand and gave it a polite shake. "May God forgive me for saying this," Shane continued, "but Grosso's death was no loss. In fact, props to whoever took him out. You know what I'm saying?"

Familiar with guilty tells from her own criminally inclined family, Mia watched Mark for signs that might hint at his culpability in Adam's murder. She picked up a slight flush under his dark skin. "I only knew the guy from the one visit to Miami. Hey, there's Ruth. We better get a table. I came straight from work and I'm starving."

"Where do you work?"

"All over. I'm a contractor. Nice to see you again."

He made a quick escape to his fiancée. "Congratulations on your engagement, by the way," Mia said as he passed by. "Make sure to check out Belle View Banquet Manor for your wedding." She turned around to see Shane staring at her with utter adoration. "What's that look about?"

"I love how you shill for Belle View even in the middle of a murder investigation." He bent down and whispered in her ear, "It makes me hot."

Mia gave him her sexiest smile. "We'll have to do something about that, won't we?" She did a one-eighty to all business, much to Shane's disappointment. "But first, we have a murder to solve."

CHAPTER 14

Mia, Shane, and Donny Junior spent the hours until closing exchanging theories implicating both Mark and Ruth. "Maybe Mark ran into Adam here in Queens," Mia said. "He was worried he'd break up his relationship with Ruth again, they got into it, and Mark killed him."

The others agreed this was a good theory. Then Donny posited another. "Maybe Ruth, not Mark, ran into Grosso. She was afraid he'd brag about their hookup to Mark and Mark would dump her, so *she* killed him."

"Another good theory," Shane said. "Or . . . maybe seeing what a threat he might be in general, Ruth and Mark *both* killed him. She hit Grosso with a car, he dragged the body into the alley."

"Nice," Donny Junior said, impressed. "Nothing bonds a couple like going in on a murder together." He saw the appalled expressions on Shane and Mia's faces. "I'm guessing!"

Mia took a minute to tap out an e-mail on her

phone. "I put all our ideas in an e-mail to Pete. He'll see them first thing in the morning." She rubbed a kink in her neck and yawned. "It's late and I still have to check out linen colors Cammie e-mailed me for our wedding."

"*Ticktock* on that," Donny said, tapping his watch. "Your wedding's coming up."

"I know. That's why figuring out who killed Adam is job one. I don't want me or Shane phoning in our vows from a jail cell."

"Won't happen," Donny said. "You two crazy kids are gonna walk down the aisle if I have to confess to the murder myself. Which, just to be clear, I have no intention of doing," he hastily added.

"We figured as much," Shane said, laughing.

Shane walked Mia to her car, where their steamy goodbye made her regret passing on a chance to take advantage of their mutual ardor. Instead, she headed home, where she analyzed the color samples sent by Cammie. She found the search uninspiring until she landed on the last option. "Tossed this one in for fun," Cammie wrote. "If you're up for a bold choice."

Mia admired the bright purple tablecloth. She scrolled to the next picture, where the zingy color peeked out from beneath a shiny gold overlay. Mia imagined an arrangement featuring her favorite flowers of lilacs, purple irises, and tiger lilies gracing the table. She got a pang recalling the bouquet Adam had tried wooing her with, then banished the image. *No! Mia, you are not going to ruin this for yourself.* She imagined the Bay Ballroom bursting with the warm, bright colors she loved. In other hands, the purple and gold theme might skew tacky. Not in Mia's. She knew how to make it fun and even hip. She e-mailed Cammie her choice and climbed into bed, happy to be thinking about anything besides murder. For a change, she was excited about her wedding instead of living in fear it might never happen.

Arguing woke Mia from her deep sleep the next morning. She threw on a bathrobe and hurried downstairs to see what was causing the ruckus. She found her mother and grandmother facing off, each holding a wedding gown. "I'm her grand-mother, she's gonna wear mine!" Elisabetta yelled at Gia. She shoved her gown in Gia's face. An over-the-top, princess-style satin gown from the early 1960s, the dress was laden with lace, sequins, and beads, and so heavy Elisabetta struggled to hold it up with both hands.

Gia shook her dress at Elisabetta. Gia's wedding gown, a late 1980s/early 1990s number, was gaud-ier than Elisabetta's, if such a thing were possible. It was mermaid style, made of ruched, bright white satin. So much beading and sequins decorated the neckline and plunging V-neck that Posi joked his mother looked like she was wearing a Rolls-Royce car grill in her wedding photos. "I'm her mother and she's gonna wear *my* dress!" Gia yelled at her former mother-in-law.

Mia surveyed the dresses, neither of which she found remotely appealing. "This is an easy prob-lem to solve. I can't wear either dress. I won't fit into them."

"You can take mine out," Elisabetta said.

"You can take mine in," Gia countered. "I was four months along with you when I wore this, so I had to go up a size."

"Or I could just sew them together and make one dress," Mia joked, heading back to her apartment.

"Yes!" Elisabetta said, hostility replaced by enthusiasm. "*Genio.*"

"It *is* genius," Gia said, equally enthused by the idea.

Horrified, Mia halted her departure. "NO. Noooo! I was kidding."

The other women ignored her. "I'll make an appointment with Lucille Giusti, the dressmaker down the street," Elisabetta said to Gia. "She can figure out how to make these into . . . what do the kids say? A mash-up."

"I know her work," Gia said. "She's wonderful. We can bring the dresses over now if she's free."

Mia waved her hands in the air in a desperate attempt to shut them down. "Stop! No Lucille, no mash-up. I'm worried about my house, which won't be my house if we don't find Dan Fee's will. I'm going to shower, then we're going across the street to start the search. So, put away the wedding dresses and put on clothes you don't mind doing some work in. I'll meet you there."

The women reluctantly obeyed, draping their gowns over the room's overstuffed chairs. Mia returned to her apartment, where she readied for the deep dive into Dan Fee's belongings. She showered and put on a faded T-shirt and her oldest jeans. She fed Doorstop and Pizzazz, then left for the comic artist's former home.

A large coterie of Circus Feeks loitered on the

sidewalk. Mia recognized a few of the fan club board members among them. "Normal person coming through," she said, cutting a path through the group. She opened the gate to the front yard.

"You're making a big mistake not taking this seriously," Thomas, the club treasurer, said.

Mia bristled at the patronizing tone of his voice. "Maybe you're the ones making a mistake by taking this too seriously."

"Ouch." Eddie, the club vice president, chuckled. "Ya burnt, T-bone. Nice one, Mia."

Mia didn't hear Thomas's reaction, but she couldn't miss the flirtatious smile from Eddie. Neither did Raina, evidenced by the daggers the fan club president shot at her from Dan Fee's tiny front yard, where she seemed to be engaged in some activity with Hannah. *The Circus Feek board is a horny viper's nest,* Mia thought. She stepped through the gate onto the front walkway of the house. "Reminder that despite your application, my grandmother owns this house," she said to the two girls. "So you're on private property."

"Some of the bouquets and notes wound up here and it's messy," Raina said. "That's disrespectful to Dan."

Hannah held up a black garbage bag. "We thought we'd clean up."

"Oh." Mia had to admit the area, not maintained by the late recluse in the first place, did resemble more of a junkyard than a front yard. "All right. You have my permission. If you want to do any weeding, I'm okay with that, too. Out of respect for Mr. Fee."

She scurried up the home's front steps.

"Don't throw anything out," Circus Mann called

after her. "We'll be going through your garbage to make sure."

Mia muttered a few choice curse words under her breath and entered the house.

She found her mother and grandmother sitting next to each other on a battered old sofa, having shoved aside piles of ephemera to make room for themselves. "Grab a pile," Gia said without looking up from hers.

"I don't know where to start," Mia said, despairing at the stacks of everything from magazines to bills. "I'd call one of those services that hauls away junk, but the Circus Feeks would probably throw themselves in front of it."

She removed a pile from a shabby wingback chair and sat down. A broken spring poked her in the derrière and she muttered a curse. She began going through a pile. After tossing aside magazines decades old, she discovered a binder. She flipped it open to reveal an intricate sketch. Mia recognized it. She held up the binder to the mural across from her, then flipped through the rest of the binder. "Wow. These are the early sketches for all the murals. They might actually be worth a lot of money."

"I'm way ahead of you." Gia held up a small clay figure of Circusman. "He also made models of his characters. A lot of them, apparently." She picked up her phone with her free hand. "I checked an auction website and bidding is up to a couple of hundred dollars for one like this."

"Let me see." Mia took her mother's phone, which was open to the website. The post showed several photos of a clay figure similar to the one Gia held. Mia noted the seller's handle:

@Rainaonme. "Huh. It wouldn't be a wild guess to think the seller is Raina, the fan club president." She handed the phone back to her mother. "My apologies to the Circus Feeks. They're right. We definitely need to take the stuff here more seriously. When we do find his will—and my lips to God's ears, we will—we don't want to get in trouble for damaging or destroying anything that might be valuable."

Elisabetta dumped a bunch of bills rubber-banded together in the box she'd designated for trash. "No one needs his old gas bills."

Gia's fingers flew across her phone keyboard. "Wrong. @Circusmann has one for sale right now and the bidding is up to fifty dollars."

Mia furrowed her brow. "I wonder how the board got access to the stuff they're selling?"

"However they got it before, they ain't gonna get it no more," Elisabetta said. "I got a call into my security guy. He's booked up on account of Adam's murder, but as soon as he's free, we're gonna wire up this place."

"Good idea, Nonna." Mia extracted a floppy Circusman doll from the trash box. Its red cape was torn, and the *C* on its chest hung by a thread, as did one of the doll's googly eyes. Sawdust wafted out of a rip in the middle of big-top tent appliqué under the *C* and Mia coughed. "We're saving this, too."

"Really?" Gia looked doubtful. "That thing is like what your pediatrician called *old stuffed animals*: dust-mite condominiums."

"It was stuffed under a pile of rags," Elisabetta said. "I only found it 'cause I went looking for something to wipe off the couch."

Mia showed her mother the doll's posterior. "Dan Fee stitched his name on the back of this. I can't imagine what that's worth to a Feek."

Mia's cell rang. She laid the doll down on what she assumed was the coffee table—it was hard to tell under the mountains of stuff—and answered the call. Her father's face popped up on the screen. The expression on his face concerned her. "Dad, hi. What's up? You don't look happy. Everything okay at work?"

"I'm not at work." Ravello flipped the image on his phone. Mia's heart sank when she saw his location. "I'm at the Triborough Correctional Facility. Your brother is back in jail."

CHAPTER 15

Triborough Correctional Facility guard Henry Marcus greeted Mia and Ravello like the friends they'd become, thanks to the combined stints of Mia's father and brother at the facility. "Make yourselves comfortable," he said after showing off pictures of his latest infant grandson, a chocolaty butterball of adorableness. "They'll bring Posi out in a minute. Congratulations on your engagement, Mia. Mrs. Marcus and I are looking forward to the wedding."

"So glad you can make it." Mia said this with excessive enthusiasm to cover forgetting that Henry was on her father's guest list. It made sense. The family had spent more time with him over the years than they'd spent with many of their own relatives.

The heavy metal door separating the visiting room from the cells opened and a guard escorted Posi into the room. He deposited him opposite Ravello and Mia, then stepped back to watch over the scofflaw.

Ravello sighed and shook his head. "Back in prison grays. Not a good look for you, son."

"Beats orange. I'm a Winter, so cool colors suit me better than warm."

Coming from a brother who proudly acknowledged his vanity, Mia knew Posi wasn't making a joke to lighten the mood. This didn't stop her from responding with a sarcastic, "I'll remember that for future gifts." She rested an elbow on the back of her chair. "So, what brings you—and us—here this time?"

Posi stroked his well-formed chin. "It involves a lady."

"I thought women weren't allowed at the halfway house," Ravello said, perplexed.

"They're not. I found a work-around."

"Of course you did," Mia said, her tone dry.

"One of the house residents was a hacker finishing a sentence for accessing other people's funds from various banks. A lovely lady who will heretofore only be known as *lovely lady* I'd been in contact with before tracked me down—"

"*Heretofore.*" Mia rolled her eyes. "Someone's spent way too much time with lawyers."

"I paid my computer friend to override the house security system," Posi continued, ignoring his sister, "so the lovely lady and I could enjoy each other's company. After curfew, I snuck out and we met up in the backyard. After we did the . . . enjoying . . . I snuck back in. Everyone was asleep. I don't know how I got busted."

"Somebody got to the hacker," Mia and Ravello said simultaneously.

"I guess so." Posi sounded hurt. "I thought he

was a friend. That's five hundred bucks I'll never get back."

Henry cleared his throat, indicating the end of their visit since they'd arrived at the tail end of midday visiting hours. Mia and Ravello stood up. "I'll get Philip on your case," Ravello said. "But I don't think you got a prayer of going back to the halfway house. The best we can hope for is that they don't extend your sentence."

"Probably better I don't go back. It'd be very hard not to clock my hacker former friend. And hey, being here means more time with my true friend, Henry."

Posi flashed his pearly whites at the guard, who chuckled. "Not gonna lie, Carina. The place is a lot duller when you're gone."

The family said their goodbyes. "For a career criminal, Posi is so naïve," Mia said to her father as the facility's beat-up elevator rattled its way down to the ground floor. "If it wasn't so aggravating, it'd be touching."

"I'm gonna give Donny Senior a call. See if he has any intel on who could've set Posi up." Ravello threaded his fingers together and cracked his knuckles. Mia knew the gesture didn't bode well for whoever got her brother in trouble.

On the way out of the facility, the Carinas got their second unpleasant surprise of the day. Heading down the front stairs, they almost collided with Detectives Pete and Ryan, who were heading up the steps to enter the facility. "Well, will you look at this." Pete pointed to himself and Ryan, then to Ravello and Mia. "Talk about a coinkydink."

"Please don't tell me you're here to talk to Posi," Mia said, sure that was exactly why they were there.

"You're welcome on me pushing CSI to get your car back to you pronto," Pete said with asperity. "And yeah, we may have a break in the case of your late husband's murder, but you won't like it. Your brother's time out during his curfew break coincides with Grosso's murder. And who would have better motivation to right a wronged sister than her loving brother? Except for her loving father and loving fiancé and loving mother and . . . there are so many suspects in this case I'm gonna steer clear of all of you before I become one, too."

The detectives passed Mia and Ravello and disappeared into the correctional facility. Mia waited until the door shut behind them, then turned to her father. "You get in touch with Philip. After Pete and Ryan leave, I'm gonna sneak back in and strangle Posi."

Ravello gave a mirthless laugh. "I'm gonna go by Philip's instead of call. You head over to Belle View. Nothing else you can do here."

"I guess not."

Mia and Ravello parted ways, heading to their separate destinations. Mia realized she'd never changed into her work clothes. She still wore the worn jeans and faded old concert T-shirt she'd put on to dig through hoarder Dan Fee's house. She got in the car and checked her schedule to see if any impromptu tours had been posted to it. Seeing none, she opted to skip going home to change. On the drive to Belle View, she thought about Posi. While she was angry with her brother, she was also sad for him. Posi seemed incapable of walking a straight path. She doubted Pete would be able to make a murder rap stick, even if he found a way to bring charges. But she feared Posi might be one of those low-level hoods who spent their lives bouncing in and out of prison.

She parked at the marina lot. Due to an early fall heat wave, the air was hot and sticky with the humidity of an incoming storm and even though it was a short walk from her car to the catering hall, Mia's T-shirt was sticking to her by the time she stepped into the lobby. She found Cammie waiting for her.

"She's here," Cammie called toward the kitchen.

Guadalupe appeared. The giantess of a woman lumbered toward them. She took one of Mia's arms and Cammie took the other. "What are you doing?" Mia resisted as they led her out of the building. "What's going on?"

"Somebody's getting married extremely soon," Cammie said, her grip on Mia's arm firm. "And that somebody's bridesmaids need their dresses, so we're going shopping for them."

"I ain't worn a dress in twenty years." Guadalupe opened the door of her camo-painted Jeep and helped Mia climb in. "I wanna get it right."

Mia stopped protesting. She decided to embrace the break from the current stressors on her life. The three women drove into Astoria, stopping in front of a shop called Your Special Day. Guadalupe expertly maneuvered the Jeep into a rare parking spot on Ditmars Boulevard and they entered the store.

Your Special Day was a fairy tale of a shop, with antiqued, artfully distressed peach-and-white display cases and a floor of Saltillo terra cotta tiles. Gorgeous party confections in a rainbow of colors filled one side of the shop; a wide range of wedding dresses filled the other. A rose scent perfumed the air. "So much beauty," Mia murmured. "I don't know where to begin."

A smartly dressed woman in her early fifties who obviously had the hearing of a bat when it came to potential customers sidled up to her. "That's where I come in. Hello, I'm Quadria. This is my shop."

Mia and her friends introduced themselves. "My friend is getting married in about a month," Cammie said, giving Mia a small shove forward. "We're her bridesmaids. We've got a short lead time, so we'll need dresses that are pretty much to size."

"Of course." Quadria smiled at Cammie. She subtly eyed Guadalupe, who had the height and build of a basketball player, and her smile wavered slightly. "We'll start with the bride. But if you know your colors, your bridesmaids can take a look at my stock to find possible choices."

"You can wear whatever you want," Mia told her friends. "All I ask is that it not clash with the purple linens."

Cammie and Guadalupe began perusing the racks of bridesmaids' gowns. Quadria studied Mia from head to toe. "Lovely figure. Average height, and I mean that in a good way. Less need to alter dress length. Let me pull a few possibilities for you."

Quadria did an expert run at a rack of wedding gowns. She stopped at one. "This."

She extracted the dress and held it up to Mia. The dress was simple yet breathtaking: white chiffon offering a snug fit through the hips and then softly flaring out, ending with a small train. A hint of glitter woven into the fabric added interest to the cowl neck that plunged slightly in the front and much deeper in the back. It was everything Mia ever dreamed of when she allowed herself to dream of marrying Shane.

An emotional Cammie cried out, "It's you!"

Mia fingered the soft, filmy material. "It kind of is."

"No kind of," Guadalupe said. "It's you."

"Why don't you try it on?" Quadria handed her the gown.

Mia hesitated. "My mother and grandmother are taking their gowns to Lucille Giusti to see if she can turn them into one dress for me."

"You know there's no way in Hades that will end well. Try on the dress." Cammie pushed her toward the dressing room. She began chanting, "Try it on. Try it on. Try it on." Guadalupe joined the chant.

"Fine," Mia said. "If it'll shut you two up, I'll try it on."

She carried the dress into the capacious fitting room, accepting Quadria's offer of assistance. The shop owner helped her into the dress. She stepped back to admire Mia. "I am so good at my job," she said with a smug smile.

Mia checked out her reflection in the three-way mirror. She swallowed tears of emotion. "It's perfect."

"I'm sure your friends will agree."

Quadria opened the dressing room door and Mia stepped out to gasps from Cammie and Guadalupe.

"Oh. Ooooh." Cammie bit her lip and wrung her hands. "You're *gorgeous.*"

Guadalupe paid Mia an even higher compliment. "That dress is so pretty, it makes me feel almost girly."

"I'll take it," Mia said to Quadria. Her friends clapped with delight. She held up a warning hand. "But . . . I don't want my mom and grandmother to know. I'm hiding it at Belle View. I'm gonna go with the theory it's better to beg forgiveness than ask permission. I'll wear it at my wedding and apologize to them after."

The others agreed to keep the purchase a secret. The shop door opened, and Teri Fuoco strode into the store. "Hope I'm not too late for bridesmaids shopping. Nice dress, Mia."

"Thank you. And you're not too late because you weren't supposed to be here in the first place. You're fired, remember?"

Teri flashed a Cheshire cat grin. "I'll be back in the mix after I share my news with you. You know how you wanted to track down the people you were with at Mingles/Singles the night you met Adam? I tracked down Rose Nunzio. And she has a secret that'll blow you away."

CHAPTER 16

Mia sat across from Rose Nunzio in the compact living room of her apartment. A box air conditioner positioned in one of the street-facing windows hummed. Next to Rose, a little boy of about four squirmed. A little boy with eyes the same shade of burnt umber as the late Adam Grosso.

"Here you go, sweetie." Mia handed Corey, the little boy, a stuffed dinosaur. Teri had provided her with a full dossier on Rose's son as well as Rose herself. Mia had rewarded the reporter in a big way. She not only reinstated her as a bridesmaid, Mia also picked up the cost of the ridiculously overpriced gown Teri picked out. Not wanting to show favoritism, Mia also insisted on paying for Cammie and Guadalupe's gowns, in addition to her beloved wedding dress. The day had proved expensive. But it was worth every penny to learn Adam had fathered a child with someone Mia once considered a friend.

Rose gave her son, who was absorbed with studying his new toy, a gentle nudge. "What do you say, baby?"

"Thank you." Corey gave Mia a sweet smile. Her heart clutched. It brought back a memory of the appeal that Adam occasionally displayed.

Rose ruffled her son's hair. "Go play with it in your room, 'kay?"

"'Kay."

Corey jumped off the couch and ran down the hallway. Rose watched to make sure he was out of earshot, then faced Mia. Her waist was thicker than Mia remembered, and her copper hair duller. She'd aged more than Ruth in the intervening years between the infamous Singles dinner and now. But Mia assumed parenthood did that to a person. Maybe more so when conception and the father's identity were closely held secrets.

Rose picked at a loose thread on the sofa. Like Ruth, she couldn't look Mia in the eye. One friend had a fling with Adam and one had been impregnated by him. And those were just the only two women Mia knew of. *Note to self, Messina Carina: Be way more careful when choosing friends.* She fixed a stare at Rose, who finally glanced up, her expression apprehensive. "I guess you wanna know what happened."

"Both yes and no. But let's go with yes."

Rose fingered the thread again. "You were home for Christmas. I think it was about two years after you got married. You and your grandma made holiday cookie platters for your friends and had Adam deliver them. When he came by me, he got here right after my boyfriend, Tulio, broke up with me—"

Mia stopped her. "Tulio? As in Tulio Longella?"

Rose gave a nod. "We met the night you and

Adam did and stayed in touch over social media for a while. We'd been dating about six months when Tulio decided I wasn't *the one.* I thought he was, so I was in a bad place when Adam showed up."

Mia pursed her lips. "With cookies and comfort."

"Yeah. Turns out I needed both. I'm so, so sorry, Mia."

"I've been hearing that a lot lately. Too much. So, Adam *comforted you,* and the end result was little Corey." Rose gave a wan nod. "Did Adam know?"

Rose gave another nod, this one angry. "He ghosted me once I let him know I was pregnant. The only way I could reach him was through you and I was too good a friend to do that."

"Wow, do we have different definitions of being a good friend. But go on."

"I hadn't seen him since . . . that night. Then all of a sudden a few weeks ago, he showed up at my door." Rose's voice rose, signaling outrage. She remembered her son and lowered it. "He gave me two choices: set up a custody arrangement or pay him not to pursue one. He was all antsy, like he was desperate."

Mia pondered this new information. For cheapskate grifter Adam to face the possibility Rose might actually force him into a custody arrangement, along with a bill for past child support, he must have been very desperate. But why? Was that the missing link to his murder?

Corey came skipping down the hall with his new present. He held it up. "I named him," he announced proudly to the women. "He's Dino." Corey climbed onto his mother's lap. The apartment front door opened, revealing a big, broad, bruiser of a man a few years older than Mia and Rose. He wore a work jumpsuit emblazoned with the name *Diego* over a logo for *Espinoza Heating and Air Conditioning*. "Daddy!"

The little boy jumped off his mother's lap and ran into the man's arms, prompting Mia to consider a new theory. Could Rose have killed Adam to protect the secret of who Corey's father was?

The man came into the room, jostling Corey on his hip. "Hey, babe." He bent down and kissed Rose.

"Hey, hon." Rose beamed at him, then said to Mia, "This is my husband, Diego. Diego, this is Mia. An old friend."

"Mia." Diego's tone indicated it wasn't the first time he'd heard her name.

He set Corey down. The little boy took his hand. "Daddy, come see Dino eat my other dinos." He pulled Diego down the hall with him.

"He knows," Rose said, as if reading Mia's mind. "We met when Corey was about one. I was honest with Diego. He begged me to let him track down Adam, but I wouldn't. As far as I knew, you two were happily married. I didn't wanna ruin it." Mia couldn't hold back a snort at the misconception. "Diego's applying to adopt Corey," Rose continued. Tears rolled down her cheeks. She used the back of her hand to wipe them away. "He's the only father my baby's ever known. Adam showing up again was gonna ruin that. I'm sorry he was murdered, but I'd be lying if I said I was sorry he's dead."

Mia faked a sympathetic nod, but her mind was elsewhere. When she compared motives to kill Adam, it was hard to top Rose and Diego's. *Maybe you're not sorry about either his murder or his death, Rose. In fact, maybe you're responsible for them. And had help from your husband.*

Diego approached them from Corey's bedroom. "Little guy lay down on top of his new dinosaur and passed out."

"Did you take a picture?" Diego showed Rose his phone. "Awww. Sweet baby. I love pictures of him sleeping. It's the cutest thing."

She handed the phone to Mia, who couldn't help softening at the image of the toddler sound asleep atop the dinosaur plushie she'd given him. She wouldn't forget Rose had slept with her husband—and had a child by him—but she would try to find it in her heart to forgive.

Mia stood up. "I better get going. Thanks for your time, Rose."

"Sure. Ruth said she was gonna check out Belle View for hers and Mark's wedding. Maybe the three of us can have lunch sometime."

"Sounds good," Mia said, knowing it would never happen—unless it offered a chance to seal the deal booking Ruth's wedding.

"Is your car the Civic with the Belle View Banquet Manor car wrap?" Diego asked. "I parked in front of you. If I didn't leave you enough room to get out, lemme know."

Mia said her goodbyes to Rose and Diego. She took the stairs from their third-floor apartment to the lobby and exited to the street. Once outside, she craned her neck to make sure neither Diego nor Rose were watching her from a window. Satisfied they weren't, she eyed the Espinoza HVAC van positioned in front of her car. Getting out of the parking space wouldn't be a problem. Her eyes alighted on an unexpected sight. She moved closer to the front of the van to confirm what she thought she saw: a dent in the right side of the front fender.

She affected a casual stroll to the coffee shop housed in the building next to Rose's. Once she knew she was out of Rose and Diego's eyeline, she ducked inside. She ordered a coffee, then retreated to the table farthest from the store entrance, where she placed a call to Shane.

"Hey," he said. She warmed at the sound of his deep voice, which had the sexy undertones of a late-night DJ. "I heard some shopping took place today. Cammie and Guadalupe came back here with big dress bags. I actually heard Guadalupe giggle. It was a little disturbing."

"I bet."

"Oh, they put one bag in the upstairs ladies' lounge closet and told me not to go in there on pain of death."

Mia recalled the image of her wedding dress and drifted into a momentary reverie. She forced herself to focus. "I need you to schedule an HVAC maintenance call for Belle View. But only with Espinoza Heating and Air Conditioning. And insist on a repairman named Diego."

"Okay," Shane said, puzzled.

Mia filled him in on what she'd learned from Rose. Shane reacted at Adam's behavior, adding color with a hefty dose of profanity. "Are you okay, honey? Learning your husband fathered a child with another woman . . . that's a lot."

Mia gave a mirthless laugh. "Understatement of the year. I'm not gonna lie. It was hard to hear. Rose joins Ruth on my burn list. But Adam." She shook her head. "He set the bar so low as a human being, it was subterranean. No—Middle-earthian." Mia checked her watch. "I gotta go. I want to call Pete and let him know about all this. Especially the fender dent."

"Go for it. I love you."

"I love you, too. Infinity much."

They spent a few minutes blowing each other kisses before ending the call. Mia gave a happy sigh. Whatever hell she'd let herself in for when she hooked up with Adam was offset by the wonders of her relationship with Shane.

She took a few sips of coffee, then placed a call to Pete. He picked up on the first ring. "Please don't tell me you have more suspects," he said in a weary voice.

"I have more suspects."

She gave Pete the same update she'd given Shane. When she was done, he gave a whistle of disbelief. "Wow. That Grosso was a piece of work. And that's putting it nicely."

"Shane put it not so nicely. And yes. So, what do think?"

"When it comes to suspects with this new cast of characters? My money's on the four-year-old."

"Ha."

"Seriously, we can't do anything about the dent without a warrant, and right now, we don't have anything a judge would sign off on. But we'll check out the activities of this Rose Nunzio and Diego Espinoza during the times in question and see if we can scare up some evidence. And hey . . . take care of yourself. It doesn't take my detective skills to figure out it was no fun learning about the kid."

"Thanks, Pete. I appreciate the concern."

Pete signed off. Mia contemplated how far she and the detective had come in their relationship. They'd first locked horns on a regular basis over his drive to prove the Carinas were using Belle View as a front for criminal activity. Now, between Cammie's demands for Pete to treat the family fairly and Mia proving she had her own well-developed instincts when it came to nailing killers, the detective and the mobster-adjacent event planner had developed a mutual respect for each other.

Mia took her coffee and headed for her car. She held on to the cup as she dug through her purse for her car keys. She finally found them, but they slipped from her hand and fell to the sidewalk. A passerby stooped to pick them up for her and she thanked him. He glanced at the Civic and did a double take. "If that's your ride, you're not gonna get far, keys or no keys."

"What do you mean?"

He pointed to the tire closest to the sidewalk. "Looks like someone took a knife to it."

"What?" Aghast, Mia saw the slash he was pointing to. A dire instinct took hold. She circled the car, examining each tire. Her blood pressure rose as the instinct was born out.

Someone had slashed all four of her tires.

CHAPTER 17

Pete kneeled by Mia's front left tire. Because the possibility loomed that the tire slashings were linked to the investigation into Adam's murder, CSI was working the scene. Technicians photographed the tires and took samples from them. They also canvassed the ground for evidence.

Pete stood up. His knees cracked and he groaned. "If this is fifty eight, I'm not lookin' forward to sixty."

Mia gestured to her car, which could now double as the world's largest doorstop. "My tires. Any discoveries? Theories?"

"I need to think on a couple. But see where they took a knife to the tires?" Pete pointed to the slash. It sat at the tire's bottom, only inches from the street. "It's a pretty good guess the perp ducked down and punched low to avoid any security cameras in the area. Which is only half helpful to them because it'd be hard to avoid being caught walking to or near the car. That would've taken a combat crawl on the sidewalk."

Mia steamed. Losing all her tires was expensive and inconvenient. But if the instigator assumed it would deter her from ferreting out who killed Adam, they didn't know who they were dealing with. If anything, it fired her up more. "I thought about how you can't check out the van without a warrant. While I was waiting for you, I took some pictures." She thumbed her phone's keyboard. "And . . . Send. I just forwarded some photographs. They might or might not include a picture of a dent. Which might or might not be useful in determining if there's any way the dent was made by the van colliding with a human being."

Pete got the not-so-subtle hint. "I always like looking at other people's pictures." He stared at her car and rubbed his chin. "You're sure this Diego guy had enough time from when you left to do this?"

"Yes. Although he is a big guy. I don't know how fast he can move."

"I'll get to meet the guy for myself because we need him to move the van so you can be towed."

Mia made a face. "I guess dinner is gonna be whatever's in the vending machine at Tony's Tires."

"Do me a fave and buzz Espinoza's apartment," Pete said. "I don't want to clue him on law enforcement being here. We get a better read on a suspect when he gets a load of us for the first time."

Mia scurried up the apartment steps into the building lobby. She pressed the apartment buzzer. After a brief pause, Rose answered. "Rose, it's me, Mia."

"You're still here?" She didn't sound happy about this.

"I bought a coffee next door. Can you send Diego down? I do need him to move his van."

"All right."

Mia left the lobby to wait with Pete. Moments later, Diego trudged out of the building and down the landing steps to Mia. "Sorry. I thought I left you plenty of room." He registered Pete and did a double take. "Wait. What's going on? Why are the police here? Are you okay?"

This came across as genuine concern for Mia's well-being, which she wasn't expecting. She pressed on. "I'm fine. My tires aren't."

Pete kept a watchful eye on the HVAC technician as Mia gave him a tour of her ruined tires. "What the hell? No. How? I don't . . ." Diego, upset, ran his hands through his thinning light brown hair. "I'm really sorry, Mia. I mean . . . this sucks."

Mia gave a curt nod of agreement. "Yup. Sure does."

"I, uh . . ." He ran his hands through his hair again. Mia wondered if the gesture was a reaction to the circumstances or a nervous habit. "I don't know what's happening to this city. Someone backed into me the other day and banged up my front fender. Did they leave a note? No. Fixing it is all on me. Anyway, I'll move the van. And again . . . sorry."

Diego got in the van. There were no other spots available on the block, so he pulled out of his current one and, after giving Mia a sympathetic wave, drove off to find one. "Did you hear any of that?" Mia asked Pete.

"All of it."

"What do you think?"

Pete crossed his arms in front of his chest and leaned on his back foot. "You're the amateur sleuth. Let's hear what you think."

"Fine." Mia shrugged off feeling defensive and took the challenge. "He seemed really surprised and not like he was acting. The fact his first instinct was to ask if I was okay tells me it was a genuine reaction. And that Rose got herself a pretty good guy. The *pretty good* versus *great* is because of this: I don't think he slashed my tires. But I think he has a feeling he knows who did. When he told me he was really sorry, it sounded more like an apology than sympathy." Pete's half grin turned into a full frown. "What?"

"I hate that you're good at this."

Mia glowed from Pete's reluctant compliment. She gave him a mock-patronizing pat on the back. "I'm on call for backup whenever you get stuck, Detective."

This earned her an eye roll and a non-knee-related groan. Pete hesitated. "Actually . . . there is something I could use your help with. Nothing with criminals. It's personal."

Mia dropped her hand and the joking attitude. "Oh. Sure. Happy to do whatever I can. Pete . . . are you . . ." Afraid the issue was a serious one about his health and not wanting to press, Mia trailed off.

"I'm fine," Pete said to her relief. "Although I'm pretty sure I'm gonna be looking at at least one knee replacement sooner rather than later. But what I wanted to talk to you about is . . . I'm gonna repropose to Cammie."

"That's great news." Mia said, smiling at him. "I'm happy for you."

"To be honest, I can't afford not to be married to her anymore. Her making me pay for what I did over and over again is gonna wipe me out. Enough already. It's time for me to put her feet to the fire. She's gotta either relieve herself or get off the pot."

"How romantic." Mia's tone could not have been drier.

"Anyway, I got a ring. I wanted your opinion on it."

Pete took a small jewelry box out of his pants pocket. He opened it, revealing an average-sized, round diamond on a plain gold band. Mia shook her head. "Bigger."

Pete sighed. "I was afraid of that."

A crime scene technician Mia had gotten to know from a slew of recent murders approached them. "Hey, Mia. Nice to see you again."

"Hi, Sarah. Weird greeting for a crime scene, but I guess what else are you supposed to say?"

"Haven't come up with anything better yet and I've been at this for twenty years." Sarah took off her mask and pushed back the hood on her plastic hazmat suit. "RIP re: your tires. All four of them."

"I figured as much," Mia said, unhappy but resigned. "Any thoughts on the weapon?"

"Only a guess until we impound these tires from Tony's, but I'd put money on a box cutter doing the damage."

Mia flashed on the interior of Adam and Annarita's apartment. She recalled the sea of boxes and an object glinting on top of one: a box cutter. Annarita didn't seem to have much going on at the moment besides her anger at Mia. *Has she been following me?* Mia wondered with a shiver. Adam's jilted ex took a dizzying ride up to the top of Mia's suspect list.

A tow truck rattled down the street and stopped in front of Mia's car. The driver hopped out of the truck and strode over to Mia. "This the vehicle?"

"Yes."

"We're gonna need the tires," Pete said. He motioned to Sarah. "We'll meet you at Tony's to supervise their removal and transfer."

"No problem." The driver faced Mia. "But the shop is closed for the night. Your car won't be ready until the morning."

He walked off to begin the process of loading the car onto the truck. "You need a ride home?" Pete asked Mia.

"No, thanks. It's an easy walk from here."

Mia left the others to their tasks. She walked a couple of blocks toward home, then made a split-second decision. She turned and headed in the opposite direction toward the Bay Manor Garden Apartments.

On the mile-plus walk to her destination, Mia formulated a plan. First, she'd check to see if Annarita was home. If she was, Mia would devise a way to get her out of the apartment for at least fifteen minutes. Posi had taught her how to pick a lock at the age of ten, so that wouldn't be a problem. And the apartment was small, so unless Annarita had unpacked, a quick but thorough search wouldn't be a problem either. Once Mia located the suspect box cutter, she'd place it in a baggie and deliver it to Sarah with an excuse about how she came by it. Pete would never believe her, but if the box cutter linked to her tires and put him one step closer to finding Adam's killer—the real goal of Mia's plan—the detective would get over any objections he might have.

Mia made a pitstop at a corner store to pick up disposable gloves and a box of quart-size plastic bags, then continued on her way. It was a pleasant walk. A hint of coolness in the air and a tint of color to tree leaves indicated fall was coming. The clock on Mia's autumn wedding ticked the date ever closer. She increased her pace. Five minutes later, she was at Annarita's front door.

Mia walked around the side of the building. She made sure the coast was clear, then tried taking a peek into the apartment's side window. No luck. The Venetian blinds were drawn. *Plan B*, she thought. She retreated to the front of the apartment. After doing a second check to make sure no one was around, she rang the bell and then dashed away to hide in nearby bushes. She watched and waited, but Annarita didn't appear. Mia waited a few more minutes, then went to Plan C. She sauntered over to the apartment and prepared to pick the lock. She placed her hand on the doorknob . . . and to Mia's surprise, the door swung open. *Uh-oh. This could be bad.* She took a nervous, tentative peek inside the apartment. Her eyes widened and she stepped inside.

Fortunately, no deceased body lay sprawled on the floor. If one had been there, Mia would have noticed instantly. Because the apartment was completely empty.

CHAPTER 18

Mia had no trouble locating the apartment complex manager. All she had to do was find an apartment-turned-office identified by a sign reading MANAGER. She opened the door and saw a harried-looking man alternating between checking a computer screen and thumbing through a huge stack of paperwork next to the older-model desktop computer.

Mia gave the door a tap to indicate her presence. The man glanced up. "Yes?" He made it sound like she was already wasting his time.

"I'm looking for one of your tenants. Annarita . . ." Mia, embarrassed, realized she didn't know the young woman's last name.

Luckily, it was distinctive enough a first name for the manager to know exactly who she was talking about. "You a collection agent? If you are, I'll pay you to lemme know when you find her. She skipped out in the middle of the night. Broke her lease and the security deposit check bounced. No more checks here at Bay Manor. I'm signing on to every cash app out there."

"I'm guessing you don't have any forwarding information on your tenant," Mia said, disappointed all three of her plans had failed.

The man gave a derisive snort, followed by a curt no, and returned to work. Mia closed the door and started a brisk walk home. She called Pete as she walked. "Breaking news: Adam's jilted girlfriend, Annarita, took off in the middle of the night. Cut out on her lease and left no forwarding information. I saw a box cutter in the apartment when I visited her a few days ago."

"You visited her? Why?"

Pete did not sound happy about this, and Mia realized she'd outed her amateur sleuthing. "I, uh, felt bad for her," she said, covering. "I wanted to share my condolences about Adam."

"*Righhhht.*" Pete's voice dripped with sarcasm.

"More important is the box cutter," Mia said to get the conversation back on track. "Our visit did not end well. She blames me for Adam breaking up with her. I hate when women do that—blame other women when it's the guy who's at fault. Anyway, you need to find an Annarita in her twenties in New Jersey. I'm betting she's my tire cutter. I know that's not a lot of info, but it's all I have."

"No worries. We interviewed her as a suspect in Grosso's murder, so I have her cell number, her e-mail address, her social media links, her parents' numbers, their address, her license plate, the make and model of the car she was driving . . . should I go on?"

"No," Mia said, embarrassed. "I'm good."

"But the box cutter sighting is new, so I'll have my Jersey contacts pay her a visit. I'm glad you called for another reason, though. I traded up on Cammie's second engagement ring. I'm texting you a picture." Mia's phone pinged a text. "What do you think?"

Mia stopped walking to examine the picture of a lovely, emerald-cut diamond sitting atop a platinum band of diamonds. "Bigger."

Pete uttered a few choice profanities followed by a big sigh and signed off.

Once home, Mia gave herself a break from the Maydays of her tires, Adam's murder, and the drama around Dan Fee's house. She spent some time using a cat wand to play with Doorstop while Pizzazz zoomed around the apartment. After a dinner of reheated manicotti courtesy of Elisabetta, Mia opened a file from Cammie containing potential favors. Cammie lived up to Mia's expectations by sharing links to a dozen choices Mia considered totally over-the-top. "No engraved champagne glasses and bottles of champagne with a personalized logo in gold," Mia muttered, clicking on the next link. "No crystal vases, no coasters made from semiprecious stones. Definitely no candle personalized with a scent that smells like a combination of me and Shane. That's just creepy."

She took another look at the champagne glasses. *Maybe etched wineglasses along with a bottle of wine from the Boldanos vineyard would work,* she mused. *Kind of over-the-top-adjacent, but not all the way there.* She e-mailed the idea to Cammie, then joined an already sleeping Doorstop in bed.

The next morning, a call from Tony's Tires informed Mia that her car was ready. She picked it up and headed to work. Cammie expressed disappointment at a favor choice she described as *mundane* and vowed to keep hunting. "Nothing from the eighties," Mia warned.

"But you're ruling out glass blocks etched with your wedding date or personalized Duran Duran CDs," Cammie said, pouting.

"You bet I am. And no personalized Cabbage Patch dolls either."

Mia left Cammie scrolling and walked down the hall. She stuck her head in Shane's office. He was absorbed by whatever was up on his computer, so she cleared her throat to get his attention. He looked up and broke into a grin, then rose to come kiss her. "Hello, the future Mrs. Carina-Gambrazzo."

She gazed up at him with a warm smile. "We're going alphabetical? I like it. What are you working on? You seem really into it. Anything I can help with?"

"No. It's from Olivia," Shane said, referring to his younger sister, who was a rising senior at New Orleans's Tulane University with a dual major in marketing and creative writing. With both parents gone, he was putting her through college and beamed with pride at the mere mention of her name.

"Is she okay?" Mia adored her future sister-in-law and worried about her like a mother.

"Great. She's making us a special wedding present." Shane took Mia's hand and led her to the computer. He had a file open to what appeared to be a book. "She's putting together a small book with our family's histories in Italy, poems she's written, and recipes from both sides."

Mia scrolled through the photos illustrating the charming volume, about fifty pages in length. "Oh, this is wonderful. I love the photos of our hometowns in Italy. And the ones with the recipes. I just had Nonna's manicotti last night." An idea came to her. "If Olivia's okay with it, I think we just found our wedding favor. We can make copies of the book for all our guests."

"That's a fantastic idea. I'll run it by her. I'm sure she'll love it."

Mia favored him with a limpid glance from her bright blue eyes. "And I love you." They exchanged another kiss, then reluctantly separated. "And thank you for having a small family that doesn't add hundreds of people to our guest list. Of course, I'm very sad you're orphans, but—"

"It's okay." Shane gently cupped her face in his hands. "I have a family now. Olivia and you. That's all I need."

"Oooh." Mia, touched, choked up. "We can't kiss again. I'll end up pushing everything off your desk to have my way with you, which would be a serious breach of Belle View sexual protocol."

Shane laughed and released her. "No prob, we'll talk business. The HVAC guy, Diego Espinoza, came by. He gave me a great bid on twice-yearly HVAC maintenance. I don't think he killed Adam."

Mia gave him a reproving look. "I appreciate your commitment to scoring good deals for Belle View, but that's not enough to write off someone as a murder suspect."

"That's not why I think he's innocent, although with the contract he offered, I'd be tempted to absolve him of any and all crimes. I made sure I walked him out and pretended to notice the dent in his front fender. I lied and told him I have a side hustle where I bump out car dents and asked to take a closer look at it. There was blue paint in the dent. I didn't see anything else. I'm not CSI or anything, but I looked pretty closely and from what I could see, it did look like another car just backed into him."

"Nice work, PI Gambrazzo," Mia said, impressed.

"It gets better," Shane said with a touch of braggadocio. "I got talking about you to Diego, and about how happy you are to be reconnecting with old friends like his wife, and it turns out the two couples—you know, Ruth and Mark and Diego and Rose—socialize. I jumped on that and said the six of us should get together. And he did not seem receptive to the idea. In fact, quite the opposite."

"Wow. This *is* better. Did you have to follow through with your claim of being a dent whisperer so he didn't get suspicious about why you were so interested in him?"

"No. I told him the damage was beyond my skill set and luckily, he believed me. But I took close-up pictures and sent them to Pete in case they're helpful. He said he already got some from you, but mine added a little more detail."

Mia glanced at her fiancé with lust in her eyes. "I didn't think it was possible, but I'm even hotter for you right now."

Shane gave her a steamy look. "I'm willing to risk breaking Belle View protocol if you are."

The two moved toward each other. Suddenly, Mia's phone erupted with a flurry of texts. She checked it and let out a despondent, "*Noooo.*"

"What?" Shane asked, concerned.

It's my mother and grandmother." She held up her phone to show Shane photos the dueling women had texted of their wedding dresses. "I have to meet them at the dressmaker in an hour. They're gonna start the process of mashing up their wedding dresses into one style nightmare—a Frankendress."

An hour later, Mia walked into the living room of Lucille Giusti's elegantly appointed first-floor home/atelier straight into an argument between her mother and grandmother. "My sleeves are better," Gia insisted, brandishing her gown.

"*Feh.* They call 'em muttonchop sleeves because they look like big hunks a' meat." Elisabetta thrust her dress in a nonplussed Lucille's face. "Use these."

"Hey," Mia barked. "Both of you, back off. Sorry about this, Lucille."

The dressmaker waved a hand. "*Fa niente.* It's nothing. But I'm glad you're here." She addressed the women with a scolding expression. "What you're doing for Mia is *molto bene,* but the dress I make will be hers. So, she gets to pick which sleeves and everything else about her wedding gown. *Voi due capite?*"

"Yes," Gia said. "Of course."

Elisabetta didn't respond. Gia nudged her. "Si," her tone a lesson in grudgingness.

"Good. Now, go. *Vai.*"

Lucille shooed them off. They kissed Mia, handed over their dresses to Lucille, and left. Mia made sure they were gone, then applauded Lucille. "Nice. They never listen to me."

"That's because they love you so much they sometimes can't hear you."

"That doesn't make sense. And yet it does."

Lucille draped the gowns over her rolled-arm sofa, upholstered in a genteel gray damask brocade. Only a few years younger than Elisabetta, there was an elegance to her born of her love for fashion. Tall and slim without being bony, she wore black, flowing pants under a tunic top of the same fabric and a minimal amount of makeup. Her pure white hair was pinned into a classy chignon. She spoke English with only the hint of an accent from her Milano hometown.

She studied the gowns with the eye of a sewing surgeon. "Marrying these two—no pun intended—will be a challenge."

"I've got good news for you. You don't have to accept the challenge." Mia adopted a conspiratorial tone. "I bought a dress I absolutely love. I'm going to wait until I put it on for my wedding to tell Mom and Nonna. They'll love it so much and be so happy I'm getting married, they'll forgive me. I hope, I hope."

"It's a plan," Lucille said, making an obvious effort to conceal her doubt.

Mia clasped her hands together in a pleading gesture. "Please don't tell them. Please."

"You're the bride, not them. You deserve to wear the dress of your dreams. Even if I didn't make it for you."

Lucille winked at Mia, who responded with a relieved hug. "A bazillion thank-yous."

"You don't have to wait until your wedding day. About a week before the wedding, I'll tell Gia and Elisabetta I failed in my attempt to combine the two dresses. They'll panic, you'll produce the *perfect* dress, and all will be well."

"*I love you.*" Mia delivered another hug.

"All I ask is that you let me make your veil."

"Done and done. I also wouldn't mind an outfit like the one you're wearing for my honeymoon. It's elegant and gorgeous. Let me know how much."

"Free. It's your wedding present."

Mia gave her a look. "You're doing this because you want to see a grown woman jump up and down."

She followed this statement by jumping up and down, much to Lucille's amusement.

Her cell rang. She stopped jumping and checked. To her surprise, the caller was Donny Boldano Senior. "Mr. B.? Hi."

"I have a small gift for you, Messina."

The head of the Family spoke in a crafty tone that slightly unnerved Mia. "Okay," she said, a touch apprehensive.

"I need you to come by Piero's. I'm here with your future husband and someone you two have been looking for: Tulio Longella."

CHAPTER 19

Piero's, the Boldano Family's go-to hangout, was a nondescript Astoria restaurant whose paneled walls, red Naugahyde tablecloths, and Chianti bottles-turned-candlestick-holders screamed old-timey Italian restaurant. Piero had been Donny Senior's chauffeur until a bout with bone cancer cost him a leg. Rather than cut him loose, the Family patriarch funded Piero's dream of opening his own restaurant. The food he served was world-class, especially his signature dish, Pasta alla Mushroom Carbonara.

At the moment, an untouched plate of it sat in front of a distraught Tulio Longella, who sat slumped in a chair. Mia was surprised to see Orlando Maladugotti standing guard behind him. She cast a questioning glance at her fiancé. "Maladugotti found him," Shane said under his breath. "Longella had camped out in his mother's old basement furnace room. She didn't even know he was there."

Shane, Boldano, and Maladugotti pulled back,

ceding the floor to Mia. She faced Tulio head-on, arms crossed in front of her chest, one leg crossed over the other, a position that telegraphed she meant business. "Glad you're over that bug you had. What was it again? Oh, right. A bad case of Avoid-Mia-itis."

Tulio placed his elbows on the table and dropped his head onto his hands. He said something, but it came out muffled. Boldano walked over, placed a warning hand on Tulio's shoulder, and the young don's head shot up. "It's all my fault," he blurted. "Adam slipped me a C-note to introduce him to you. If I hadn't done that, none a' this would've happened. You wouldn't have married, he wouldn't have cheated on you, Adam wouldn't have come back to life and then died again, and none of us would be suspects in his murder."

"Not gonna lie," Mia said. "Some of this is on you. But Adam was a flirt and a professional con artist. He really didn't need you to be his wingman. He knew how to fly all by himself."

Tulio sniffed. He ran a tattooed hand over his shaved head, where another tattoo read, *Bald Bro.* "I feel a little better."

"Don't." Mia uncrossed her legs and planted both feet on the floor. She leaned into him. "I'm not done with you. I wanna know everything about every single contact you had with him after we got married. I know you did, so don't try and tell me you didn't."

"I won't." Considering the hulking brute of a guy Tulio was, Mia took silent pride in the fact she seemed to intimidate him. His passive-aggressive tactic of disappearing until tracked down ticked her off. "I was as shocked as anyone when Adam suddenly showed up again in Astoria," the lug continued. "I heard he was here but didn't see him until the night of the Mets game. He called and said he was gonna get back with you if it was the last thing he did. Which it kinda was."

"No *kinda* about it," Boldano pointed out.

"He said if I didn't help him, he'd tell everyone he paid me to introduce the two of you. I didn't wanna get involved, so I stalled. Told him I'd think about it."

Mia scowled at him. "How handy he died and you didn't have to give him an answer."

Longella shook his head with vigor and waved his hands back and forth. "No, I swear, it wasn't me. If it makes you feel any better, it didn't sound so much like it was about love for him. More like he was desperate for money. Maybe he heard how good things at Belle View are going and wanted to cash in. Or he heard your grandma had a way with day-trading. Anyway, hope that makes you feel better."

Mia pressed her lips together. The depth of Tulio's cluelessness astounded her. "Somehow, the fact that my late husband was more interested in me for money than love does not make me feel better. But I can buy him being desperate. He obviously got himself in trouble in Florida. It was bad enough for him to create a fake identity and still have to get out of town. What I want to know is what happened. Any ideas?"

Tulio shook his head. "He didn't say nothing to me except he had to have you back."

Mia gave an inward groan. After all the mystery surrounding Tulio, the goombah was a dead end.

"We're done here. But I'm not gonna let you off the hook for breaking Rose's heart. As far as I'm concerned, she traded up. Even if her husband might be the guy who slashed my tires."

"Huh?" Tulio looked mystified.

"Never mind. Just go."

"You got it," Tulio said, relieved. "I just need to get my carbonara to go."

Boldano gave him a whack on the side of the head. "Get outta here!"

"I'm going, I'm going." Tulio jumped up.

"Wait!" Mia picked up Tulio's plate. "I can't stand seeing Piero's carbonara go to waste." She handed the plate to the Family underling. "Have Piero pack it up. *Then* get outta here."

"Maladugotti, get him home," Donny Senior instructed. "In one piece."

The underling gave his boss a small salute. "Sir." Maladugotti clapped a hand on Tulio's shoulder. "*Vieni*, loser." He pushed Tulio toward the kitchen and through its swinging doors.

"Nice," Shane said to Mia, impressed. "You handled that like you run the Family. No offense to you, sir." He hastily directed the last line to the senior Boldano.

Boldano waved off the comment. "None taken. I agree. I gotta hand it to these Carina women. Her mother's knocking my socks off, too." He slid into the booth across from Mia. Shane followed his lead. "Sorry about that *stronzo*. I'll take care of him."

"You don't have to do that, Mr. B.," Mia said, alarmed. "It's all good. Really."

Boldano made a face. "I don't mean that in the way you're thinking. Longella's just gonna get a firm lecture on how to behave in a professional manner even in a difficult situation. I could also use someone to sort through the Family garbage for recyclables and that seems like a good job for him. Unpaid. For a long while."

"Ouch, but I'm sure he'll get the message." Mia tapped a number into her cell phone. "I need to touch base with Pete Dianopolis."

"My detective friend," Boldano said. "Words I never thought I'd say."

Mia smiled at him. "I know he does appreciate the help you've sometimes given him, even if he has to pretend it never happened." The detective answered her call. "Hi. I wanted to give you a heads-up that Donny Boldano located Tulio Longella." She repeated the little Tulio had to share. "The only useful thing he offered was that Adam seemed desperate for money. I wondered if you've been able to dig into his finances."

"Not very deeply. The guy made an obvious choice not to leave a paper trail. We're figuring he went old school and paid cash wherever he could, which is getting tougher for criminals like him because a lotta places don't take cash anymore. I had to download some cash app just to buy a cup of java the other day. What's up with that?"

"Adam's finances?" Mia prompted.

"Right. Near as we can tell, his dark web ventures earned him enough to get by. But there's no sign they'd get him in trouble with anyone but the feds and the IRS."

Neither had anything else to add, so they ended the call. "We need to know what happened in Florida," Shane said. The others nodded in agreement.

"I stayed clear of that scene," Boldano said. "You mess with someone else's turf, it gets ugly."

"Some of my dad's *coworkers* are still around," Shane said. Something he and Mia had in common, whether they liked it or not, was that both their fathers were *connected*, Mia's in New York, Shane's in the Sunshine State. "I'm gonna reach out and see if one of them can do a little digging and find out what Adam was up to. But they won't talk to me over any form of electronics. If they learn anything, I'll have to fly down to hear it in person."

"You're not going alone," Mia said. "Adam had a whole life on the side I knew nothing about, but I'm guessing someone down there was in on his secrets. When I left Miami, I swore I'd never, ever go back. But the time has come."

Shane took out his phone. "I'll handle travel plans."

He excused himself and moved to another table. The restaurant front door opened and the mailman entered carrying a nice-size box. He greeted them, then asked, "Is Piero around? I wanted to hand deliver this. It says, *Handle with Care.*"

"Piero, you got a box," Boldano yelled to the kitchen.

The restauranteur-chef came out of the kitchen. He had a slight limp engendered by the prosthetic leg that replaced the one he'd lost to cancer.

Piero took the box and thanked the mailman, who departed. "Go ahead and open it," Mia said. "We're all curious now."

"Sure."

Piero ripped open the brown wrapping paper,

revealing a gift box. He opened the box and a large bouquet of paper flowers erupted from inside while the Wedding March played under a voice-over Mia instantly recognized. "The pleasure of your company is requested at the wedding of Messina Bellissima Carina and Shane Pacino Gambrazzo," Cammie intoned. "Please scan the QR code for details and to RSVP for this joyous occasion."

Mia, aggravated, shook her fists at the heavens. "Cammie! I'll kill her."

Boldano got a text alert. He checked and held up his phone to Mia. "That's Aurora. We got our invitation, too."

Mia growled. Boldano got up to call his wife and Mia banged out a number on her phone. "Camilla Dianopolis," she said the minute Cammie answered, "I told you, nothing fancy!!!"

"Mia Carina, I thought you knew me well enough to know I can't do anything not fancy," Cammie said, hurt. "You might give me a little credit for not going 1980s. Do you see mauve, aqua, or peach anywhere on the invitation? No, you do not."

"That's true," Mia admitted.

"Plus, I got the invitations at cost. The vendor has been dying to try out the QR code and voice-recording combo and couldn't get anyone to bite. Now he's got a sample video for his website."

"Wow. Well . . . I'm sorry I snapped at you." Mia glanced at Piero, who was admiring the bouquet. "I have to say, the invitations are amazing. Thank you."

"You're welcome. Now, onto your floral arrangements."

"Remember, nothing—" Cammie was already gone. Mia finished the sentence to the air. "Fancy."

Shane came toward her. "Did you see the wild wedding invitation Piero got? It talked. I couldn't hear what it said, but I'm guessing it was, *Hi, I've got too much money and too little class.*" He chuckled at his own joke. "It was weird, though. The voice sounded kind of familiar."

"More about that later," Mia said with a grimace. "Any news on our travel plans?"

"Yup," Shane said with a nod. "My dad's old *paisan* Rocky Genovese is already doing some sniffing around. Go home and throw a bikini into a carry-on. We got an eight a.m. flight to the Magic City."

CHAPTER 20

The instant Mia and Shane deplaned at Miami International Airport, she was assailed by memories of her past in the city—none of them good.

Shane noticed the anxious expression on her face and placed a comforting arm around her. "You doing okay?"

Mia shrugged. "Been better. The last time I was here, Miami PD barely released me as a suspect in Adam's disappearance. Now, here I am, only it's worse. I'm a suspect in his actual murder."

"At least you're not the only one this time," Shane said, pointing to himself.

"Why doesn't that make me feel better?" She asked this with a bemused expression.

The couple made their way to the MIA Mover, which took them to the airport's Car Rental Center where, upon Mia's insistence, they rented separate cars. "No way am I staying overnight. You go your way, I'll go mine, and we'll meet up at the departure gate to compare notes."

"Yes, ma'am." Shane gave a mock salute, then bent down and kissed her. "We're gonna get through this. And get married. And live in the circus house. And have the best life any two people ever had."

Mia fought back the urge to burst into tears. "I love you so, so much." She grabbed Shane and planted a kiss on him that earned whistles from people waiting in line for their cars.

They picked up a couple of compact sedans and headed in separate directions. The exit alone from the airport reminded Mia that when it came to speeding and tailgating, Miami drivers gave New Yorkers a run for their money. *Then again, half of them probably* are *New Yorkers.*

The car's GPS chirped directions she didn't need to the Tutta Pasta that Adam managed before his mysterious disappearance. Slowed by the usual heavy traffic between the airport and North Bay Village, it took Mia twenty-five minutes to travel the eleven-mile route. She pulled into the half-empty parking lot and stared at the restaurant's logo: a giant, politically incorrect caricature of an Italian chef holding a smiling, anthropomorphic vat of steaming pasta. She exited the vehicle and was immediately assailed by a blast of Miami's notorious humidity. The restaurant entrance was only a few yards away, but perspiration already dripped down her cheeks by the time she got to the front door. She steeled herself, then pulled it open.

Mia stepped inside the restaurant . . . and didn't recognize the place. It had been completely remodeled, its original kitschy décor replaced by an attempt at a more upscale design in muted silvers and grays. Mia took in the changes. "It's like when they clean up after a crime scene," she muttered.

"Excuse me?"

This came from a hostess Mia hadn't noticed. "Hi. Yes. I haven't been here since you remodeled. When Adam Grosso was the manager." She eyed the young girl, who appeared to be about nineteen, with a perky energy that made her a good fit for the job. "You didn't work here then, did you?"

The girl shook her head. "No. But I know who you're talking about. I've heard the stories." She said this in a conspiratorial whisper.

"I bet you have," Mia said, her tone wry. "I'm looking for anyone who was around when Adam ran the restaurant. I used to come here a lot," she added by way of vague explanation.

"Ah. Got it. Unfortunately, the last employee who knew him quit a few days ago. Skye was our bartender. She's moving to New York to be a mixologist. That's better than a bartender."

"Yes, I know," Mia said, although in her book they were synonyms, with the only difference being those who claimed one title insisted on a higher hourly rate when she booked them for events.

Having shown up at Tutta Pasta an hour before lunchtime, business was slow, allowing the hostess time to gossip. She leaned an elbow on her hostess stand and began dishing. "Skye had a *lot* to say about Adam. She left here to go into business with him in a new restaurant. Then he and her investment disappeared. She had to come back to Tutta Pasta and start over. She was *not* happy."

"I bet," Mia said, her internal buzzer going off, alerting her to a new suspect.

"When the police declared him missing at sea,

Skye didn't believe it for a moment. She said he probably changed his name and took off for a new city. A new country, even. Like one of those where they don't send you back to America if you get arrested."

Skye, you have no idea how close you were to the truth. Mia tapped her lip with her index finger. She adopted a thoughtful expression. "Skye. I remember her. She was cool. Do you have contact information for her?

The hostess hesitated. "I do, but I don't know if I should give it out."

Mia dropped the act and fixed a look on the girl. "Here's the deal. I'm Adam's wife, now his widow. And I got a lot to say about him, too. Especially because he was murdered."

"What?" the girl exclaimed, shocked. She grabbed a pad from the shelf of her stand and scribbled numbers on it. She tore off the top sheet of paper and handed it to Mia. "Her cell. Do me a favor and don't tell her you got it from me."

Mia pocketed the piece of paper. "Thanks. I won't."

"Do they know who killed him?" the hostess asked, nervous.

"Nope. They're still on the loose." Mia patted the girl's arm. "But don't worry, honey. It wasn't me. Even though I was tempted to many, *many* times."

The nondescript, slightly shabby midcentury apartment building where bartender and wanna-be mixologist Skye lived was only two miles from Tutta Pasta. Mia found a spot directly in front of the building, which was built in the style of a

1960s' motel, with separate entrances for each small apartment. Skye's soon-to-be-former home was on the first floor. Mia ID'd it immediately. The front door was wide open and boxes were piled on either side of it.

Mia approached the apartment and took a tentative glance inside. Taping a box closed was a woman in her late twenties who looked vaguely familiar to Mia, although she couldn't figure out why. Even sitting on the floor with legs akimbo, Mia could tell Skye was tall and rangy. Her long hair, pulled into a high ponytail, was dyed black, but halfway down the ponytail transitioned into a rainbow of colors. Her arms were covered with tattoo sleeves, her ears and face sporting a myriad of piercings.

Skye looked up from her task and noticed Mia. "Hi," she said, her tone polite. "Are you looking for someone in the building?"

"Yes," Mia replied, cutting right to the chase. "You. I'm Mia Carina. Adam Grosso's wife. Well . . . his widow."

Skye stared at her. She put down her tape gun. "I'm so sorry. On every level. You better come in."

Mia did so. She took a seat on what appeared to be a foldout couch. It was the only piece of furniture in the studio apartment. "The hostess at Tutta Pasta gave me your address and number. Don't be mad at her. I didn't give her much of a choice."

"Not surprised. They basically pay Jeneice to gossip."

"Along those lines, she told me you were going to go into business with Adam, but he and your money disappeared."

"Truth." Skye looked down at the box between

her legs. "Full disclosure: I owe you an apology because I also slept with him. Only once. He moved right on to Felicity, the bee-you-tee-ful blond cocktail waitress all the guys were hot for."

"The one they found dead in his boat."

"Yup. Adam never liked that I was taller than him. Tall girls run in my family."

Mia examined her. "You're, what? Five-eight? Five-nine? I'll trade you five inches for the platforms I have to wear to get within eye range of my current fiancé."

Skye released a genuine laugh. Her cell rang. She checked the number and her face lit up. "Hello? Yes, hi. I'm so glad to hear from you."

Mia stepped outside to give the girl privacy. She stood in the shade of a giant hibiscus bush covered with bright pink flowers and texted what she learned about Skye and Adam's ill-fated business venture. He wrote back: **Put her on the list. Still with Rocky. Getting great intel.**

Mia pocketed her phone. She peered through the window to Skye's apartment and saw the bartender was off the call and appeared downcast. "Are you okay?" Mia asked, stepping back inside. "You look like you got bad news."

"I did." Skye pushed aside the box she'd been working on and moved on to another with dampened enthusiasm. "I was up for a position as a mixologist at a new restaurant opening in Manhattan. But they give it to someone with more experience than working the frozen margarita machine at Tutta Pasta."

"That sucks." Mia felt for the girl. Skye may have had a motive to kill Adam, but she didn't come across to Mia as someone who'd be vengeful enough to do it. She seemed more like the type who'd get angry, then cut her losses and move on—exactly like she was doing now. An idea came to Mia. "I run a banquet hall in Queens. We job in bartenders, and we can up the price if we call them mixologists." This earned Mia a smile from Skye. "I don't know where you'll be living, but if it's not too far from Belle View—my place of business, not the psychiatric hospital—I'll hire you for events."

All gloom disappeared from Skye's uniquely pretty face. "You will? That's awesome. I'll have my car, so I can go anywhere. I'll be staying with my cousin Annarita and her family in Jersey at first, but—"

Mia's jaw dropped. "*Stop.*" In a state of shock, she issued this as an order. "Did you say Annarita? From Jersey? Is your *cousin?*"

Thrown by Mia's reaction, Skye responded with a small, wary nod.

Mia collapsed onto the couch. It dawned on her why Skye looked familiar. Yes, she'd probably seen her a couple of times at Tutta Pasta. But that wasn't why she struck a note with her. Strip away the tats and piercings and dyed hair and Skye could twin with Annarita—Adam's vindictive former girlfriend.

"You know Annie?" Skye asked, pulling Mia out of the vortex of theories swirling around inside her brain. "She's going through a rough time. I helped her get a job at the Edgewater Tutta Pasta. Annie hooked up with some customer she met there named Gerald Katzenberger after, like, three dates, and they moved to Los Angeles so she could work at the first Tutta Pasta in California.

She was excited because it was in Hollywood—California, not Florida. I feel bad for her. She and Gerald moved to New York, and when his ex-wife found out he'd fallen in love with someone else, she was so angry, she killed him." Skye's face darkened with anger. "And she's gotten away with it, the beeyotch."

"Is that what Annarita told you?" Mia, nonplussed, stared at Skye.

"Yeah. Wait . . ." A horrified expression colored Skye's face as the reality of what she was saying dawned on her. "No. It can't be. You said *widow*. Not *ex-wife*. It's not you. Or is it?!" She grabbed her tape gun as if it were a weapon and backed away from Mia.

Mia pinched the bridge of her nose, then released a doleful sigh. "Skye, my friend, put down the tape gun and tell me you haven't packed away your booze. You're gonna need it."

CHAPTER 21

Fortunately for Skye, she hadn't packed away her liquor. She downed several shots of whiskey while Mia detailed the story behind "Gerald's" real identity, disappearance, and subsequent death. The bartender and former Adam flame cursed him out with a string of profanity that made Mia's ears burn. "I swear, if someone hadn't offed him, I would've done it myself," she declared, glowering.

"You have no idea how many people have said the same thing," Mia said. Mindful of the drive back to the airport, she reluctantly took only a small sip from the unbelievably delicious mango mojito Skye had made her, then carried the almost-full glass into the kitchen. "I better go. My fiancé and I have a plane to catch."

Skye stood up, swaying a little from the whiskey she'd imbibed. "I'm gonna have a long talk with my cousin. This is *so* not your fault." She threw her arms around Mia. "You da best. And I'm super-excited about working for you at Belle View."

"I'm sure our clients will love you." Mia pulled

away and eyed Skye with concern. "You're not hitting the road today, are you? Because I wouldn't recommend driving right now."

"No worries. I'm leaving tomorrow." She gave Mia a boozy wink. "I overserved myself. But if there's anyone who knows how to dodge a hangover, it's a mixa-cologist. I mean, a mixologist."

After making sure Skye drank several large glasses of water, Mia took off. She left Pete a message to bring him up to speed, then hopped in her car and started for the airport. Her cell rang and she answered the call via the car's connection. "Somebody's getting an ess-ton of RSVPs," Cammie said in a singsongy voice.

"Not too many, I hope," Mia said with the fire code in mind.

"So many I can't even keep up. It's the QR code. Makes it easy to respond. Your wedding is gonna be the event of the year."

Mia gave a snort. "For the gabagool crowd, maybe. I don't think *Vogue* will be doing one of their wedding spreads on it."

"Maybe not. But that new local hot sheet, A-Story-a, wants to do one. That title is so smart. Who knew you could turn Astoria into *A-story-a?* Oh, I almost forgot. Between your wedding and the rest of the Belle View events, I got so much going on that I turned your wedding shower over to Teri. She's thrilled, natch."

A feeling of dread suffused Mia. "Oh boy. Teri? Warning: If there's a stripper, I'm never speaking to either of you again. They're the guy version of #MeToo."

"I'm not making any promises, but I'll do what I can to keep Teri in line."

"Please. Oh, and I'm texting you contact information for a bartender to job in for upcoming events. Her name is Skye Terrasanti."

Mia ended the call. "*I'll do what I can* sounds a whole lot like a cop-out," she muttered. Traffic on the Airport Expressway came to a dead stop. Mia gave her horn a loud honk, accompanying it with some choice words for Miami traffic. She knew the gesture was useless. But it felt good.

Mia returned her car to the rental company and took the MIA Mover back to her terminal. She blessed TSA PreCheck for moving her through security at a much faster clip than the standard security line. Shane was already waiting for her at their designated meeting place, the outpost of a popular Cuban restaurant. Mia exchanged a quick kiss with her fiancé, then got in line to order. "I haven't had time to eat," she said after ordering a hot Cuban sandwich with a side of plantain chips, along with two iced lattes.

Shane patted his stomach. "Rocky's wife, Marie, made homemade gnocchi di Sorella with fresh everything. Basil, her own tomatoes, fresh mozzarella. I got a to-go container for you, but it's packed away."

"No problem. I like to eat local in airports." Mia retrieved her tray of food and the couple sat down at a set of the eatery's utilitarian table and chairs. In between large bites of her sandwich, she filled Shane in on her conversation with Skye.

"I can't believe she's Annarita's cousin," he said, shaking his head in disbelief.

"I know, right?" Mia speared a fried plantain with her fork. "I told her I'd throw some work her way at Belle View. A—we can keep an eye on her, because she could still be a suspect in Adam's death, even though I doubt it. And B—she makes a killer drink, no pun intended. Did you know there's such a thing as a mango mojito? I do now, and there's no going back." Mia devoured the plantain, then continued. "I'm sure Adam's sketchy friends were covering for him while he figured a way out of Miami. He only got a couple of grand out of Skye, though. That's a day's grift for him. Not enough to force him out of town and into a new identity."

"I can fill in the blanks, I think." Shane took a swallow of his latte. "Rocky came through for us. He called in a few favors for leads and learned Grosso borrowed from some connected people. He blew most of the money on online gambling, panicked, and was trying to escape to the Caymans with his waitress girlfriend when his boat crashed into another boat, which happened to be making a delivery of contraband Cuban cigars to Miami. His girlfriend, who was drunk and in the middle of a sexual act at the time, hit her head and died in the accident. Adam jumped into the smugglers' boat to save himself. Before the smugglers could kick him out, a patrol boat from the Bahamas appeared and started a chase. Adam used some of the money he had left to pay the smugglers to sneak him back into Miami."

"Wow," Mia said, appreciative. "Bravo, Rocky. We owe him."

"Rocky knows this because his Family, the Genoveses, were the recipients of the cigars—for their own pleasure, not to sell. The guys driving the boat figured they'd be much better returning

Adam's money to the Giardinos, since it was theirs to begin with, and telling them the truth about what happened."

Mia mulled this over as she took a big bite of her sandwich. "So, they got about half the money. How much did he still owe?"

"About five grand."

"Hmmm."

"Hmmm is right."

With their similar Family backgrounds, Mia and Shane knew $5000 was not enough money to kill over. Rough someone up to send a message, yes. Spend a year tracking them down and then offing them, like someone had done to Adam? Not gonna happen.

"But," Shane posited, "Grosso would still be freaked out, thinking his life was in danger, and wanna get out of town. So he gives himself a new name and lays low in Miami while he figures out a plan. He meets Annarita and learns she's moving to LA to work at the first Tutta Pasta they're opening there. He comes on strong to Annarita—"

"Annarita is hot for him," Mia said, picking up the story, "and they move to the California Hollywood. But why did they leave Los Angeles? I don't buy it's because Annarita was homesick for the East Coast and her family. I met her. She's not exactly a dainty flower."

"Inept con artist Grosso tries pulling some other stunt that gets him in trouble and he has to book it from LA."

Shane shared this with a tinge of self-satisfaction that Mia found endearing. When she daydreamed about a soul mate, she never imagined it would be someone with whom she bonded over murder investigations. Yet here she was—madly in love with a partner in solving crime.

She placed a hand on top of his and favored him with a knowing look. "Are you thinking what I'm thinking?"

He eyed what was left of her sandwich with lust. "That I should get one of those Cubans for the plane ride home?"

"Yes. They're incredible. Except . . . get two. Because instead of New York, we're gonna get on a plane to Los Angeles."

CHAPTER 22

It only took minor recalibrating to change their outbound flight from New York to Los Angeles. With the three-hour time difference, they would arrive in the City of Angels by early evening.

The couple hunkered down for the long cross-country flight. When the plane reached cruising altitude and beverage service commenced, they opted for nonalcoholic beverages. Dealing with the time change would be stressful enough on their systems. They didn't need anything else interfering with their mental acuity.

Mia took a sip of the seltzer she'd requested from the flight attendant and thanked her. She waited for the attendant to move on, then said to Shane, "I've been thinking. Maybe Adam running into me at the wedding expo wasn't such a coincidence. He knows about my position at Belle View. Early on in our relationship, I even talked about both of us running it someday. All you have to do is look at our website to find out I'm working there now. Plus, the wedding expo was on the events page."

"I can see that," Shane said. "But I don't see how both of you being at the Mets game was anything but a coincidence."

Mia pondered this. "Actually . . . Adam knows if there's an afternoon Mets-Dodgers game, I always go to it because less people attend afternoon games and it's easier to get out of the parking lot when it's over."

"Ha," Shane said with a laugh. "You sound like an Angeleno, not a New Yorker. Dodgers fans are famous for leaving early to beat the traffic out of Dodger Stadium."

Mia gave him a playful swat. "Take that back! I'm a native New Yorker. It's my birthright to hate Los Angeles."

"Or move there. Those are the only two choices for a New Yorker when it comes to LA."

"True." Mia resumed analyzing Adam's machinations. "He knows I like to sit in the upper deck behind home plate, so that's why he was in that section of the stadium. He wasn't sitting when I saw him. He was walking. He could've been looking for me."

"But if he was looking for you, why did he disappear both times? And why was he looking for you when he was with his girlfriend? She thought they were gonna get married. That's not a casual relationship."

Mia pulled a face. "I can bet why he was looking for me. He wanted to make sure I was still attractive."

Shane sat up straight, his quick move causing

him to knock into his tray table, sending his cola sloshing out of its cup. "*Excuse me?*"

Mia winced. She hated having to articulate her late husband's Neanderthal views. "Adam had a theory that women start losing their looks once they turn thirty. Him sharing this outrageous and completely insulting theory was the beginning of the end for our relationship. My guess is he ended up at the ball game because he didn't get a good enough look at me at the wedding expo. I saw him and he had to make a run for it. He found out the Dodgers were in town and took his chances he'd see me there, which wasn't a big reach. When we popped up on the Jumbotron and he saw I'm still relatively presentable, he felt safe making a move on me."

Shane inhaled and exhaled through his nose like a bull getting ready to charge. He clenched his fists. "Oh, how I wish that guy would come back to life," he said through gritted teeth, "so I could personally off him. If I told that story about him thinking women lose their looks over thirty, not only would I get off on a murder rap, I'd be a national hero."

Mia patted the hand closest to her and Shane unclenched his fists. "Luckily, someone took care of Adam for us, so we don't have to worry about that. Why don't you take a nap? You'll need all your strength for driving in LA. I've only been there once, but I still wake up in a sweat sometimes from a nightmare about their traffic. Adam was right about one thing: their freeways make the Long Island Expressway look like an empty country road."

Shane gave a nod. He put on his noise-canceling headphones and leaned back against his seat. He soon fell asleep. Mia was too wired to nap. They'd been fortunate enough to snag a row with an empty seat. She moved over to the window and gazed out. A light cloud cover only allowed for peeks at the land below, which appeared flat, brown, and devoid of human inhabitants. The emptiness depressed her. She pulled down the window shade and returned to the seat next to Shane. She leaned her head against his broad shoulder and, lulled by the plane's humming journey, she drifted off to sleep.

Mia and Shane woke up to the pilot announcing the flight's arrival in Los Angeles. The plane taxied to the gate, where they met with the usual slow crawl of passengers deplaning into the terminal. Mia realized she'd forgotten to take her phone off airplane mode, so she and Shane detoured to a nearby row of seats. She extracted her phone from her purse and made the adjustment. It instantly pinged with an incoming text. "It's from Pete."

"Maybe he's got news," Shane said, hopeful.

"Here's hoping." Mia checked the message to see a photo of yet another engagement ring, this one a larger version of the previous ring Pete had run by her. She texted back what was becoming her usual response: **Bigger.** Her phone pinged a response: a tears emoji and **I may have to rob a store. But then I'd have to arrest myself.** Rather than send another text, Mia responded to the detective with a phone call. "Relax, Pete. If you haven't found the perfect ring by the time I get home, I'll go shopping for one with you."

"Thanks. I obviously need help on this. I heard you're in Florida doing some snooping, which of course I don't support. When are you due back?"

"We're not in Florida anymore. We're in Los Angeles."

"You flew to LA from Miami? For the love of God, why?"

"I didn't have a chance to fill you in on everything we learned in Florida." Mia updated Pete with the information Shane gleaned from Rocky Genovese. "We think whatever happened to Adam here in LA could have led to his murder."

"You flew all the way to LA for that?" Pete chortled. "Talk about a long flight for nothing. We've learned *Gerald Katzenberger* sold a pitch about his life as the husband of a Mafia princess, took the money, and never delivered. Unfortunately for him, he sold it to an Armenian mobster who wants to be a producer, like everyone out there. Needless to say, the mobster was not happy about his bad investment. But he has an ironclad alibi for the time of Grosso's death."

Mia released a frustrated groan. "Argh. I'm such a dummy. I should have checked with you before we flew here. I wish you'd called me with this news."

"If you'd gone through the academy, spent three years walking a beat, took enough tests to work your way up to detective, and were assigned as my partner, I would have."

"Got it," Mia said, sheepish. "I'll let you know when we're back in Queens."

"No rush. The largest police force in the country *is* working this case. You can take a day and go to the beach."

Pete signed off. "I could hear Pete through your phone," Shane said. "The LA portion of our investigation is a wash, huh?"

Mia dropped her head in her hands "It's all my fault. I'm really sorry."

"It's not all your fault. You didn't hear *me* say, *Hey, let's check in with Pete,* did you?"

Shane bent down. He placed an index finger under her chin and gave it a gentle lift upward. "I know LA pretty well from my modeling days. We're gonna take the night off. I'm renting a convertible and we're driving up the coast to Malibu." He pulled Mia to her feet. "Let's go, Astoria Barbie."

Her spirits revived, Mia gave him a flirtatious grin. "I'm all yours, Queens Ken."

The trip up Pacific Coast Highway proved to be the break Mia didn't know she needed. She breathed in the salty sea air as they zipped along and drank in views of the spectacularly blue Pacific Ocean. Eventually Shane made a left and they navigated a narrow, two-lane road that ended in the parking lot of a small, casual restaurant tucked away in a coastal cove. Shane asked the hostess for a table by the water and she showed them to one with much batting of her long, false eyelashes.

He and Mia settled into white plastic chairs positioned around one of the tables set up on the restaurant's beach. Gentle waves lapping on the shore provided the soundtrack to their meal, which was delivered by a waitress also besotted with Shane. "That girl was so busy staring at you she almost dropped my fish and chips in my lap," Mia said. "I guess I better get used to it."

"Maybe I won't age well," Shane offered. "I hear guys lose their looks after thirty."

Mia reacted with an appreciative chuckle. "Ha. Nice one. Don't let the female employees of this establishment know you're not just gorgeous, you have a sense of humor. They'll throw you in the trunk of our convertible and make you their prisoner of love." She dabbed a fry in ketchup. "I'm so furious at Adam for using our relationship in one of his scams. His—" Mia made sarcastic air quotes—"*Life as the husband of a mob princess.* What a load."

Shane rested an elbow on the arm of his chair and sat back in the sand. He fixed a thoughtful glance on Mia. "I still can't wrap my head around the fact that you married this grifting loser. You're so talented and smart and fantastic. And he was so . . . none of that."

Embarrassed, Mia focused her attention on her fries. "First of all, thank you. As to the mystery of my attraction to Adam . . . Pete once gave me a compliment, believe it or not. He said I would have made a good detective. I told him I understand crime because I grew up with it. You'd think Adam would have set off every alarm bell when I met him. But the thing is, he didn't come off like a braggy show-off. You know, like a lot of the guys in the Families, who throw around money and act all tough and are all about bella figura—doing better than the next guy in the Family and impressing people more. Adam came across as a little shy. A little sensitive. His sense of humor was . . . what's the word I'm looking for? Self-deprecating. His hook was that he made you feel like you were the one woman in the world who was meant to take care of him."

"Wow." Shane planted all four chair legs back down in the sand. "Now I get it."

"You want to finish my fries?" Mia asked, motivated by a strong desire to change the subject.

Shane gave her the side-eye. "Not if you're trying to fatten me up so the lady waitstaff can't fit me into the car trunk."

Mia gave a fake gasp and clutched her heart. "*What?* Me? Never."

The couple shared a warm smile. Shane reached across the table and took Mia's hands in his. "I love you. You're the best thing that's ever, ever happened to me."

Mia squeezed his hands, overcome. "You took the words right out of my mouth, Queens Ken."

The two finished dinner. "Good timing on our part," Shane said. "It's sunset." He pointed toward the ocean, where the glowing yellow orb had begun a spectacular descent, filling the sky with an impressionistic painting of pinks and golds.

"It's so beautiful," Mia said, marveling at the sight. She stood up. "I can't leave California without putting my feet in the Pacific."

They walked hand in hand to the water's edge. Mia shed the utilitarian sneakers she was wearing and took tentative steps into the water. She shivered. "Oooh, that's cold."

"It's the Pacific. Much bigger body of water than the Atlantic, so it's colder."

"Look at you, knowing all this ocean stuff," Mia teased. She retreated from the water to the shore.

She brushed off sand from her legs and feet and slipped on her sneakers. "I have to say, Southern California is pretty cool. I can see why people live here."

"I could never," Shane said. "Not enough Italians. All the times I came here, I could never find a legit good red gravy."

Mia tore herself away from the last of the sunset and followed Shane back to the car. The miserable traffic on the highway and freeway were enough to make her take back her pronouncement that she could see why people lived in sunny SoCal, along with the migraine-inducing sea of cars and humanity at the infamous LAX, an airport that seemed ridiculously small for the country's second-largest city. A mad dash through security and the terminal got them to their gate barely in time to board a red-eye flight home. "Hey, get this," Shane said as they buckled in for the ride.

"What?"

"When we land at six a.m. tomorrow, we'll have traveled from New York to Miami to Los Angeles and back to New York in less than twenty-four hours."

Mia gaped at him. "*No*. Really? You're right. You wanna know something else?"

"Sure."

"It was our first time traveling together as a couple." She followed this with a kiss on Shane's cheek. "Here's to our next trip being for a honeymoon and not a murder investigation."

Worn out by their triangulated crossing of the country, the couple slept most of the flight home.

They woke up in time to get the last round of coffee from the flight attendants, which they paired with their Cuban sandwiches, which had miraculously survived the journey from Miami to Los Angeles to New York.

The plane made a smooth landing and, after deplaning, Mia and Shane headed straight for the exit to catch a cab. They'd opted for a nonstop, which deposited them at JFK rather than their airport home turf of LaGuardia. But a cab proved unnecessary. As they headed for the terminal exit, they were stunned to see neighbor and Carina family lawyer Philip pacing as if anxiously waiting for someone. He saw Mia and Shane, stopped pacing, and strode toward them.

The serious expression on his face concerned Mia. "Philip? It's six thirty in the morning. No one wants to make a JFK run any time day or night, but especially not at dawn. Why are you here?"

Philip faced them. "There's been a shooting."

Mia turned white. Dizzy and fearing she'd faint, she clutched Shane. He put an arm around her waist for support. "Oh, God. Is it Nonna? Mom? Dad? I'm sure a few of his old enemies are still around, but—"

"It's no one in your family," Philip said, cutting her off. "It happened across the street. At the Dan Fee house. One of his fans. A guy who called himself Circus Mann."

CHAPTER 23

On the drive to the police station, Philip didn't have much to share about the shooting. "One of the victim's fellow fan club board members called it in. No one's sure who. What they were doing at the house in the middle of the night I have no idea. Elisabetta is at the station because she's technically the homeowner."

"She can't have been happy about that," Mia said. "A murder at the house is bad enough. But Nonna is *not* a morning person."

They arrived at the utilitarian building serving the Astoria precinct and Philip parked. He led Mia and Shane into the lobby. Mia took a moment to appreciate that neither she nor any family member was there as a suspect for a change, then went to her grandmother. Paying deference to the solemnity of the occasion, Elisabetta wore a solid black velour tracksuit. "*Madonna mia*," the octogenarian said after exchanging hugs with her granddaughter. "I heard the shot. I thought it was a car backfiring."

"Do cars even do that anymore?" Mia wondered. "It seems kind of old-timey. Have the police told you anything about what happened?"

Elisabetta shook her head. "Only that one of them called 911." She gestured to a small cluster of Circus Feeks huddled together in a corner of the room, then sat back down, rested her head against the wall next to her chair, and fell asleep.

Mia eyed the Feeks. All looked pale, which she attributed to their lack of outdoor activity. They also appeared petrified, which she assumed came from finding themselves in a police station due to the murder of a friend. She identified the Feeks as club VP Eddie, treasurer Thomas, and secretary Hannah. Mia wondered where their leader was, a mystery solved by Pete and Ryan, emerging from the hallway that led to interrogation rooms on either side of Circus Feek fan club president Raina.

The young woman, face red with fury, pointed an accusing finger at Eddie. "*You.* Thanks to you, I'm a suspect in Mann's murder."

Eddie gave her a blank stare. "What are you talking about? I haven't done anything. I wasn't even at the house last night."

"Can we not fight?" Hannah implored, weepy. "One of our friends is dead."

She began to cry. Thomas laid a comforting hand on her back. Raina ignored her. "I told the detectives I was at the house because Circus told me he was going to break into Dan's house and I followed him to stop him, but they don't believe me." Raina whipped her head back and forth between the detectives and the fans so fast that her long, dyed-red ponytail whipped her in the face.

"Circus dropped his gun, and I thought it was the toy one you gave him where a flag pops out that says *Bang!* when you pull the trigger. But you traded it for a real gun! You set me up so you could hit on *her.*"

This time, Raina whipped around to point an accusing finger at Mia, to the event planner's shock and chagrin. "Whoa. How did I get mixed up in all this? I was in Los Angeles until about two hours ago. With my fiancé, *who I love very much.*"

"We're each other's lovers *and* alibis," Shane said, pulling Mia toward him protectively.

"Maybe skip the lovers part," she whispered to him.

"Raina and Eddie are kind of a couple," explained Thomas of the unwashed hair. "They're always breaking up and getting back together. But Eddie's been talking about how hot you are a lot lately, which really ticked her off."

"Flattered," Mia said, "but so not interested."

"You better not be," Raina said, glaring at her. "I didn't kill Circus, but my dad hunted and I know how to use a gun. I'm a *great* shot."

"Oh boy, oh boy, oh boy." Philip gritted his teeth, his lawyer buttons pushed. "I'm not your lawyer, but I *am* a lawyer, and I can't stop myself from telling you it would be in your best interests to stop talking right *now.*"

Eddie leaned back against the hard waiting room bench. The smirk on his face telegraphed that he was enjoying being the recipient of Raina's ardor, murder accusation or not. "Raina, I love ya, but this is wacko. I've never owned a gun in my life. The one I gave Circus was a one hundred percent licensed toy. How he ended up with a real one I don't know. But I do plead guilty to finding Mia hot."

He shot her what must be his definition of a sultry expression, which looked more like he was having a ministroke. "You don't take a hint, do you?" Mia said. Sensing Shane was about to deck the guy, she placed a warning hand on his arm. "I'll spell it out for you one last time. A. Hard. Pass. N-O, *No*. And, like Raina, I'm a great shot."

Philip released an aggravated squeak. Pete gave an eye roll. "Way too much gun talk for a bunch of people claiming their innocence," the detective said. "Hinkle and I'll be back in a few minutes. We need coffee. Nobody leaves here without confirming their contact information with the desk."

The detectives reversed their trajectory, disappearing behind the closed doors that led to precinct offices. Raina collapsed onto one of the lobby's hard aluminum chairs. "I'm so tired. I've been up all night. I told the police exactly what happened. It's so frustrating they won't believe me."

"What did happen?" Mia asked, phrasing it in a way that indicated she'd accept Raina's story.

"I went to the house to stop Circus from breaking in. I saw someone running away after I heard the shot and went to help Circus. Someone all in black."

She shared this eagerly, as if repeating the story might finally get someone to take it seriously. "Did you notice anything else about this person?" Mia asked Raina.

"Like I told the police, it was someone skinny and not super tall. Maybe five-seven or five-eight? I couldn't tell if it was a man or a woman. All I know for sure is it wasn't me."

Hannah shed more tears. "This is awful. All for a bunch of junk."

Thomas dropped his hand from her back. "Junk?" he repeated, horrified. "How can you say that? The murals alone belong in a museum. Any museum, not just one dedicated to Dan Fee. What is wrong with you, Hannah?"

Hannah did a one-eighty from weepy to angry. "People are dying because of that stupid old dump of a house. I'm sorry, but I don't think whatever's inside is worth it. And you keep going on and on about those stupid murals. They aren't even his best work. In fact, they suck. They're already peeling."

Club vice president Eddie cast a suspicious glance at Hannah. "How exactly do you know that?" He rose to his feet and planted himself in front of her. "You've been inside the house, haven't you?"

Hannah, frightened, took a step back. "No. Never. I know from the pictures in the website article. Blow them up for yourself. You'll see what I'm talking about."

The expression on Eddie's face telegraphed to Mia that he didn't believe Hannah. Mia got it. She didn't believe the club secretary either.

A thought suddenly occurred to her. "I have a question. How exactly did you all get the things from Dan Fee you're selling on the Internet? And don't say you're not doing it because your sellers' IDs include your real names." Mia failed to keep a triumphant hint of *gotcha!* from her voice.

"Those were all gifts from Dan," Thomas said,

unperturbed. "A lot of celebrities like him pay people to run their fan clubs. Dan didn't have that kind of money, so he'd give us things to auction off."

"Oh," Mia said, embarrassed by his simple, sensible response.

"I'm tired. I'm leaving." Raina rose from her chair. The other Feeks followed suit. She glowered at Eddie. "I don't want you anywhere near us. You're dead to me."

"Nice word choice," he said, unfazed.

He gave Mia his version of a sexy wink as the group passed by, heading for the exit. Sick of his ham-fisted cluelessness, she reacted by pretending to stick her finger down her throat. Shane turned a literal red with anger but managed to restrain himself from throwing a punch at the fanboy.

Philip made sure the group was out of hearing range, then let out a loud, aggravated grunt. "Thank God they're gone. It was torture listening to that girl incriminate herself. I'd offer my services as her lawyer, but that fan club is all kinds of crazy."

"Tell me about it," Mia said, pursing her lips.

Pete opened the hallway door. He held a coffee cup in one hand. He crooked a finger at Mia. "I need to ask you a few questions about the items inside the Dan Fee house. I already went over this with your grandmother, so she can keep sleeping."

"No problem."

Mia started after Pete. "I'm coming with you," Shane said, sticking close to her.

"Me too," Philip said, "to provide counsel if you need it."

The three followed Pete, squeezing into his

small office. Mia took the one chair. Shane and Philip stood behind her. "You look like Secret Service agents," Pete said. "You should come up with a code name for Mia, like the Secret Service does for the president and his family. Hey, I've got one: Nosy."

Mia shot him a look. "Tough talk for a guy who wants me to go engagement ring shopping with him."

"Apologies." Pete said this without sounding remotely apologetic. "I'd offer you all coffee but something's wrong with our machine. Every pot tastes like it was made three days ago. Usually it tastes like it was made only two days ago."

"We're good," Mia said. "Before we talk about what's inside the Dan Fee house, I have a question: Annarita fits the description of whoever it was Raina saw. Do you think the killer could have been her? Maybe she was coming after me and picked the wrong house. She hates my guts. If her grief and anger over Adam kept building; it could have sent her over the edge into murder mode. Also, the club secretary, Hannah, is about the same height. There's something hinky about her. I can't figure out exactly what, but I don't think her fellow board members trust her anymore and I don't blame them."

"Oh, goody. More theories from the sleuthing desk of Mia Carina. I'll add it to the list."

"Cammie doesn't find sarcasm attractive."

"Thanks for the reminder," Pete said. "I'll stick to being sarcastic around you." He tapped on his computer keyboard, bringing his screen to life. "Now, let's talk about any items of value you found at Dan Fee's house."

"Considering his devoted following, I think any item associated with him is a potentially valuable item. I mean that seriously, not sarcastically." Mia closed her eyes to replay the discoveries she'd made with her mother and grandmother when they began the arduous task of combing through the comic artist's belongings. She ran through a list Pete typed into a file on his computer.

"That's it?" Pete asked after a few minutes.

"That's all we got through. There's tons more. *Tons.*"

"If you're right about the value of this guy's stuff, you need security at his house."

"Nonna's regular guy is booked for the next couple of weeks," Mia said.

Shane held up his cell phone. "I put a call into a new security company."

"I'll help you get them to expedite installation."

"My client has answered your questions to the best of your knowledge," Philip said. "I assume we're free to go."

"Sure." Pete hit Save and closed his file. "Why not?"

"One last thing," Mia said, earning a groan from the detective.

"If it's about this Annarita girl," Pete said, "yes, I will verify her whereabouts for the evening and FYI, her parents informed us she never left the house the evening of Grosso's murder."

"A parental alibi isn't much better than a spousal one," Mia said. "My question is, do you think there's any chance Circus Mann's murder is tied to Adam's? They both happened on our block. My family's kind of connected to both guys, although only distantly to Circus because Nonna bought the house for me and Shane. I'm not saying any of us did it," she added hastily. "It's just weirdly coincidental. And I was brought up to believe there are no coincidences. Well, at least not when it comes to crime."

"It feels like a reach," Pete said. "But we'll be examining both murders from every angle."

"Thanks, Pete. I do appreciate you considering other suspects besides ourselves and our loved ones."

"You got it. And I hope you'll keep my consideration in mind when it comes to helping me find a flippin' ring for Cammie." Pete rubbed his eyes. Mia noticed the circles under them were darker, the bags puffier. The unsolved murders were taking a toll on everyone.

The three visitors to Pete's office stood up to leave. Mia's phone rang out a text alert. She checked and her heart lifted. "It's from my dad. He says Posi has an alibi for the time of Adam's murder. He sent a couple of videos to prove it." Mia pressed Play. She made a face. "Ugh, it's a sex video."

This motivated a quick rise on Pete's part from behind his desk. He came around it to view the video over Mia's shoulder. Shane joined him and Philip as well, but with much less interest.

The video showed a couple engaged in the kind of activity usually reserved for adult movies. "I can't even tell if that's Posi," Mia said. The man in the video turned and she recoiled. "Ugh, it is. I can't watch my brother having sex. I'll never unsee it." She was about to close her eyes when she caught a glimpse of Posi's partner. She let out a yelp of surprise. "OMG, that's Cimmanin."

"Who's Cimmanin?" Philip asked. "And what kind of name is that? I can't place its ethnicity."

"That's because it doesn't have one. It was supposed to be Cinnamon, but nobody could spell it right. She used to date one of the Koller brothers; you know, from the Manhattan real estate company. We met when my dad was accused of killing this stripper who I found dead in the cake she was supposed to jump out of at a bachelor party. I was trying to figure out who the real murderer was and thought it might be one of the Koller brothers.* I know Cimmanin and Posi were in touch through social media, but I didn't know it was this kind of *in touch.*" She squinted warily at the video. "Are they done . . . doing it?"

"Yes, sweetie," Shane said. "It's all over. Wait— whoa. I did not know humans could bend their bodies into that position."

Mia whimpered and squeezed her eyes shut. The men stared at the video, stupefied. Finally, Philip said, "*Now* it's over."

"I kind of forgot to check the time stamp on the video to confirm it gives Carina an alibi," Pete admitted sheepishly. "I need to see it again." This prompted more whimpers from Mia.

Her phone pinged a second alert. "Dad sent another video. I can't watch." She thrust the phone into her fiancé's hand.

Shane pressed Play. "This isn't a sex video." Pete impulsively released a disappointed grunt and Mia glared at him. "It's only Cimmanin. I think you should listen."

Mia leaned in. The flaxen hair extensions and

*For more on this story, read *Here Comes the Body.*

enhanced breasts that were Cimmanin's marks of distinction filled the camera frame. She'd added eyelash extensions to her heavily made up repertoire. They fluttered up and down like antsy caterpillars as she spoke to the camera on her phone. "Hi, all. It's your fave influencer Cimmanin here." Mia noted she'd given up trying to sound like an upscale Manhattanite. Her heavy Queens accent was back in full force.

"You're not gonna believe this, but you know the guy in my new sex tape?"

"New?" Philip gave his head a disbelieving shake. "Yikes."

"I just found out this guy Posi I was doing it with—oh, before I forget, you can follow him at @hotconvict. That's what he is. A superhot convict. Lucky me, huh?" Cimmanin giggled and gave an exaggerated wink. "Anyhoo, it turns out Posi was what the police call *a person of interest*"— Cimmanin highlighted this with exaggerated air quotes—"in a murder investigation." She widened her eyes and gave a theatrical gasp. "But . . ." She drew herself up proudly. "I am here to tell the world that Posi Carina is innocent of all charges. When whoever the guy who got murdered was murdered, Posi and I were really busy f—"

"Stop!" Mia covered her ears. "I don't need to hear the rest. Or any of this. What's important is that *you* hear it, Pete."

"Heard it, watched it. I'll track down this Cimmanin chick." Pete frowned. "These *influencers* gripe my keister. They'd rather make a video and share crucial information with a bunch of vidiots than do the responsible thing and contact the authorities who can actually get a suspect off the hook."

"I don't have her contact information," Mia said. "You'll have to slide into her DMs. Her handle is @yourfavoritespicecimmanin."

Pete picked up his pad and wrote this down. "What a name. I could never spell the word *cinnamon* in the first place."

"Neither could her mother," Mia said. "Or anyone else awaiting her birth."

Mia, Shane, and Philip left Pete's office for the lobby. A kind officer had unearthed an emergency foil blanket for Elisabetta, and she happily snored away beneath it, the lobby's fluorescent lights reflecting off the blanket's foil. Mia gave her grandmother a gentle shake. "We're done, Nonna. Andiamo. Let's go."

Elisabetta mumbled words in a mix of Italian and English Mia couldn't make out. She opened one sleepy eye, then closed it and went back to sleep. "I'll carry her," Shane said.

He easily lifted up the tiny octogenarian and transported her to Philip's car. They delivered Elisabetta to the comfort of her bed at home, then Philip left to drive Shane home.

Mia went upstairs to her second-floor apartment, where Doorstop waved a lazy paw from his prostrate position on the top of his cat tree. Pizzazz tweeted a cheery greeting. Mia let her out for a quick fly around the room, then showered and replaced the clothes she'd been wearing for over twenty-four hours by that point. After feeding her animal babies and providing much affection, which was returned—at least on Pizzazz's part—

Mia headed out. But not to Belle View. She first made a detour to the Triborough Correctional Facility.

Guard Henry gave her a warm welcome. "Posi already has a visitor, but I'm gonna make the call that he's allowed to have two this morning."

Puzzled, she glanced at the seating area to see who else might be waiting for Posi. The visitor's wiry black hair confirmed she was looking at the back of Donny Junior's head. "Donny?"

He turned around. "Oh, hey, Mia."

She came over and took a seat next to him. "What are you doing here?"

"My dad sent me."

"Mr. B.?" Mia said, worried. "Why?"

Before Donny could answer, a guard brought out Posi. He took a seat across from them. The expression of pique on his face mystified Mia. "Hello, brother dear. I stopped by to congratulate you on alibiing out on Adam's murder. I expected you to look a lot happier."

"You can barely see my face on the sex video," he griped. "It's uscless."

"Um, *it did help you dodge a murder rap*," Mia said. Annoyed, she laid heavy emphasis on each word.

"So? It did nothing for my brand."

Mia released an exasperated exclamation. She dropped her head in her hand, confounded by her brother's breathtaking obtuseness.

"What's your problem?" Donny Junior sounded as grumpy as Posi. "You got to have sex with the hottest girl around. I've been following Cimmanin since she broke up with that *stronzo* Koller brother. I even slid into her DMs. I thought I'd be the one to hook up with her, not the jailbird that is you. Was it worth it, bruh? Getting kicked out of the halfway house and sent back here?"

Posi didn't say a word. He just smiled.

"Oh, great. It *was*." Donny Junior cursed and gave the table a pound with his fist, earning a warning from the room's two guards.

Mia held up her cell phone. "While you two were having a you-know-what measuring contest, I DM'd Cimmanin." The cell rang. "That's her. She's FaceTiming me."

Cimmanin's face appeared on the phone screen. "Mia! Hi. Long time, huh?"

"Yes indeedy."

"I heard you're engaged." Cimmanin gave Mia a thumbs-up. "And another guy you know was murdered." She turned the gesture into a thumbs-down. "Can I do a video with you where we gossip about it?"

"No."

"'Kay. Hey, I'm with a friend of yours right now." Cimmanin scanned over to reveal Pete, who responded with a baleful glower at the camera. The two were in his office. "Tell Posi I'm really sorry I used him to increase my visibility."

"I'm right here." Posi leaned toward the phone, earning a warning from his guard. Mia flipped the camera around to show him. "I don't care about that, Cim. But I'm hurt you can barely see me in the video. I don't get nothing out of it. Except, of course, a very lovely evening."

"My bad on that," Cimmanin said. "I'll get my editor to cut a new version where we can see you more. Oh, and I got a new sponsor. Good Vibration Sex Toys. I'll negotiate a cut for you. It's only fair."

"I appreciate that. You're a good person, Cim."

"Aww, thank you."

"Hey! I'm here, too, Cimmanin." Donny Junior twisted his body to try to get in on the video call, earning himself a warning from Henry. Mia sighed and turned the camera toward him. "Donny Boldano Junior."

Cimmanin gave him a flirty smile and waved. "Hi, Donny. I saw you in my DMs. Sorry I haven't gotten back to you. My phone's been blowing up since the video with Posi."

Posi did a victory fist pump and puffed out his chest. Mia, Henry, and Posi's guard exchanged a three-way eye roll.

Donny Junior leaned toward the phone. "Seeing as how you were just using my cousin Posi and are not into him, I feel comfortable asking you this. If you're not doing anything on September 25, wanna be my date to Mia's wedding?"

Mia gaped at him. *Seriously?* she mouthed. He ignored her.

"Love to. I'll DM you my cell. Byceee!"

Cimmanin gave another flirty wave and ended the call. Mia put away her phone. "If you two are done living up to the stereotype of being total *cafones*, a reminder that if we don't find Adam's killer and the police home in on one of us as the prime suspect—"

"Not me." Posi did a little victory dance in his chair. Mia gave him a cold stare. He instantly stopped. "Sorry, sis," he said, contrite. "As long as I'm in here, I'll sniff around my jail compadres and see if anyone knows or heard anything. Lotta ears to the ground here at the Tri."

Donny Junior placed his hands on Mia's shoulders and looked her square in the eye. "Messina Bellissima Carina: I swear on all that is holy, we're gonna find the *coglione* who killed Adam Grosso. Your wedding *will* happen. I have a date with Your Favorite Spice Cimmanin and nothing, repeat, *nothing,* is gonna get in the way of making that dream come true."

CHAPTER 24

When Mia found herself dozing off as she waited for a light to change, she decided a few hours' sleep made more sense than heading straight to work. She returned home and texted Shane and Cammie. She didn't hear back from Shane right away, a mystery Cammie cleared up. "He's passed out in the upstairs bridal lounge. Your gallivanting around the US of A caught up with him, too."

Mia was suffused with the warm glow of love for her man. Bouncing from one city to another and then another in their cross-country quest to find Adam's killer had bonded the two even more if that were possible. "Unless there's an emergency, let him sleep."

"That was my plan."

"I haven't had a chance to check the wedding RSVPs yet. Have you?"

"You betcha. Not a single Regrets."

"*No*," Mia said, upset. "We need Regrets. I built a ten percent attrition rate into the guest list. If everyone shows up, we won't be able to fit them all into the room. I don't want my own wedding to be the event that gets us shut down because we violated the fire code."

"Relax. We haven't heard back from everyone. We can always say we overbooked, like with the airlines."

"Oh, and we know how well that goes over. There aren't a million news stories with people screaming they're gonna sue because they couldn't get on a flight."

"We'll be okay. Worse comes to worst, we'll rotate family members in and out of the room that night to keep us at the limit."

"Please tell me you're kidding."

"I'm kidding." The tone in Cammie's voice belied this.

Too tired to brainstorm alternatives, Mia shelved concern about her guest list. She napped for a few hours. After a light lunch, she decided to go for a rejuvenating bicycle ride. She rode up and down the streets of the neighborhood, the ride turning the late summer/early fall air into a crisp breeze. She passed seamstress Lucille's house, which made her think of her secret wedding dress. A frisson of excitement coursed through her as she imagined herself wearing the beautiful gown and walking down the aisle into the arms of Shane.

Her reverie came to a crashing halt as she biked past the far end of the alley behind her house. She got off her bike and walked it to the spot where Adam's body had been found. A feeling of sadness overwhelmed her. For all Adam's indefensible behavior, he didn't deserve to be murdered, she thought to herself. Jail for sure. A nice, long sentence. But murdered? No.

Mia hopped back on her bike and quickly pedaled away from the literal scene of the crime. She turned onto her block and rode to her house. Glancing across the street, she saw Elisabetta supervising a team installing security equipment at the Dan Fee house. She could hear her grandmother barking orders at the browbeaten workers and chuckled.

She made two right turns, which took her to the garage, where she parked the bicycle. After a quick change of clothes and an application of makeup, she headed down the stairs and out the front door. She came to a halt at the sight of a black Cadillac Escalade idling in front of her house. The back passenger window descended, revealing Donny Boldano Senior. "Hello, bella Mia. Come for a ride with me."

Mia took a slow walk down the front steps. "Those words are never good coming from you, Mr. B.," she said warily.

He responded with a loud guffaw. "You and that sense of humor." He opened the door for her. "I have some news. I prefer not to deliver it over electronics, hence my visit. *Vieni*. Come."

Mia got into the black leather backseat of the Escalade. The chauffeur pressed a button and the dark-tinted window rose until it closed. They drove off, the ride so smooth Mia wasn't sure the car was actually moving. "Water?" Boldano asked, gesturing to an open console between them.

"Yes, thank you."

"Plain or *con gas*?"

"Carbonated."

Boldano handed her a small bottle of Pellegrino. "I wanted to let you know we got to the bottom of who paid off the halfway house hacker to set up Posi. Turns out it wasn't to make your brother a suspect in Adam Grosso's murder. It was to get him back in jail and, hopefully, have his sentence extended to remove him as a possible contender to replace me."

"Replace you?" Mia, not sure what Boldano was implying, repeated this.

The Family head hunched his shoulders. For the first time in Mia's memory, he looked his late-sixties years. His dark hair had given up and gone completely gray. His commanding presence had shrunk, along with his height. Once described as wiry, he now teetered on the edge of physically going soft. "I'm thinking about retiring," he said. "Frankly, it's a miracle I've lived long enough to do it. I don't wanna press my luck. It's time. Some of my underlings have smelled blood in the water. They're undercutting and backstabbing each other to try and position themselves as my successor. One of those is the *stronzo* who betrayed your brother. Orlando Maladugotti."

Hearing the name filled Mia with ire. "I knew it. I never completely trusted him."

"You have good instincts. Better than mine these days." The *capo di tutti capo* delivered this with sadness. "When Maladugotti saw how beloved Posi is with all of us, he felt threatened. He got word out to the halfway house residents they should let him know if they saw anything that would get your brother in trouble. Maladugotti lied and said the order was coming from the

Boldano Family and we would pay well for the information. The hacker living in the house knew that Posi and Cimmanin had been, what do they call it? Sexting. Like texting but with sex." Boldano's tone indicated his disapproval. "On behalf of Maladugotti, the hacker manipulated Posi into a romantic evening with her, knowing Posi would have to break the house rules to make it happen. The hacker set him up, then snitched on him."

Mia, furious, clenched her fists and mimed boxing. "Oooh, would I like to take these to that Maladugotti."

"Don't worry. He and the hacker have been taken care of."

Mia released her fists. She cast a wary glance at Boldano. "Every time you say *taken care of*, I get worried, Mr. B."

Boldano let out a laugh. "You never have to worry, Mia. At least not anymore. The punishment handed out is all aboveboard. The hacker was reported to the authorities. He's out of the halfway house and back in full-way jail. And Maladugotti is flying to Italy at this very moment, on a very legal one-way ticket." Boldano gazed out the window. "I've done bad things in my life," he said, sounding wistful. "But I've also done good things. If someone I trust doesn't take over the family enterprise, a lotta people I care about will be outta work. And finding other employment won't be easy for them. I'll do my best to make them whole. Probably sell off my legitimate businesses. But still . . ."

He paused. Then he gave himself a shake, as if to physically rid himself of the melancholy mood. "Anyway, speaking of Italy . . ." He handed Mia a manila envelope. "A wedding present from the missus and me."

"Oh, Mr. B." Mia opened the envelope. She extracted a black leather travel portfolio embossed with gold script reading "Honeymoon Itinerary for Mr. and Mrs. Carina-Gambrazzo."

"Donny Junior told me you're combining your last names," Boldano said, bemused. "It takes work keeping up with you kids today."

Mia removed a document from the portfolio. In beautiful gold calligraphy, it informed her that she and Shane were being gifted with a three-week, all-expenses-paid Italian honeymoon at the best hotels in each location. Mia's eyes filled with tears. "I don't know what to say. This is . . . incredible. Thank you and Mrs. B. so, so much."

"You're the daughter I never had, Mia." His voice was husky with emotion. "I always hoped you'd marry one of my sons. Donny Junior, not so much."

"Never!" Mia blurted, to the older man's amusement.

"My money was on Jamie. I could see the two of you happy together. But he's got a beautiful wife who's gonna make me a grandpa, God bless. And you'll soon have a beautiful husband. And I mean that sincerely. The guy looks like a Michelangelo sculpture come to life."

"He really does."

"Stop worrying about Grosso's murder. Pete Dianopolis knows what he's doing. He'll nail whoever did it, if he's not distracted by the other crimes happening in this crazy city every five minutes." He rubbed his forehead like he had a headache.

Mia eyed him with concern. "Mr. B., you sure you're okay?"

He unfurrowed his brow, his expression immediately lightening. "I'm good. Nothing to worry about. Only questions about the future bothering me."

"You need to do what's right for you, Mr. B. The rest of us will manage."

The SUV pulled up in front of Belle View. Boldano patted Mia's cheek. "Here we are. Now go. Make us all some money. In an honest, legitimate way."

"Will do." Mia hugged the man who was her godfather, in addition to being an actual Godfather.

Mia exited the Escalade feeling inspired. Once inside her office, she checked Shane's schedule. Seeing he was booked all day giving tours, she texted him the news about Maladugotti and the Boldanos' incredibly generous wedding gift. He responded with rows of fist bumps and hearts, along with his avatar blowing her a tornado of kisses.

After tying up loose ends for a few upcoming events, Mia took a break to concentrate on her own nuptials. She opened a file from Cammie with photos of sample centerpieces, one more ornate than the next. All featured her favorite flowers, so she picked one that wouldn't take up half the table and approved it. Next, she called the publishing house producing Olivia's lovely book of memories, family recipes, and poems and confirmed delivery of the wedding favors the following week. Mia then confirmed details of the reception menu with Dream Events, the caterer Cammie had hired for the wedding in order to free up the Belle View staff to attend as guests.

Having checked off her list of tasks for the day, Mia decided a trip to a local clothing store was in order to pick up a few items for her honeymoon. She texted Cammie to let her know she was leaving for a dose of retail therapy. Cammie texted back: **Budweiser Clydesdale horses are going to be in town around the time of wedding. Can I hire them to bring you and Shane to the reception?** Mia texted back one word: **NO**, followed by several rows of exclamation marks.

Mia cabbed over to Ditmars Boulevard and Panache Boutique, the latest addition to the gentrifying street. The shop was still having an end-of-summer clearance sale, and she snagged two bathing suits, shorts, tops, and a couple of flowery, flowing dresses for Italian alfresco dining.

Celebrating her good fortune as she exited the store, Mia just missed literally bumping into two women walking down the street holding coffee drinks. "Sorry," she said—and realized she was talking to Ruth Behling and Rose Nunzio.

"Mia. Hi." Ruth's cheery tone didn't mask her obvious discomfort. Rose managed a smile but didn't say anything.

"Hi there, you two," Mia said. Sensing something was off, she responded by plastering on her own fake smile. "I asked my friends to pass on bridal shower invitations to both of you. They're keeping the whole thing a surprise, so I have no idea when it's happening, but I'm looking forward to seeing you there."

Ruth made the kind of face that indicated an

awkward situation. Rose seemed rooted in place. She remained silent. "Bad news," Ruth said. "Rose couldn't find a sitter and I'm drowning in all this prep stuff for my own wedding. You can relate, right? *So* sorry. We'd love to be there and are totally bummed we can't make it." She affected an expression of disappointment Mia didn't buy for a minute.

"I'm bummed, too." Mia mirrored Ruth's expression, adding a touch of mockery out of spite. "We'll just have to get together another time. All six of us." Mia tossed this out knowing it was a nonstarter. Ruth's bald lies annoyed her, so she allowed herself a moment of watching the women squirm.

"Absolutely!" Ruth said, upping the level of her insincerity. "Great running into you, we have to go, bye!"

She gave Rose a push that almost sent the woman toppling over from her still-as-a-statue pose and the two hurried off.

Mia shot the evil eye at their backs. They turned a corner, and she whipped out her cell phone to call Pete, who picked up on the first ring. "Hi. I just saw my two ex-friends: Ruth, of the boyfriend she cheated on with Adam, and Rose, who was knocked up by him. They acted very weird, like they wanted to avoid me, and it made me remember my slashed tires. Did you guys ever find any leads to who did that?"

"To be honest, we got sidetracked by the fanboy's murder. I'll put Hinkle back on it. I was gonna call you. I'm at Forever Yours Jewelry on Steinway. I'm sending you a picture of a ring."

A photo of an obscenely large emerald-cut diamond popped up on Mia's phone. "That's the winner."

"I was afraid you were gonna say that." Pete's voice sounded shaky with nerves. "If I tell you the price, I'll bust out crying. I hear there might be an opening at the top of the Boldano Family. I may have to claim it so I can afford this thing."

The call over, Mia stepped to the edge of the sidewalk. She put her hand up to hail a taxi. A limousine came to a halt in front of her. Not having called it, Mia waved it away. But the limo didn't move. The passenger door opened. To Mia's surprise, Cammie stepped out. "Cammie? What are you—"

She didn't get to finish the sentence. Someone suddenly grabbed her from behind, threw a hood over her head, and shoved her into the limousine.

CHAPTER 25

"Happy wedding shower!"

Mia recognized Guadalupe, Cammie, and Teri's voices. She made a move to remove the mask, but one of them stopped her. "Nuh-uh," Teri said. "The mask comes off when we get to our destination."

"This was your idea, wasn't it?" Mia said, peeved. "Cammie, I told you to rein her in."

"I did," Cammie said. "You should hear the ideas I shot down."

The limo drove around for half an hour. Mia tried to use her hearing to determine where they were going, but she gave up as any clues were drowned out by women chattering and the early 1990s soundtrack playing over the limo's sound system—"We're using music from the year you were born," Guadalupe said with pride. Mia accepted a glass of champagne from Cammie, drinking it by straw through a hole in her mask, and gave in to the fun in store for her.

The limo finally came to a stop. "We're here," Teri announced.

The women helped Mia out of the car. They whipped off her mask to reveal the wedding shower site: the Belle View Banquet Manor. "Nicely done," Mia said, amused by her friends' good-natured trickery.

"Cammie said we should hold it at the best place in the city," Teri said. "So we are." She clapped her hands together. "Ladies, it's go time!"

The women went in and scurried up to the second-floor Bay Ballroom. Teri threw open the ballroom doors to the deafening scream of "Happy Wedding Shower!!" delivered by dozens of Mia's nearest and dearest female friends and family. They converged on her with hugs that left her breathless. "Back! Back!" Teri cried out, fake-beating them off.

"Thank you all," Mia said, overwhelmed with emotion. "This is the best day of my life."

"Until your wedding." Elisabetta enveloped her granddaughter in a hug.

"Mia sandwich!" Gia came at her daughter from the other side, putting Mia in the middle of the two women.

"Let go of me," Mia said, laughing. "I need to say hi to everyone."

Elisabetta and Gia released her and Mia made the rounds of her guests. She marveled at how far along her pregnant friend Nicole was and exclaimed at how little Madison was showing her own future offspring, a well-kept secret at her wedding months earlier. "I hope you're okay I'm here," Cimmanin, an unexpected guest, said. "Donny said it'd be okay. I bought a great gift in case it's not."

"Of course it is," Mia said in all sincerity, and the two exchanged a hug.

"Hi, Mia."

She turned to see another unexpected guest: Larkin Miller-Spaulding, heiress to a fortune and daughter of extremely questionable parents.* A pretty but mousy brunette around Mia's age with zero interest in a makeover, she wore her stick-straight hair in a bob and her usual uniform of gray tunic over black leggings. Her tortoiseshell glasses slipped down her nose and she pushed them back. "Larkin! Hi. I'm so glad you came."

"Of course. I'd never miss my best friend's wedding shower."

Mia, who'd known Larkin for maybe a week in total, responded to this statement from the odd duck with a hug.

Teri stuck two fingers in her mouth and issued an earsplitting whistle. The room quieted. "Ladies, get a drink, then we'll kick off the shower activities. It's time to par-tay! Woot, woot!"

The guests availed themselves of the champagne glasses being passed by the waitstaff. Mia saw a face she recognized among them. "Skye. Hi. Welcome to New York."

Skye picked out the fullest flute on her tray and handed it to Mia, along with a grateful smile. "Thanks to you, I do feel welcome. I really appreciate the soft landing."

Mia held up her flute to toast the bartender. "Here's to this being the first of many jobs at Belle

*For more on Larkin and her sketchy parents, please see *Long Island Iced Tina.*

View." *As long as you provide the occasional intel on your sketchy cousin.*

Usually far more comfortable in the background of other people's events, Mia allowed herself to be the center of attention for a change. She welcomed the break from stressful recent events weighing on her. After about twenty minutes of mingling, Teri emitted another piercing whistle. She held up a roll of toilet paper. "We're playing a shower game. Here's how it works. Everyone, divide into teams of two. You'll get a roll of toilet paper you have to turn into a wedding dress. We'll do a runway fashion show of the dresses and Mia will pick the winner. Mia, you can play, too, but only for fun."

Teri tossed toilet paper rolls to the guests, who were busy counting off in twos. Nicole raised her hand. "I'll be Mia's partner. I might not be around for the fashion show. You never know when your water's gonna break."

"If it does, this will come in handy." Mia held up her roll of toilet paper to roars of laughter.

The guests paired off. Nicole began draping toilet paper around Mia to form the semblance of a wedding gown. "I'm so happy for you, Mimi." She gestured for Mia to spin so the toilet paper could wrap her waist.

"Mimi. No one's called me that in forever. I think you're my oldest friend here. I mean, like you're the friend I've known the longest."

"I know. All the way back to elementary school at Our Lady of Perpetual Anguish."

The two women shared a smile. "Speaking of old friends," Mia said, "you know who I ran into? Ruth Behling and Rose Nunzio. I'd already seen each of them on their own and things seemed fine. I even forgave Rose for having a kid by my husband, which I think is pretty generous of me. But when I saw them today, they made it clear they don't want anything to do with me."

Nicole paused. Her smile disappeared. She wrapped a swath of toilet paper around Mia's arm. "Darn, it broke."

She began wrapping again. Mia held out a hand to stop her. "Stop. You know something. Tell me."

"I don't know," Nicole said, conflicted. "I don't want to hurt you."

"Please. Do *not* worry about that. With all that's happened over the last couple of years, I've developed a hide so thick it would make a rhinoceros jealous. Hit me with whatever it is you're hiding."

"If you say so," Nicole said, sounding unconvinced. "It's just a rumor. I can't swear to it. But the Astoria gossip grapevine says that when Rose found out she was pregnant, she begged Adam to leave you and marry her."

"Really," Mia said, more angry than wounded. "I take back forgiving her for having sex with my husband."

"She's not a bad person. I think she was just scared and in a panic. Luckily, she found Diego. He's a good guy. Superprotective, though. So's his brother, Mark."

Mia gaped at Nicole. "Wait, Mark? As in Ruth's fiancé? He's Diego's brother?"

"Half brothers. They have the same mother. They're really close. It's how Rose met Diego— through Ruth."

"Which all happened after I moved, so I had no

way of knowing," Mia said, digesting the revelation. "Nic, when you say they're superprotective,
what exactly do you mean?"

"Only that when it comes to anything with their
family, you don't want to cross them. My brother
Joey belongs to the same gym they all do. Some
guy tried hitting on Ruth and Mark went after him
with a barbell. He never came back to the gym.
Joey heard another story about how both brothers
had a talk with the father of a kid who was bullying
Corey. Joey knows the dad, who was a bully himself. But not after Mark and Diego got through
with him." Nicole resumed creating Mia's toilet
paper wedding dress. "Enough. This is your shower.
No more gossip."

"Uh-huh," Mia responded absent-mindedly, every
cell of her brain analyzing this new information. It
obviously hadn't reached Pete and Ryan, who'd
been thrown off course from the slashed-tire investigation by Circus Mann's murder. "Great job,
Nicole. I love it."

"I'm not done. I want to make a train."

"I'm not a train kinda bride."

Mia left her bewildered friend and hurried off
to the privacy of the ladies' room lounge, trailing
toilet paper from her arms and waist. She called
Pete. "I have news," she said in a whisper, not wanting to attract the attention of her guests.

"It's your wedding shower. I know because Cammie billed the expenses to my credit card. Enjoy
the cake. Those are genuine gold flakes on it."

"This is way more important than my shower."
Mia recounted every detail of what she learned
from Nicole. "Adam refused to dump me for Rose,

and then he suddenly showed up again in her life, threatening to sue for custody if she and Diego didn't pay him off. Talk about motive. And Diego and Mark . . . overprotective hotheads. It doesn't look like Adam's murder was premeditated. More of an impulsive act. Any of these three—or all of them—could have done it."

"Mia?" someone called from the ballroom. "Has anyone seen our guest of honor?"

"I'm on the toilet!" Mia yelled.

"Classy," Pete said, his tone dry. "That Shane's a lucky guy."

"I gotta get back out there. You're welcome for the leads."

Mia started to leave the lounge. She stopped and did an about-face. She opened the door of the room's closet. It contained a single item: Mia's wedding dress. She unzipped the garment bag to take a peek at the beautiful gown. "I cannot wait to wear you," she murmured. She closed the bag, taking care not to catch the gown's delicate chiffon in the zipper, then exited the lounge.

A cluster of women draped in toilet paper awaited her in the ballroom. "Time to judge," Teri said, steering Mia to a chair.

One by one, women paraded past Mia, modeling their TP wedding finery. She raved about the "gown" Cammie and Larkin had created, a mini-dress festooned with paper ruffles. "Larkin, I think you could actually wear that somewhere."

"Thanks," Larkin made an awkward pirouette. "We had help."

"You weren't supposed to tell her," Cammie hissed.

"I'm not lying to my BFF. My advisers recommended I invest in Hillary Marks's company. She's a designer. I FacedTimed her for some input."

"Hillary Marks?" Mia repeated, her voice a squeak. "She's not *a* designer. She's the hottest one around right now."

Larkin held up her phone, revealing Hillary Marks, who waved to Mia. "Hi, and thanks for the compliment. Larkin, send me pictures of the dress. I can use it as a prototype for my new bridal line."

"Sure."

"And for the last time, Larkin, please let me do a makeover on you." Hillary clasped her hands together in prayer. "I'll give you any clothes you want from my line for free. All I ask is that you let me burn your gray tunics."

"No, thank you." Larkin ended the call and faced Mia. "Are we disqualified?"

"'Fraid so," Mia said.

Cammie, grumbling, led Larkin off. The fashion show finished with Mia awarding the Golden TP, a trophy Teri created, to the creative efforts of Cimmanin and Guadalupe, who got extra credit for incorporating the chef's paper toque into the duo's veil design.

The rest of the party was equally entertaining. Dream Events, the caterer handling Mia's wedding, provided a delicious meal for the shower. Evans insisted on making the cake, though, a spectacular almond cream cake decorated with the pricey gold flakes Pete mentioned. A second party game involved guests writing down ways Mia and Shane might spice up their marriage if they fell into a rut. Everyone wrote *have sex* except Elisabetta, who wrote *fare sesso—have sex* in Italian.

Mia's shower gifts ran from the practical to the salacious: a see-through corset, courtesy of Cimmanin, along with a hefty gift certificate to sex toys from Good Vibration, her new sponsor. "Boy, does my set of mixing bowls look dull," Madison said. "I'm glad we added the month of cooking classes."

"Considering what a bad cook she is, Shane will be grateful," Elisabetta said to laughter from the others.

"Thanks a lot, Nonna." Mia gave her grandmother a jokey side-eye. She opened an envelope from Larkin and took out a letter. She scanned it. "This is from the New York City Landmarks Commission. It says they're going to take a very close look at the Circus Feeks' application for having Dan Fee's house designated a landmark and evaluate whether the request was made in good faith. Oh, Larkin . . ." Mia choked up.

"I heard there was a problem with your new house and did what I could to help fix it as my gift to you." Larkin looked puzzled. "Isn't that what friends do? Use their incredibly high-priced legal teams to work connections at the highest level of government?"

Cimmanin put an arm around Larkin's shoulder. "It sure is. When the party's over, I got a couple of lawsuits to run by you. Some copyright infringement. Invasion of privacy. Nothing major."

The shower ended shortly afterward. Mia said goodbye to her guests, each of whom left with a high-end designer candle, which she assumed was courtesy of Pete's credit card. She exchanged a warm hug with pal Jamie Boldano when he showed up to pick up wife Madison. He gestured toward an empty corner of the room. Mia got the hint he wanted privacy and the two strolled over together. "Dad told me about Maladugotti," Jamie said in a low voice. "His betrayal was a wake-up call for Dad. What a dumb, arrogant thing for that guy to do."

"And insecure when you think about it. He didn't trust his own ability enough not to be threatened by someone else."

"Maybe you're the one who should become a therapist, not me," Jamie said with affection. "You're right. In the end, it worked out for the best. Dad considered him the Family heir apparent. But it would have been a disaster. Maladugotti would have reversed the current direction away from criminal activity back toward more of it."

"And I would have had to put up a fight, along with everyone else here, because no way will I ever let Belle View become a front for crime."

Jamie gave a somber nod of agreement, then switched gears. "I've been working on your wedding service." Mia and Shane had opted for a civil service in New York, followed by a convalidation ceremony for just the two of them at a Catholic church in Italy on their honeymoon. They'd asked Jamie Boldano to officiate the civil ceremony. He'd earned a license online, figuring it might tie in well with his future practice as a marriage and family therapist. "I'm truly honored you asked me to lead it."

"Just make sure you leave plenty of time for our personal vows. I have so much I wanna say to Shane, mine are turning into more of a novella."

Jamie and Madison left, and Mia finished her

goodbyes to the other guests. Before departing, she went into the kitchen to thank the catering and waitstaff for a marvelous event. She missed one of them, a kitchen worker, only catching her back as the girl disappeared down the rear staircase. Something about her triggered a feeling of recognition, but Mia couldn't place what.

She stepped outside Belle View to find a purple Tesla waiting for her. Shane got out of the driver's side. He wore a chauffeur's cap that he removed as he bowed to her. "Your carriage awaits, madame."

"You scared me when you said carriage." Mia gave her fiancé an affectionate grin. "I thought Cammie went ahead and booked the Clydesdales and they were gonna pull up behind you. Where'd you get the cap?"

"A guy in my building lent it to me. It's from when he was in the chorus of *Annie*." Shane opened the door and Mia climbed inside. He got in, started the car, and they drove out of the parking lot. "How was the shower?"

"Wonderful. I couldn't have asked for anything better."

"Wanna tell me about it?"

Mia considered this. While she wanted to share Nicole's dirt on Mark and Diego with Shane, it would disturb the afterglow of the wonderful evening. She rested her head against the back of her seat. "I'll fill you in on everything tomorrow. All the champagne I knocked back is starting to hit me. I'm ready for a good night's sleep."

Unfortunately, this goal proved to be wishful thinking. Only four hours after rolling into bed, the incessant ringing of her phone roused Mia from a deep sleep. She fumbled around for her phone. Seeing the caller was Evans, she pressed Accept. "Hey," she said, her voice groggy. She checked and saw it was six a.m. "What's going on? Is there a problem with the Kiwanis Club breakfast? I checked the Marine Ballroom before I left last night, and it was all set up for them."

"It's not that." The tone of the sous-chef's voice alarmed Mia. She sat up, now wide awake. She'd never heard Evans sound so upset. "I got here early to try out a new recipe for the club, breakfast calzones. I heard running water and went upstairs. Someone turned on the shower in the ladies' lounge. It was on all night. The Bay Ballroom is completely flooded. It's unusable."

"No." Mia fought back tears. "I'm on my way."

Mia threw on clothes and raced over to Belle View, where she met up with her father, Shane, Cammie, and Pete. "He was with me, so I made him come," Cammie explained.

The five hurried up the stairs to where Evans and Guadalupe were waiting on the second-floor landing, grim expressions on their faces. The two chefs opened the doors to the ballroom. The flood had overtaken at least half the room's carpet, turning it into a soggy, unsalvageable mess. It had also saturated the surrounding baseboard.

The group surveyed the damage in silence. Ravello finally spoke. "This much water, the damage won't only be cosmetic. It's gotta have damaged the ceiling underneath and whatever pipes are there, too."

"I'll get a structural engineer out here as soon as I can," Shane said. "I'll let them know it's an emergency."

"Let me take a look at the shower," Pete said.

"I'll show you," Evans said. "But walk carefully. The carpet is soaked through."

Pete followed Evans. Each step they took was accompanied by the unpleasant sound of the drenched floor covering squishing beneath their feet.

Mia covered her face with her hands. "This is a disaster." She dropped her hands. "Focus, Mia. Focus." She shook off her emotions. "Okay. Since this room is in the west corner of the building, any damage below it would affect our offices and a small portion of the kitchen. It won't affect the Marine Ballroom, so we don't have to cancel events scheduled for it. Luckily, we're light on bookings in this room for the next couple of weeks. I can see how many I can switch to downstairs, and we can also put up the party tent to enclose the patio. I'll offer a generous discount to anyone we have to move. None of the scheduled events hit numbers that would bump up against the fire code. Except one."

"Our wedding," Shane said. Mia bit her lip and nodded. He took her hand and gave it a consoling squeeze. "I'll get the engineer here this morning, even if I have to kidnap him. I can get guys over to start ripping out the carpet in an hour. We'll have the place up and running in a few days."

Mia gave him a wan smile. She appreciated his optimism but didn't share it. The sight of Evans and Pete sinking into the carpet as they walked sent an ominous message about what might await workers when they tore out the carpet and accessed the waterlogged floor and first-floor ceiling below it. She was afraid with good reason that what they discovered could take weeks to fix.

Pete and Evans emerged from the ladies' lounge where the shower was housed. "The on-off valve is working, so it's not like someone couldn't turn it off after they turned it on," the detective said. "Which is suspicious."

"But there's a giant wet rag on the floor, so someone may have tried to sop up the water, then panicked and ran," Evans said.

Mia's heart dropped. She felt sick to her stomach. She pushed past the others and hurried to the lounge, ignoring the cold water on her sandaled feet. She saw the sodden mass of fabric Evans referenced and lifted it off the floor, confirming her worst fears. Mia held up her once-beautiful wedding dress, now a viciously slashed and sodden ruin.

"No," she murmured.

Then, unable to control her emotions any longer, she lost it.

CHAPTER 26

With Pete already on-site, the Bay Ballroom quickly morphed into a crime scene, adding a dose of intrigue that the arriving members of the Kiwanis Club considered a welcome change from their usual boring meetings.

Cammie, Evans, and Guadalupe oversaw the event while the others retreated to Ravello's office. Ravello turned over the job of comforting Mia to her fiancé and took the lead on hunting down a structural engineer and the necessary repairmen.

"I'm being punished," Mia declared. Having already wept her way through one box of tissues, she extracted one from a second box to wipe her eyes. "Mom and Nonna wanted Lucille to combine their wedding dresses into one for me. Lucille and I came up with a plot where I was gonna lie to them and say she couldn't find a way to do it so I could wear the dress I wanted to. And now I have *no* dress to wear. Because I'm a bad person and don't deserve one."

This engendered another round of sobbing. Shane held her in her arms. "Bella, it's gonna be all right. Nothing's gonna stop us from getting married. I don't care if you walk down the aisle in your underwear."

"Good, because that's what I may end up wearing. But where's our reception gonna take place? We're kidding ourselves if we think the Bay Ballroom will be ready by our wedding. Where else are we going to find a place we can afford that'll hold five hundred people on such short notice?"

Shane paled. "Five hundred?" he repeated with a gulp.

Mia nodded. "And that's with the list pared down."

"Wow. Okay. Well . . . don't worry. It's gonna be okay. We got this." Shane sounded less convinced with each platitude.

Pete appeared in the doorway. "The crime scene unit will be done pretty soon. We've got a case of second-degree criminal mischief here."

"This wasn't some cutesy, mischievous prank," Mia said, ire raised. "It was sabotage."

"Don't let the name fool you. Second-degree criminal mischief is classified as a felony. Whoever did this is looking at some serious time."

"Oh." Mia sniffled. "I feel a little better."

Pete took one of the chairs Ravello kept on hand for client interviews and positioned it across from Mia and Shane. "I want you both to know that I feel a personal connection to this case. I was planning to capitalize on the magic of your event to repropose to Cammie, so to have your wedding destroyed by some sicko makes me very, very angry. Mia, close your eyes and think over your shower. Did you see or hear anything that would help us nail the perp?"

Mia wiped her eyes and closed them. She took her time running through every moment of the event, from arrival to departure. "Skye Terrasanti. The bartender. She moved to New Jersey from Florida and got a job working my party. She's Annarita's cousin. You know, Adam's girlfriend and—" She flashed on an image of the sole kitchen worker she hadn't personally thanked, the girl she only saw from the back, running down the stairs to make her escape. Mia's eyes popped open. "Annarita! Who hates me. It had to be them, the two cousins. They were in on it together."

Pete slapped his hands on his thighs. "Now, that's what I call a lead." He stood up. "I'm gonna head over to the station to write up a report and bring in the cousins for a li'l chat. I'll keep you posted."

Mia and Shane thanked him and he left. Ravello hung up his desk phone. "An engineer's on his way. Donny Senior's sending over his contractor with a crew to assess the damage and start in on repairs. Once everything is completed, we'll have to get a building inspector out here to sign off on everything." He sighed. "I miss the days when you could find one on the take."

"I'll call anyone booked into the Bay Ballroom and discuss alternate arrangements," Shane said.

"If you're doing that, what should I do?" Mia asked.

Shane placed a comforting hand on her cheek. "Do whatever you need to take care of yourself.

That's job one for you right now." He kissed her on the forehead. "I love you."

"I love you, too."

Before Mia could embark on any form of self-care, she faced another task—an onerous one. She steeled herself for it.

"I have a confession to make," she told Gia and Elisabetta. The two sat across from her, next to each other on Elisabetta's sofa. She drew a deep breath, then shared the plot she'd hatched with Lucille. "I'm so sorry. I should have been honest with you. This is payback for sneaking around behind your backs."

"Oh, sweetie." Gia got up from the couch and came over to give her daughter a hug. "We're the ones who owe you an apology. It's *your* wedding. You should be able to get married in your undies if you want to."

"Funny you should say that," Mia said with a wry expression. "At this point, that may be my only option."

"*Sciocchezza*," Elisabetta said with a dismissive wave of her hand. "Nonsense. No granddaughter of mine is gonna parade down the aisle in her panties. Call the store where you bought the dress. Maybe they got another one."

"I did. They don't."

"Then go over there and buy a different one."

Mia shook her head. "No. The universe sent me a message: Go with the original plan. I talked to Lucille and she's going to do her best to create a wearable mash-up of both your wedding gowns."

"*Bene*," Elisabetta said. "If that doesn't work, I'm sure she can alter my dress for you."

"Or mine," Gia said.

Elisabetta made a face. "Nobody's gonna be able see her under all that ugly fabric."

Gia glared at her. "If she wears your dress, she's gonna look like one of those toilet paper cozy dolls."

Elisabetta let out an angry gasp. "*Riprendilo!*"

"No, *you* take it back!"

Mia left her mother and grandmother arguing and tromped upstairs. *Toilet paper seems to be a theme in my life these days,* she pondered. *I wonder what the message behind that is?* She checked the time on her phone and did a double take. "How can it only be nine a.m.?" she wondered out loud.

Doorstop, unaffected by the morning's dramatic events, roused himself from his beauty sleep. He yawned and meowed a request for breakfast. Mia removed the cover from Pizzazz's cage and let the parakeet out. After feeding them both, she collapsed on her bed. The day loomed long and miserable. "My dreams about planning my wedding never included murders and vandalism and no wedding dress or reception venue," she said to Doorstop, who'd jumped on the bed and curled up next to her after scarfing down his breakfast. "Maybe I'm getting the wrong message from the universe. Maybe it's telling me not to get married at all. I effed it up once. What if I effed it up again?" Doorstop gave a sympathetic meow and nuzzled her with his head. She petted his silky golden-ginger fur.

The lack of a good night's sleep began to get to Mia and her eyelids fluttered shut. Her phone

rang and she ignored it, letting the call go to voice
mail. A few seconds later, it rang again, and she si-
lenced it. A few more seconds later, it vibrated in-
sistently. "Someone really wants to talk to me,
Doorie. Ooh, maybe Pete made an arrest."

The phone rang a fourth time and she answered. But the caller wasn't Pete. "Why don't you
get married at my house?"

"Larkin?" Mia said, surprised to hear from her.
"Hi. You heard about the Bay Ballroom already?
Who told you?"

"It's the lead story on the *Tri Trib* website."

Mia went to her phone's search engine and
called up the website. Photos showing the damage
to the ballroom courtesy of Cammie were accompanied by a story from editor Teri Fuoco, excoriat-
ing the criminals who vandalized the facility and
urging anyone with information on the crime to
come forward.

"I mean it," Larkin said, insistent. "You can get
married here."

Here happened to be a massive stone mansion
and grounds on the edge of the Long Island
Sound that made the estates extolled in classic
books like *The Great Gatsby* look like shacks. "It's a
gorgeous location," Mia said, tempted.

"Please. It'd be fun to throw a wedding. I'll
open up the Miller Art Collection to everyone. I
have a new installation. It's called *Naked Pieces*. It's
very sensual. The artist is also a porn star. She's
very talented in both areas."

"Maybe we'll keep the guests away from the artwork. Weddings can get rowdy. I'd feel terrible if
anything was damaged." Knowing Larkin's pre-
dilection for bizarre art, Mia thought separating it

from older, more conservative guests like the elder Boldanos was a wise move. "If you really mean it—"

"I do, I do. Oh, I said *I do*. That's funny. I want *you* to say, *I do* at my house." Larkin sounded pleased at her own cleverness.

"Then, I say *I do* to moving our wedding to your *house*."

"Yay!" Larkin enthused. Mia could hear the quirky girl clapping with delight. "I have to call Cammie and Teri and tell them their idea worked." The heiress ended the call.

"Of course it was Cammie and Teri's idea." Mia rolled her eyes at her friends' machinations. Still, she had to admit it was a wonderful pivot. She lay back on the bed. *Dare I get excited about my wedding again?* was her last thought before drifting off for a nap.

CHAPTER 27

The first thing Mia did when she awoke from her nap was call Shane and share the news about their new wedding venue. "If it makes you happy, I'm happy," was his kind and generous response.

"I'm texting you some photos I took of Larkin's place the last time I was there." Mia did so.

There was a pause. "Um . . . is it appropriate to go *hubba hubba* over a house?" Shane asked.

"If there was ever a time to bring back that old expression, along with a wolf whistle, it's for the Miller-Spaulding estate. Not to diss our terrif place of employment, but we've definitely traded up."

"Then, hubba *hubba!*"

Mia laughed. "I've gotta go. I'm meeting with Lucille, the dressmaker, to see if she can cobble together a gown for me to wear for the wedding. I've come to terms with the fact I'll be wearing Frankendress."

"You'll look beautiful in anything you wear."

Mia's heart overflowed with love for her gallant fiancé. "Here's hoping you still feel that way when you see me heading toward you down the aisle in whatever she manages to come up with."

The couple blew kisses to each other before hanging up. Mia pulled on a T-shirt over leggings and slipped on a pair of sneakers for the walk down the block to Lucille. Her phone rang with a FaceTime from Teri. "I got news," she said, her face sporting a glow that Mia had learned came with the reporter landing a big scoop.

"I'm about to leave for a wedding dress salvage project, but if this is about the Bay Ballroom, I can be late."

"It is. Not to brag, which of course means I'm gonna brag, but getting people to reveal stuff they shouldn't is my superpower. I badgered Pete for an update on the sabotage and finally broke him down. All I ask is that when Pete calls you with an update on the case, act like you didn't hear it from me first."

"He'll know I did, but we can play pretend. Hit me."

"The cops tracked down Skye and Annarita. Skye was genuinely clueless about what happened. She was only guilty of getting her cousin a job working for the caterer in the kitchen for your shower. She fell for Annarita's sob story about how Adam left her broke."

"I think that's probably true, not that it justifies what I assume she did."

"The Jersey police picked up Annarita and delivered her to Pete. She panicked and admitted everything. You know how you saw her running down the stairs? She didn't leave the building. She hid until everyone was gone. Once she was alone, she took a box cutter to your dress—"

"I knew it! I remembered seeing the box cutter and put it together with my dress." Mia allowed herself a moment of pride in her deduction skills.

"And then she turned on the shower and somehow snuck out of the building without triggering the alarm."

"Hmmm. I think when the security company is done with the Dan Fee house, we need to hire them for an upgrade at Belle View."

"She's been charged with second-degree criminal mischief. If she cuts a plea, they may reduce charges, but she's still in trouble."

Mia thought of Adam and what he'd put Annarita through. It didn't excuse her vengeful behavior. But it did reduce the onus a bit. "Maybe we can help with the reduction of charges. She needs to at least take responsibility for her actions, but I blame Adam for pushing her over the edge. I know he fed her lies about me and our relationship, making himself out to be the victim and me the wicked beeyotch who seduced him."

Teri chuckled. "Mia Carina, wanton temptress." She laughed even harder.

"It's not *that* hard to believe," Mia said, a little annoyed.

Mia finished with Teri. She texted the news about Annarita to her father and fiancé, with a warning to play dumb with Pete, although she thought to herself, *if he can't figure out we're all covering for Teri's big mouth, he should turn in his badge.*

Mia finally made her way to Lucille, offering an apology for her late arrival. "Not a problem," Lucille said. "Since I retired and only take the jobs I want, I don't go by a clock anymore."

This time, the elegant seamstress wore a flowing silk tunic patterned with teal and terra-cotta flowers over slim black pants. "Put that outfit on my honeymoon list," Mia said. "But I'm paying for it." She playfully wagged a finger at Lucille. "Enough freebies, you."

Lucille responded with a sphinxlike smile. "We'll see. But on to the task at hand. Now that we're serious about Frankendress, I need to confirm your measurements. What you're wearing is formfitting enough for me to get an accurate take on them. You don't need to remove anything." Lucille took a tape measure out of the antique carved walnut chest of drawers that held her sewing supplies and wrapped it around Mia's bustline. She followed this with her waist, abdomen, and hips. "I've been thinking about how to marry the two different gowns—no pun intended—and I think I can come up with a dress that won't embarrass either of us."

"That would be a dream come true."

Mia's phone alerted her to a video call from Larkin. Lucille gestured for her to take the call and Larkin popped up on the phone screen. "I had a couple of ideas for your wedding and ran them by Cammie. She loved them."

"Uh-oh," Mia said under her breath, to Lucille's amusement.

"My next-door neighbor just had a yacht delivered. I'm sure he'd let me borrow it. What if it picked you and Shane up at Belle View and brought you across the Sound and that's how you arrive for the wedding?"

"Let me think about it," Mia said, waving her

hand behind her back in a vigorous *no* gesture, to the amusement of Lucille.

"Also, I'm one of the principal donors to the New York Philharmonic. I checked and they're dark the night of your wedding. I thought they could play the Wedding March for your bridal processional."

Lucille's eyes widened. She mouthed *Wow!* and covered her mouth to hide a laugh.

Mia did her best to control herself. "Uh . . . That's such an amazing offer, Larkin. Thank you so much. But I was kind of leaning toward something simpler. Like, just a flautist or cellist."

"Ah. Got it. One last idea. What about for the Viennese dessert hour, I import a real Viennese pastry chef?"

"Love that," Mia said, genuinely enthusiastic. "Go for it."

"Yay! Talk to you later. Oh, I almost forgot. My lawyers got in touch with my friends at the Landmark Commission. They're denying the Circus Feek's application for Dan Fee's house being declared an historical landmark."

Mia placed a hand on her heart. "OMG, Larkin. I can't tell you what a relief that is. I'm so grateful to you. We owe you big-time."

"I wish I could take credit for it, but I can't. They were going to deny it anyway. It doesn't meet their criteria. They did say you could put up a plaque acknowledging he lived there if you want."

"We might. He meant a lot to his fans. It would be a nice way to honor his legacy without going all the way to making his house a tourist attraction."

"I'll let them know." Larkin signed off.

"You heard all that, right?" Mia asked Lucille, who nodded.

"Yes, and I'm so glad we won't have to worry about all those fans spilling over the sidewalk and street anymore." Lucille wrapped up her cloth measuring tape and returned it to the dresser drawer. "The theme song they sang made me *pazzo*. It worked its way into my dreams. I was hearing it from a radio in a dream the night your poor husband was murdered. I remember because the thump from him being hit by a car woke me up."

Memories of the awful night came flooding back to Mia, from her altercation with Adam to the sight of his bruised body. She suddenly flashed on one specific declaration he made during his ill-fated attempt to rekindle their marriage: *"I'm gonna win you back, Mia Carina. And no one, repeat no one, will stop us from moving into the circus house and making it our forever home."* His emphasis on Dan Fee's house didn't make sense to her at the time, so she ignored it. But now it felt like the final link in the chain of events leading to his death.

Mia stared at Lucille, her instinct for sniffing out crime on high alert. "Lucille, did you mention hearing the song that night to the police?"

"No. I told them about the thump waking me up, but I didn't tell them about the dream. I didn't think it was important."

"If it was a dream, it wouldn't be," Mia said. "But . . . what if it wasn't a dream?"

CHAPTER 28

Mia erased the whiteboard on the office wall she usually used for laying out event schedules. Instead, she put it to work mapping out a criminal investigation, her suspicions having been buttressed by a good old-fashioned online search.

"I have a theory about who might have killed Adam," she told Shane, Teri, and Cammie, who were all crammed into her small office. "But before I share it with anyone, especially Pete, I want to establish a timeline of Adam's reappearance in my life. And why I think his death might be tied to the Dan Fee house."

"You think?" Cammie sounded doubtful. She furrowed her brow. "It feels like those are apples and oranges. Although I never got why that's such a popular example of opposites. One's an apple, one's an orange. Big deal. They're both fruit."

"You know what throws me?" Teri said, "That tomatoes are a fruit and not a vegetable. That will never make sense to me."

The others concurred. Mia cleared her throat to get their attention. "Focus, people."

"Sorry," Teri said. "As you were."

Mia wrote *Wedding Expo—Adam Sighting One* on the board. "This was my first Adam sighting, which happened before we found out my grandmother bought Dan Fee's house. Adam was hard up for money. He knew I was running Belle View, so I think he brought his girlfriend/kind-of-fiancée Annarita to the expo under the pretext of checking it for themselves when he was really checking out me and my business."

Cammie gave a derisive snort. "Who has a *kind-of-fiancée?* She either is or isn't."

"Adam played by his own loosey-goosey rules. Woe to any woman who ignored the bazillions of red flags they waved and the alarms they set off, like yours truly." Mia wrote *Mets Game—Adam Sighting Two* on the board. "Second sighting is at the Mets game, which is also the second time Adam disappears. What do these sightings have in common? Adam flees after knowing I saw him. He wants to check me out—that's a whole other story I won't go into right now—"

"He thought women lose their looks after thirty," Shane interrupted with a glower, igniting outraged protests from Cammie and Teri.

Mia whistled to regain everyone's attention. "Again, focus! To repeat: at sightings one and two, Adam wanted to check me out but didn't want me to catch him checking me out."

Mia wrote *Adam Confronts Me—Sighting Three* on the board. "This is when Adam showed up at my house to say he wanted me back. Now, what happened between Sighting Two and Sighting Three?"

Teri thrust her hand in the air like an eager third grader, bouncing up and down on her folding metal chair. "Oh, oh, I know, I know!"

"I hated kids like you in school," Shane said, scowling at her.

Teri ignored him. "Between Two and Three, I wrote a breaking story about how the house your grandmother bought was the longtime residence of comic artist Dan Fee. Sidebar: I got so many likes and shares on that story we increased our ad revenue by twenty percent. Yay me."

"That's right," Mia continued, "at least time-linewise, although congrats on the story's success, too. Teri breaks the news about Dan Fee's house. Crowds show up. And a few days later, so does Adam, begging me to reconcile." Mia drew an arrow pointing upward between sightings two and three and wrote *Dan Fee Breaking Story* above it. "The story implied the house was full of valuable memorabilia, which it is."

Mia snapped the top back on the dry erase marker and transitioned to using it as a pointer, aiming it at the arrow. "Lucille told me a detail she never shared with the police because she didn't think it was important. She said she dreamed she heard the dumb Circusman theme song on the radio the night Adam was murdered. That reminded me of what he said when he was trying to get me back: no one would stop us from living in the *circus house*. It sounded like that was really important to him . . . and that someone was trying to stop it from happening."

"So, you think maybe Lucille really did hear the

song, but it was playing from a car radio or an electronic device funneled through a car," Shane said.

"Exactly," Mia said. "Adam susses me out. He hears about how much the contents of the Dan Fee house might be worth, which makes me even more financially desirable than just being an event planner at Belle View. I think he connected with the Circus Feek board members, who were all over the house as soon as the story broke and that somehow led to his murder. Maybe he offered them some kind of deal based on what he figured he'd be entitled to from selling memorabilia we uncovered in the house. *If* he and I resumed our lives as husband and wife."

"He could have pitched a side hustle," Teri said. "Sneaking stuff out of the house without you even knowing and splitting the proceeds of sales with the board members if they were all in on it. If they weren't, then whoever he was dealing with."

"Good one," Mia said. "I can totally see Adam doing something so sneaky."

The others nodded agreement.

"Based on my interaction with the Feeks, I have a theory about who Adam's contact might be," Mia said. "But before I bring it up to Pete, I wanted to run all this by you and make sure I don't sound like a nutjob. What do you think?"

"I think what we have here," Cammie said, "is apples and apples."

The support of her friends gave Mia the confidence to share her theory with Pete. Cammie helped her sell it to him. Mia didn't have to ask how. The glow on his face after a weekend getaway answered the question. "I had Hinkle check alibis on the fan club board," he told Mia when he dropped Cammie off at Belle View post getaway. "A couple of the Feeks provided alibis for one another, and you know how much stock I put into friends and lovers cutting each other a free pass for a crime timetable—a giant goose egg, as in zero."

"This is going to sound very TV cop show," Mia said. "But what about a sting? Put the most logical suspect in a position where they incriminate themselves?"

"We generally do those a lot less than you see on TV because they're pricey. Oh, to have the budget of a *Law & Order* episode. But this case might warrant it. I'll run it up the flagpole at the precinct and see if my superiors salute."

"Great." Mia eyed his off-duty weekend togs of Bermuda shorts, slip-on sandals over white socks, and a T-shirt that read *Party Till the Check Liver Light Comes On.* "But you might wanna go home and change first."

Pete got a yes for a sting operation that would hopefully entrap Adam's killer, and possibly Circus Mann's as well. But when Mia offered herself as bait in the operation, she got a resounding no from the detective. Shane seconded that and offered himself up for the job. Mia did manage to wrangle approval to join Pete, his partner Ryan Hinkle, and other NYPD operatives in monitoring the sting.

They rendezvoused in the surveillance van at

around one a.m. the next morning. The vehicle was battered and nondescript on the outside, except for the logo of a pest extermination company. Inside, it was kitted out with a variety of computer equipment that would enable the law enforcement officials to view and record Shane as he engaged with the suspect inside the Dan Fee house. "Props on the logo," Mia said to Pete, who was busy attaching a wire to Shane's impressively developed chest. "Do the criminals you target ever figure out they're the pests you're trying to exterminate?"

"A couple have gotten the joke after we cuffed them and stuffed them into a patrol car. All done." He delivered this to Shane and handed him a pullover sweater.

"Good thing the weather's gotten colder," Shane said, pulling on the sweater. "Easier to hide the wire. I had a lotta problems with that in Florida. Try hiding this thing under a T-shirt, or a muscle tee, or even a button-down you sweat through the minute you step outside."

Mia gawked at her fiancé. "You've worn a wire before?"

"A few times." Shane delivered the revelation with remarkable casualness. "Once for my dad, when he needed to get incriminating evidence for sketchy associates he thought were skimming money from him. Once for the feds, when they wanted to bust a competing Family. And once not for real, during my only acting gig when I played an informant on an Italian cop show, *Blocca o lo Otterrai.*"

"*Freeze or You'll Get it,*" Mia translated. "I know that show. Nonna watches it on the Italian cable channel." She flashed Shane a sexy look. "Look at me, engaged to a TV star. I learn something new about you every day."

Shane returned the look, adding some smolder of his own, to the annoyance of Pete. "*Hello*. Crime operation in progress here. Save the flirty stuff for later."

"Yes, sir." Shane adjusted his sweater. "Okay. I'm good to go."

Pete pulled open the van side door facing the sidewalk. "Keep hunting for Fee memorabilia to sell from the house and keep the suspect talking. Chances are pretty good they'll blabber until they get themselves in trouble with us."

Fear assailed Mia. Nervous about dislodging Shane's surveillance apparatus, she clasped his hands in hers instead of hugging him. "Desperate people are dangerous. Be careful."

"I will."

Mia and Shane exchanged a kiss she prayed wouldn't be their last and he jumped out of the van onto the sidewalk. Mia shut her eyes, mentally following the route mapped out for Shane to distance him from the van. First, he'd cut through a neighbor's yard to access the alley, making sure not to trigger a security light. Once in the alley, Elisabetta, who was all in on the plot, would let him into her first-floor abode so he could exit out the front door, offering the illusion that he'd come from Mia's apartment to meet with the person in question at the Dan Fee house.

Finally, after an agonizing wait that felt like an hour but proved to be less than three minutes by the clock app on Mia's phone, Shane appeared on a feed from security cameras on her house, covertly adjusted to film the front of the Fee house. The van occupants watched as the suspect stepped out of the shadow of a tree on the sidewalk's easement to greet Shane. "Do you have the key?" Shane held up the home's front door key. "All right. Let's do this."

Shane and the suspect disappeared into the house. The van fell silent, waiting for the feed from Shane's wire kicked in. "Do you hear that?" Ryan said. "It's picking up his heartbeat."

"Actually," Mia said, embarrassed, "that's mine. I'm really nervous, so it's thumping loud."

Pete released an aggravated grunt. "Take a pill or do yoga, Carina. That heartbeat of yours is distracting."

"Sorry."

Mia tried calming herself with deep-breathing exercises. Balancing this with listening to the anxiety-producing feed from Shane's wire proved a daunting task but she did her best, managing to reduce her heart's thumping to barely audible.

The sound of footsteps on the tile of Fee's entry transitioned to the wooden floors of his living room. The footsteps stopped. Mia and the NYPD detectives heard Shane say, "Before I do anything, I've been thinking about the split."

"We already went through this."

The suspect sounded angry, alarming Mia. She knew Shane was taking a chance changing the terms of the deal he'd already struck, but it was the best way of getting compromising evidence recorded.

"Yeah, but I'm the one with more at stake here,"

Shane continued. "My fiancée finds out what I'm up to, she'll dump me. So I was thinking we go sixty-forty, my favor."

The suspect let a few profanities fly. "Man, you're as bad as Grosso. If he hadn't crossed me, he'd still be around."

"Are you saying you'd kill me like you killed him?" Shane managed to imbue this with a touch of doubting arrogant thug.

"You try to change our fifty-fifty split, yes. Be scared, bruh, because that's exactly what I'm saying."

"Nicely done, Gambrazzo," Pete said, impressed. "You can tell he's a pro at this. An amateur would say *Are you saying you would kill me?* which would clue in any perp to a sting."

"I don't need the analysis," Mia snapped. "You got a confession. Can we get Shane out of there?"

"It's not airtight," Pete said. "A defense attorney could get a jury to write the statement off as bragging. We'll give it a couple more minutes to see if Gambrazzo can get the words *I killed Grosso* on tape."

The van quieted. The wire picked up sounds of papers being shuffled, then Shane coughing. "The back on this old doll ripped and stuffing's coming out. It's falling apart."

"If we can't sell it, toss it."

"Okay. Wait." There was a pause. "There's something inside. A piece of paper." They heard a paper being unfolded, then an exclamation from Shane. "It's a will. Dan Fee's."

"What?! Let me see that."

The two fell quiet. Mia's assumption they were

reading the will was proven correct when Shane said, "Wow. That's the executor? Interesting choice."

"Give me that."

"Whoa. Take it easy." There were muffled sounds Mia couldn't identify. Her heart resumed thumping loudly. "Hey! Gimme back the key. What the— That's one of those Circusman fake guns, right?" The concern in Shane's voice didn't sound manufactured.

"There's a gun!" Mia said, grabbing Pete's arm.

"Why'd you have to find that stupid will? If whoever the executor is finds out they're the executor, they'll get everything. That'll ruin my plan."

"*Our* plan. Right? I'm in on this, too, you know."

"Not anymore. I've got the key to the house. I don't need you. Now, all I have to do is make sure no one ever, ever knows about the will."

Mia couldn't take it anymore. She threw open the van door. Before anyone could stop her, she ran across the street at lightning speed, beating the SWAT team already moving in on the house. With the strength of a mother lifting a car off her child, Mia threw her body at the front door, breaking it down. She stumbled, then regained her balance, and rushed into the living room.

The commotion distracted fan club treasurer Thomas. He turned toward the front door, giving Shane the split second he needed to tackle him. He took down Thomas, whose gun went flying in Mia's direction. She grabbed it and trained it on the fanboy. "Touch a hair on my fiancé's incredibly gorgeous head and you're a dead man," she growled.

The SWAT team burst in, along with Pete, Ryan,

and the officers from the surveillance van. Pete did the honors of cuffing Thomas and leading him to a waiting patrol car. Despite the late hour, every house on the block seemed ablaze with lights and residents poured into the street to observe the police action. Elisabetta strode across the street, Mia's bat in hand. She brandished it in Thomas's face. He appeared more terrified of the feisty octogenarian than the phalanx of law enforcement officers clad in full SWAT gear. "*Figlio di puttana!*" she yelled at him. "You coulda ruined my granddaughter's wedding!"

"Put away the bat, ma'am," the burly team commander said to her. "We got this."

"You better," Elisabetta said, gesturing at him with the bat, unfazed.

Evans, who lived on the other side of the block and down a few houses from Mia, made his way through the crowd that had gathered. Mia saw Teri elbowing her way over behind him. "Teri was over," the chef said to Mia. "She saw the extermination van out my window and got suspicious something was up."

"You can tell the perp's an amateur," Teri said, casting a derisive glance Thomas's way. "Every criminal in the city's onto the cutesy *Pest Exterminators* logo."

"I'll give Pete a heads-up about that," Mia said. She winced. The aftereffects of her heroic door-busting were catching up to her.

Shane separated from the police officers he'd been conferring with and came to them. Teri whipped out her phone. "Awesome timing, Shane. I can interview you right now, write up the piece, and get it online by five a.m."

Evans placed a warning hand on the phone. "Put the phone away."

Teri instantly caved. "Yes, sweetie." She pocketed the phone, batted her eyelashes, and blew him a little kiss.

"I can't stay to talk anyway. I need to go to the station and give a statement." He kissed Mia on the top of her head, then gazed at her with affection and admiration. "Are you okay? That was some bold move you pulled. If Dan Fee was still alive, I think he'd have to introduce a new character: Circus*woman*."

Mia managed to smile, despite the pain. "Circuswoman, Circuswoman . . . Nope. Can't come up with a song for that."

CHAPTER 29

Mia spent the next few days recovering from the injuries she incurred breaking down the Fee house front door. While age and neglect had weakened the door's hinges and it was on the flimsy side to begin with, Mia's slight frame still suffered the consequences of her heroic action. She sported an almost dislocated right shoulder, a massive bruise on her hip, plus pain from a couple of banged-up ribs.

On the plus side, the injuries garnered even more love and attention from Shane, if such a thing were possible. It also gave Mia an excuse to luxuriate in the whirlpool bath at the clinic providing the physical therapy her doctor prescribed.

That was where Pete found her when he had updates on the case to share. Not in the whirlpool but in the waiting area post appointment. He was dressed in his detective togs of jeans, button-down white shirt, and black blazer jacket. "I was on my way to talk to the events planner at the Ditmars

Bookshop about doing a signing for my next Steve Stianopolis mystery, *Reality Unchecked*," he explained to Mia. "Cammie said you were here, so I thought I'd grab a minute with you on the way."

Mia dropped the towel she'd used to dry her hair after her whirlpool session into a bin marked *Laundry*. She pointed to a paperback in Pete's hand. "And I assume you also stopped by to see if I'd put in a word for you with the bookstore events planner, since they usually don't do signings for self-published books."

"That too. The book's inspired by everything that happened when *The Dons of Ditmars Boulevard* shot its pilot in Astoria.* The murders, the love affairs. How you once again helped solve the crimes."

Mia gave him a knowing look. "Buttering me up, huh? No worries. I'll give the bookstore a call and see if I can work my magic, from one event planner to another."

"Thanks. I appreciate it."

"So," Mia said as the two made themselves comfortable on a couple of the room's white pleather chairs. "Whatcha got for me?"

"The handy thing about noncareer criminals is they tend to blab things without a lawyer present. Eventually all the TV cop shows they've watched kick in and they remember to ask for one. Lucky for us, it's usually after they blather something self-incriminating, like *Yeah, I killed him and I'd do it again. But, but—*" Pete imitated a suspect blurting

*For more on this, see *Four Parties and a Funeral*.

this out, then realizing his mistake. "*I want a lawyer!*"

Mia grinned. "Add acting to your many talents."

Pete took a mock bow, then resumed the update. "Our murder suspect, Thomas Berger, is a good example of what I'm talking about. Oh, how he blabbed. He admitted to killing your Adam Grosso—"

Mia held up a hand. "Calling a foul. Never, ever refer to Adam Grosso as *my* anything. Even when we were married, he wasn't mine. All the therapy in the world will never get to the bottom of why I hooked up with him in the first place. I look back and think, was I that insecure? Did I need verification of my own attractiveness so much that I ignored every red flag and just went for it? Or was it a subconscious way of getting back at my dad and brother for feeling like the secrets they kept from me in terms of their illegal behavior were a form of betrayal?" She gave Pete the side-eye. "Are you recording me?"

"Sorry." A sheepish Pete put away his phone. "It's great stuff for Steve Stianopolis mystery number twelve. I don't have a title yet, but PI Steve meets his match when he teams up with a smart, hip Astoria event planner."

"Pete, I already told you I'd talk to the bookshop. You can take a break on the buttering."

"I'm not buttering. It's a good character. I'm having fun writing her."

"Fine. I get to read it before you publish to make sure you got me, I mean *her*, right. Now, back to the case."

"This Berger mook verified your suspicions about your hubby. After Grosso read Fuoco's first piece in the *Tri Trib* about the Fee house, he did a little Internet surfing and saw what Circusman memorabilia goes for. He sniffed around the fan club board members and ID'd Berger as the best mark for milking whatever goods they found in the house, which Grosso knew would be easy if you and he were an item again. Otherwise, they were looking at breaking into the house on a regular basis, which would be A—risky and B—only net a small haul of things they could sell."

Mia pursed her lips. "Nothing like knowing all you are to a man is a paycheck."

"*Associates* of the Los Angeles mobster-wannabe-producer Grosso tracked him down to New York and he was facing a world of hurt if he didn't cough up the money he'd ripped off from the guy. Hence his desperation. Even though pretty much all the board members are a greedy bunch, he thought Berger was the smartest, which is why he landed on him as his partner in these crimes." Pete noticed a bowl of nuts and dried fruit put out for guests. "These up for grabs?"

"Help yourself."

Pete did so. He chomped away on a handful as he continued the update. "Grosso underestimated Berger. He wrote him off as a weak techie. He didn't get that the guy had a lethal side. When Grosso tried changing the split of their deal from a fifty-fifty split to seventy-five/twenty-five, Berger balked, they got into a fight, and Berger hit Grosso with his truck. He claims Grosso scootered in front of him and he couldn't stop in time. We think that was BS and he was playing the Circusman theme song to rev himself up into doing what he needed to do to end the *partnership*."

Mia rose from her chair. She went to a small fridge containing water bottles and extracted two. She handed one to Pete, who was coughing on a wrongly inhaled nut. "I'm assuming I was right about Adam being stuck commuting on scooters because he lost his license to DUIs." Pete nodded. "Any symbolism to the murder happening at the end of my alley?"

Pete shook his head. "Our guess is that your hubby was heading back to you for another crack at winning you back when he and Berger met up. Once we lined up Grosso's dire financials with the discovery of Fee's trove of valuables, we were circling all the board members as possible cohorts. But I'm curious. What made *you* zero in on Berger?"

"He was the first one to tell me I was underestimating the value of Fee's memorabilia. And he said it more than once. Thomas was the fan club money guy. It was right here in his club bio on their website—the degree in accounting, plus the experience freelancing with auction houses pricing different superhero and graphic artist memorabilia. My late husband was nothing if not street-smart. I can see him homing in on Thomas as the person who could parse out the most valuable items in Fee's house."

Mia picked out a few dried cranberries from the bowl of nuts and dried fruit, then continued. "Plus, Thomas worked a little too hard at making himself innocuous. That made me suspicious. After that, it was about ruling out the others. Raina seemed like a logical choice but almost too logical as the club president. Knowing Adam, he would have aimed more under the radar. Plus, I couldn't see him taking on a woman as a partner. He wasn't one to separate sex and business, and sex always came first with him. Eddie didn't seem bright enough to pull off any of this, and I never got a greedy vibe from Hannah."

"Did you get a lying vibe? She faked the alibi for Berger because they were *kinda sorta dating*. Which is apparently enough to justify obstruction of justice."

Mia took her ice-cold water bottle and held it against her injured shoulder, which had begun to ache. "I thought Circus Mann and even Raina might be Adam's possible accomplices, but his murder and her reaction to it kind of ruled them out."

"You were close." Pete unscrewed the cap on his water bottle and guzzled it. "I may have some acting chops, but I'm not the star performer Raina Turnikan turned out to be. She had everyone convinced she was doing her best to protect the Fee stash from a sticky-fingered Circus Mann. However, thanks to the security system your grandma installed at your house, we have Turnikan arriving at the Fee house *before* Mann. We think he showed up at the house to stop *her* from stealing anything."

Mia sighed and shook her head. "Annarita, Adam's ex-fiancée, was taking up so much space in my head, I went right to her when Raina described the person she was trying to point to as Circus Mann's killer. But now I realize the description was vague enough to apply either Hannah or Thomas. Nothing like making your *friends* scapegoats for a murder you committed."

"The superhero collectibles market is through the roof thanks to all the movies about them," Pete said. "The NYPD's art cop has added original work by comic book creators to his list of valuable art to police."

"Really? Wow." Mia moved the water bottle from her shoulder to the bruise on her hip, wincing when the two made contact. "I'll need to get in touch with Fee's lawyer again. Nonna's the official homeowner, but the estate still owns everything else. I wonder why Fee made Hannah the executor. My money would have been on Raina. Then again, maybe Fee knew something about her we didn't—that his fan club president was capable of murdering to get what she wanted." Mia paused as a new thought occurred to her. "His death isn't suspicious, is it?"

"Nope. Fee died of a massive heart attack. There's no record of the guy ever seeing a doctor. I guess his health finally caught up with him. So, the only mystery left is how the mousiest board member wound up winner takes all. But that one's for you, not NYPD. I've got a fresh batch of homicides waiting for me back at the station."

Mia rose. Pete did the same, saying, "I'll walk you to your car."

They exited the building and made a left toward the adjacent parking lot. Pete uttered an annoyed grunt. "I left my book inside. Be right back." He did a light jog back to the clinic.

"Mia! Hey, Mia!" someone called from a construction site across the street. Mia glanced over and saw Mark Giuseppe, Ruth's fiancé, waving to her. He darted across the street, deftly dodging oncoming traffic.

"Wow. You must really want to talk to me." Mia framed this as a joke but wondered why he'd made such an effort, considering Ruth was hell-bent on avoiding her.

"Um. I do." Mark broke eye contact. He scuffed a foot back and forth on a gritty patch of the sidewalk. "It's about your slashed tires. Diego and I are gonna pay for them."

Mia raised an eyebrow. "Go on."

He released a heavy sigh. "Here's the deal. I saw Adam Grosso coming out of the barber shop on Steinway. Ruth told me about how he came on to her that time we visited you in Miami, and how they hooked up. I confronted him, we got into it, and I took a fist or two to him."

"So that's where Adam's bruises came from. I wondered."

"Yeah. That was me." Mia picked up a hint of pride in the construction worker's voice. "Diego called me while you were with Rose. When he heard you snooping around about Adam, he got nervous you might be trying to get info you could use against him and Rose and Corey for money, the way Adam was trying to."

Mia, angry, folded her arms in front of her chest and stared Mark down. "Diego doesn't know me, but Rose does, and so does Ruth. So do you. How could you all jump to such a horrible conclusion?"

Mark gave a helpless shrug. "No one had seen you for a few years. How did we know Adam hadn't changed you? Like, you know, taken you to his dark side?"

Mia calmed. "That's a little dramatic. But I can buy it."

"Anyway, Diego called me all upset and worried. Ruth and I live across the street from him and

Rose. The only thing I could think of doing was send a message to back off by slashing your tires. I would've come clean sooner, but I was afraid I'd be a suspect in Adam's murder. Anyway, I'm really sorry. We all are, for ever thinking bad of you. I wanna make things right."

Mia turned to examine the construction site across the street. A large sign marked it as a project under the watchful eye of Mark Giuseppe, General Contractor. "You're a contractor, huh? We're looking at a big remodel of the two-family my grandmother just bought. How about you come by and give me a very competitive bid? I'm not looking to take advantage here, so one where you still do okay. But you could at least cut us a little bit of a deal."

"That doesn't sound like me making it right," Mark said, confused but relieved. "More like bidding on a job. But you got it. I'll be sure to throw in some extras." He extended a hand, and they shook on it. "And again, I apologize. I know slashing your tires was a stupid thing to do. But I'm a fan of this suspense series called the Steve Stianopolis Mysteries, and the guy is *awesome*. He once cut a criminal's tires to stop them from escaping, so it gave me the idea."

"*Ahem.*"

Pete, who had come back outside but maintained a discreet distance from Mia so as not to intrude on her conversation, cleared his throat. Mia waved him over. "Mark, this is my friend—NYPD Detective Pete Dianopolis."

Considering that Mark *had* slashed her tires, causing her financial stress and general inconvenience, Mia allowed herself the brief satisfaction of watching him turn white. He gulped. "Did you . . . did you hear any . . . ?" Mark trailed off and gave Pete a beseeching look.

"I heard all of it," Pete said. "Since you seem to be making it up to my pal Mia here, I don't think she's gonna be pressing charges." He draped an arm around a nervous Mark's shoulder. "But tell me more about how awesome Steve Stianopolis is."

CHAPTER 30

Mia's eyelids fluttered open. She yawned and stretched, happy to emit only a slight groan of pain. A few days of PT and whirlpools were already paying off.

"'Who's gettin' married in the morning'?" She said this in a sing-song voice to Doorstop, who she swore responded with a smile. "Technically, I'm getting married tomorrow night, but I like singing it the other way better."

She threw off the covers and hopped out of bed, both terrified and excited by her first task of the day: the one and only fitting of Frankendress. She'd bravely resigned herself to wearing whatever Lucille managed to concoct. If the dress turned out to be a total disaster, Mia's backup plan was to "accidentally" delete any unflattering wedding photos.

She adjusted the showerhead to Massage and focused the water on her sore shoulder. After the shower, she slipped on black leggings and an oversize forest-green pullover sweater that would ward off the early fall chill without necessitating a coat over it. She fed her pets and let Pizzazz out for a quick zoom around the apartment. Then she went downstairs to meet her mother, her grandmother, and her wedding gown fate.

The three walked to Lucille's in silence. Mia sensed the dress reveal was weighing heavily on Gia and Elisabetta, too. They'd apologized multiple times for pressuring her into wearing their gowns, each subtly laying blame with the other until Mia told them if they didn't stop, she'd turn the joke of getting married in her underwear into reality.

Mia caught a glimpse of Lucille watching for them through the small window on her front door. *I think she's as nervous as we are,* she thought. A moment later, the door flew open. Lucille greeted them with a wide, slightly forced smile. "Ciao. Here we are. The big day. Come in, come in."

She ushered them into her living room. "I'd offer espresso, but I thought we should save all liquids until the dress is packed and out of harm's way."

"Good idea," Mia said.

Lucille clapped her hands together. "So. Here we go."

She disappeared into her sewing room. Mia fought a losing battle against scrunching her eyes shut. Gia and Elisabetta grabbed each other's hands and held them tightly. Mia heard her grandmother mumble a repeated prayer under her breath. She heard both women gasp and let out a worried whimper.

"Ooooh. *Che* bella." Gia spoke in a voice filled with emotion.

"Si. Si." Elisabetta's sniffle indicated she'd succumbed to tears.

Mia slowly opened one eye, then popped both open. It was her turn to gasp. "Lucille. I can't . . . I never . . . How did you . . ."

The gown the dressmaker held up was a vision. Barely there sleeves fell off the shoulder. The bodice, now corset in style, featured the sequins, beads, lace, and pearls of Gia's dress arranged in a delicate pattern. The waist came to a point, from which flowed the silken fabric of Elisabetta's princess-style gown. Lucille had used additional lace and fabric from Gia's wedding gown to add the length needed to compensate for the height difference between Mia and her grandmother. "What do you think?" Lucille asked. Her hands shook slightly as she waited for the verdict.

Mia swallowed. "It's the most beautiful wedding dress I've ever seen."

The pressure off, her mother and grandmother joined Mia in heaping effusive compliments on Lucille. "You're a genius," Gia said, blowing her kisses.

"A gift from *Il Dio.*" Elisabetta pointed heavenward and crossed herself.

"I'm not going to lie," Lucille said with a relieved laugh. "This was the hardest assignment of my career. I panicked I wouldn't be able to make it work. So, I reached out for help."

"Surprise!"

Designer Hillary Marks jumped out from behind the sewing room door. The women shrieked with delight.

"Standing ovation for both of you," Mia said, leading the way by standing up herself.

Hillary and Lucille took mock bows, Lucille making sure not to let her stunning creation drag on the ground. "Larkin, the rich girl, connected us after she heard your dress was ruined," Lucille explained. "I can't thank Hillary enough for the input she gave me on incorporating both dresses into one design."

"I'm the lucky one here," Hillary said. She gave Lucille an appreciative pat on the back. "She's a find. A fabulous artisan. I can't wait to do future projects together. If you're okay with it, I'd like to do a version of this dress to end my next runway show. Or a version of the toilet paper dress. I can't decide which."

"I have a few thoughts on that," Lucille said, keeping her tone polite as she mouthed *No toilet paper dress* over Hillary's head at the others. She handed the wedding gown to Mia. "You need to try this on. We have just enough time for me to make any necessary alterations."

Mia gently caressed the gown. "It's incredible. I bet you won't have to change a thing."

She and Lucille disappeared into the sewing room. The dressmaker and Hillary helped her into the gown. Mia was right. It fit perfectly. "You're gonna be a beautiful bride," Lucille said.

"Thanks to you." Mindful of her gown, Mia gave the dressmaker the gentlest of hugs.

She stepped out of the sewing room and modeled the gown to applause from Hillary and tears and whoops of joy on the part of her mother and grandmother. "I'm taking pictures for my website," Hillary said, snapping away with her phone. "Don't be surprised if a modeling agent calls you. Or *Vogue,* asking to cover the wedding."

"I don't care about any of that," Mia said, admiring the dress's reflection in the three-way mirror. "All I want is to walk up the aisle in this incredible dress as Messina Bellissima Carina. And walk back as Messina Bellissima Carina-Gambrazzo." She made a face. "Yikes. I never said that out loud before. It's a mouthful."

Mia returned to the sewing room, where she changed back into her daywear. Lucille slid a protective cover over the gown. Gia and Elisabetta then lent Mia a hand transporting the gown to her apartment, where it would spend the night before her wedding in the second bedroom.

On the walk up the street, Mia happened to glance at the Fee house and notice a full mailbox. After hanging up the wedding dress, she made a trip across the street to empty the mailbox before Circusman fans descended upon it to snatch up souvenirs. She retrieved the contents and returned home, where she poured a cup of coffee and cut up half a cantaloupe for breakfast, saving her appetite for the massive amount of food she was sure Piero would serve at the evening's rehearsal dinner.

Mia nibbled on melon and sipped coffee as she went through the Circusman mail. Most of it was junk mail she felt comfortable tossing in her recycle bin. As she did so, an envelope encased in plastic and marked *Damaged* by the postal service dropped out from inside a grocery store flyer onto the floor. Mia bent down to retrieve it and a letter fell out of the envelope. She couldn't resist a quick glance at it. Her eyes widened as she took in the letter's surprising contents. She picked up her phone and made a call.

Circus Feek board member Hannah sat on Mia's plastic-covered couch, head down, hair falling in front of her face. Her hands were in her lap, and she kept folding and unfolding them like the gesture was a nervous tic.

"Would you like a glass of water?" Mia asked in the gentlest voice possible. She knew the girl never expected her secret to be revealed.

Hannah shook her head. "No, thank you." She spoke so softly Mia could barely hear her.

"How long did you produce Mr. Fee's artwork for him?"

"Only the last five years." Hannah finally lifted her head up. "I sent him fan art when I was a junior at art school. It was no big deal. A lot of people sent fan art. But he thought mine was closest to how he drew, so he asked me to meet him at his Vermont house. But keep it a secret. He had one of those sicknesses where your hands shake, so he couldn't draw anymore. His mind wasn't working too well either, so I pretty much did everything. Stories. Storyboards. Communicating with production to get the comics out."

"The murals. You painted them. That's why you shot down people like Thomas when they insisted the murals were extremely valuable."

Tears rolled down Hannah's cheeks. "Toward

the end, he got really sad and said he wished he could live in the world he created. So I painted the murals. And I made him Circusman. He got to be the amazing character he created. At least in paintings."

"He was more than grateful. The first will Shane found in the Circusman doll made you Dan Fee's executor." Mia pointed to the damaged letter. "This second will makes you heir to everything in his estate. There's also a press release officially designating you as his artistic successor. The letter was only returned to sender because he was such a recluse, he didn't know postage had gone up."

"He was a really nice man."

More tears coated Hannah's cheeks. Mia handed her a tissue and she wiped them away. "Final question. Are you the board member who reported Circus Mann's shooting?"

Hannah gave a small nod. "I didn't know there would be a shooting. Circus Mann told us all he'd heard your grandmother was going to put in an alarm system, so we had one last chance to grab anything of value from the house before we could get caught. He insisted Dan owed us. I didn't know anyone would actually go through with breaking in. That people I thought were my friends were so horribly greedy. When Mr. Fee died, they went from being fans to thieves. It's awful."

"I know," Mia said with much sympathy. "But it's over now."

Hannah inhaled a shuddering breath, then exhaled it. She sat up straighter. "I'll work with a lawyer to move everything up to Mr. Fee's house in Vermont. I used to meet him there until he couldn't go anymore. It's beautiful and will make an awesome museum dedicated to his work. I also need to go public about how I covered for him the last five years. Just putting out the press release isn't enough. I want people to know the story behind it."

Mia smiled. "I happen to know a very enterprising reporter named Teri Fuoco who would be beyond happy to share your story with the world. Or at least Queens."

CHAPTER 31

Miller Manor, the majestic mansion resembling a British castle that Larkin Miller-Spaulding called home, looked particularly spectacular the evening of Mia and Shane's wedding.

The mid-October weather was crisp but comfortable. With Jamie Boldano officiating, the couple would exchange vows under a bower that had been set up at one end of the estate's verdant lawn, with a vibrant twilight of golds, pinks, blues, and yellows providing a spectacular backdrop. After the ceremony, everyone would move inside the gilded-age mansion for the reception.

Mia and her bridal party readied for the ceremony in the mansion's opulent library. Dressmaker Lucille aided Mia in putting on her gown. Bridesmaids Cammie, Teri, Guadalupe, Shane's sister Olivia, who was Mia's maid of honor, and Larkin, a last-minute addition after Mia talked her into it out of gratitude for her generosity, donned a variety of rich purple gowns. Each had chosen a design suited to their body type. Grandmother of the bride Elisabetta wore a lavender evening gown and a matching bolero jacket adorned with crystal beads. Mother of the bride Gia was clad in a deep green chiffon gown with long sleeves and a flattering boatneck collar.

They all watched world-famous beauty expert Rylie Kenner dust a light layer of powder over Mia's face to set her makeup in place. The celebrity's presence at the wedding was yet another gift from Larkin. Rylie leaned back and admired Mia. "You look gorgeous." She turned to Mia's bridesmaids—who were waiting with her in the mansion's opulent library, along with Gia and Elisabetta. "You all do."

The older women responded with starstruck giggles. Olivia, the only Gen Zer in the room, exchanged an amused look with her peer, Rylie.

Mia stood up. She studied her reflection. A beautiful young woman glowed in the mirror. Rylie's artistic touch brought out Mia's bright blue eyes and accentuated the striking contrast between her pale skin and dark hair, arranged in a soft chignon. "I may cry," she whispered, overcome.

"Don't," Gia said. "You'll ruin your makeup."

"You never have to worry about that with my products," Rylie said with a confident wave of her hand. "My whole line is waterproof."

There was a gentle rap on the door. "Sis?

"Posi!" Whether her brother would be able to perform his role as Shane's best man was a question mark up until the final hour. But family friend and lawyer Philip had struck a deal that allowed Posi to attend the wedding in the care of his guard, Henry Marcus, who was already coming to the wedding with his wife as guests.

Gia opened the door to her son. He came into the room, looking dashing in his black tuxedo, which hid the ankle monitor on his left leg. Mia noticed Larkin staring at Posi with a dreamy expression she'd never seen on the girl's face before. She'd also never seen the heiress dressed up and wearing makeup for a change. Rylie Kenner had even talked Larkin into trading her heavy, black-frame eyeglasses for contact lenses, revealing eyes a beautiful shade of lavender enhanced by her silky, deep purple bridesmaid's gown.

Posi ignored his mother. "Hey, sis, question: Who owns the incredibly rare Lamborghini Veneno in the driveway?"

Elisabetta gave her grandson's arm an angry swat. "*Stronzo!* It's your sister's wedding night and that's what you come in here for?"

Larkin stepped forward. Her eyes locked on Posi's. "The car is mine."

Posi drank in Larkin. He returned her lustful gaze. "They only built fourteen Venenos."

"And I own four of them."

Posi clutched his heart and swayed. "Don't even think about stealing one of those cars," Mia hissed at him.

Posi formed a heart with his hands and placed it on his chest. "The only thing stolen around here is my heart." He gazed at Larkin with soulful eyes. "I'd consider it the highlight of my life if you went out with me."

"Yes, oh yes," the heiress murmured.

"Full disclosure. It'll be a little bit down the road since I still have six months to go on my prison sentence."

"I'll wait," Larkin said, enraptured.

Colin Cowie, the celebrity party planner Larkin hired to run the wedding, stuck his head inside the room. "It's showtime, folks."

Posi snapped out of his lovestruck stupor. "Oh, Mimi, I almost forgot. I saw Donny Senior. He wants to talk to you after the pictures and before the reception. He says it's important."

Posi left to join the groomsmen, a foursome that included Evans, along with a few of Shane's oldest friends. Lucille clipped on Mia's veil and Cammie joined her in adjusting it. Mia noticed a giant diamond glittering like a disco ball on Cammie's finger. "Pete did it. He reproposed. And you said yes. Oh Cammie, congratulations."

"Thanks."

Mia gestured to the ring. "Impressive."

Cammie shrugged a *meh*. "Not bad for a starter ring. Or re-starter in my case."

The women filed out of the library into the massive, Gilded Age living room, where they paired up with their grooms. Ravello, distinguished in a tuxedo with tails, brought up the rear. At the sight of his daughter, he choked up. "Bambina. Bellissima. *Non ho parole.*"

Mia kissed her father on the cheek. "You don't need words to show how much you love me, Dad. You never have."

He sniffed and nodded. Then he offered her his arm. "It's time for me to give you away to a very lucky man."

The wedding party traversed the path from the house to the site of the ceremony, which buzzed with an excited hum from the guests. Mia and her family waited as the bridesmaids and groomsmen made their way down the aisle, a couple at a time, as Larkin's close friend Yo-Yo Ma played Bach's "Cello Suite No. 1" in G major. Cowie nodded to Elisabetta, who had chosen neighbor and friend Philip to walk her down the aisle. He gallantly extended his arm, and they headed off.

Cowie handed Mia her bouquet. She closed her eyes and inhaled a deep breath. Yo-Yo Ma switched to playing Mendelssohn's "Wedding March." Mia opened her eyes. The guests rose to their feet. Gia hooked Mia's other arm in hers and she started down the aisle with her parents.

Mia beamed at friends and family as the three walked. She saved the biggest beam for the man who would be her husband in a matter of minutes. Shane, looking next-level handsome in his tuxedo and tails, wiped away tears with the back of his hand at the sight of his beautiful bride.

She and her parents reached the bower. Ravello and Gia each kissed her on the cheek. They took their seats, as did the rest of the guests. Jamie gave them a warm smile. "You two ready?" he said under his breath.

"You have no idea," Mia said. Her groom stifled a laugh.

Jamie addressed the guests. "Shane and Mia, along with their families, want to welcome you all and tell you how much it means for them to share this special night with you. And considering recent events, they also don't want to take any chances of some kind of drama interrupting the big event, so let's get to it." The guests laughed and applauded. Jamie opened the gilt-edge journal he was holding and began to read. "'Dearly beloved, we are gathered together here to join this man and this woman in holy—'"

"Oh my God!"

A concerned rumble surged through the guests. Mia and Shane turned to see the cry came from Jamie's wife, Madison. She was standing, clutching her pregnant stomach, a panicked expression on her face.

Jamie dropped his journal. He stared at his wife in shock. "Sweetie—"

She extended a desperate hand to her husband. "Jamie . . . My water broke!"

CHAPTER 32

"Somebody call 911!" Mia yelled to her guests as Jamie ran to his wife.

"So many people are calling we're tying up the lines!" Finn Barnes-Webster, Philip's husband, yelled back, holding up his phone.

"Is there a doctor in the house?" Shane called out. "Or the lawn? Or anywhere?! A nurse? Anyone who's taken a biology class?"

No one responded. Mia scanned the crowd. "Five hundred guests and no medical professionals? Seriously? We need to widen our circle of friends."

Madison moaned. "This can't be happening."

Mia hiked up her wedding gown and began issuing orders. She waved concerned guests away from the mother-to-be. "Shane, Posi, help Jamie take Madison inside the house. We need to make her comfortable until the ambulance comes."

"We'll go with her," Gia said, motioning to herself, Elisabetta, and Aurora Boldano.

"We've been there," Aurora said. "We've all had babies. And that's my grandbaby coming."

Mia grabbed Colin Cowie's arm as he hurried past her, trying to corral the guests. "Open all the bars. Start passing the hors d'oeuvres. Do whatever you can to keep the guests happy and occupied."

"Of course," the event planner said. "I told *Vogue* they should cover this wedding. I'll be dining out on this story for *years*."

Mia and her bridesmaids hurried after Madison and the men. Madison let out a howl. "Oh my *God*. I think the baby is coming! It's not supposed to be like this. I'm supposed to be in labor for hours."

"Sometimes they come quick." Elisabetta gestured to Ravello. "I popped out this big guy in twenty minutes."

"And I went through under an hour of labor with both you and Posi," Gia said to Mia.

Pete Dianopolis exited a restroom attached to the building on the estate housing the Miller Art Collection, Larkin's pride and joy. He hurried to them, tucking his shirt into his pants. "Did I miss the ceremony? My bad. But nature called."

"You lucked out," Cammie said. "Jamie's wife, Madison, went into labor before the *I dos*."

Another howl from Madison confirmed the statement. Jamie cursed. "Where's the damn ambulance?"

Pete waved to him. "The house is too far. Get her in the bathroom here." He pointed to one of the two attached to the collection. "You." He pointed at Larkin. "This is your digs, right?" Intimidated, she nodded. "Get me blankets and towels. Lots of 'em. I need the husband with me. Also the mamas. You can coach her." He clapped his hands. "Let's go, people. Move it!"

He started for the restroom, Cammie on his tail. "Pete, what are you doing?"

"Delivering a baby." He flashed a cocky grin. "Part of my training. They don't call us New York's Finest for nuthin'."

He led the way for the others, including Cammie. "I'm coming with you. OMG, I get to watch you deliver a baby!" She sounded like a besotted tween.

They disappeared into the restroom. Mia, Shane, and the rest of her bridal party paced anxiously outside. "I'm so sorry my concierge doctor isn't here," Larkin said. "He hitched a ride back to the city with Rylie in her helicopter."

"You're hot and you have your own helipad." Posi clasped his hands together in prayer and gazed upward. "Thank you."

"Did you say hot? About me?"

Larkin staggered slightly. Mia put out the hand not holding her bridal bouquet to steady the heiress. "If we're gonna pray about anything right now, it should be the baby," she scolded Posi. "It's being delivered in a *bathroom.* By *Pete.* He's a good detective but would not be my first choice for midwife." She cast a worried glance up the half-mile graveled drive separating the estate from the road running past it for any sign of an ambulance.

"Shhh." Guadalupe held up a hand to quiet everyone. "Sirens. You hear them?"

"Maybe." Teri stopped typing on her phone. "Yes. They're getting louder."

"Are you sending this into the *Tri Trib*?" Mia, feeling irascible, said this through gritted teeth.

"Uh-huh." Teri resumed typing. "Great human-interest story. It'll be picked up everywhere. Maybe even *Vogue.*"

"Mia!" Donny Boldano Senior called to her as he hurried through the grass to the group huddled by the restroom. He'd broken out in a sweat. Considering the increasing chill in the air, Mia attributed this to nerves. "I don't care if Aurora ordered me not to do anything. I can't wait any longer. What's happening?"

The sirens' wail grew louder. But another wail drowned it out. Aurora threw open the restroom door. She was weeping. "It's a girl! I'm a grandma! Donny . . ."

She held out her arms to her husband, who ran to her. They embraced, then disappeared into the restroom.

Seconds later, two ambulances screeched into the estate's circular drive. EMTs loaded mother and child onto a gurney for the drive to the hospital. Jamie hopped in with them. "Sorry about the ceremony, you guys," he said to Mia and Shane, not bothering to hide his ecstatic happiness. "I'm a daddy!"

The wedding party whooped and cheered. But the celebration was suddenly interrupted.

"Wait! Hold the other ambulance!" Mia's pregnant friend Nicole struggled toward it, helped by her husband, Ian, who sported the same terrified expression Jamie had on his face only shortly before.

Mia gaped at her. "Nicole . . . No. Don't tell me."

Nicole grimaced and nodded. "Oooh. Ouch!"

"Breathe, baby, breathe," Ian panic coached. He

waved frantically to the second ambulance's paramedics, who rushed to the couple's side.

"Sympathy water break, I guess," Nicole said, allowing the EMTs to help her onto a gurney. "Anyway, congratulations, you two." She blew them a kiss as she was wheeled away and loaded into the ambulance.

"Wow." Mia watched the ambulances drive off. "I have to say . . . I did not see any of this coming."

While the wedding guests mingled, nibbled, and imbibed a boatload of booze, Mia and friends and family desperately tried to find a new officiant. Even Larkin's connections weren't coming through due to a few galas sapping the locale populations and a few local clergy who didn't respond kindly to her avant-garde art installations.

Event planner Cowie pulled Mia aside. "Just an FYI that your guests are teetering on the edge of being overserved. I know it's been . . . a night. But as Hollywood's foremost party planner to the stars—*People* magazine's designation, not mine—I recommend you cut to the reception."

"Give me five more minutes," Mia said, pleading.

"All right." He hailed Larkin. "Larkin, honey, we need to plunder your wine cellar."

Larkin led the planner off. Shane fixed tender eyes on Mia. "I know this isn't the wedding you dreamed of. It's not my fantasy wedding either. But we have the convalidation in Italy. Instead of only validating our marriage, we can turn it into a real ceremony. For just the two of us."

Mia swallowed tears. "Maybe. But I'm not ready to give up tonight."

"One of the many things I love about you. You're a fighter."

Shane kissed her, then continued the hunt.

Donny Junior sauntered up to the couple. He had an arm around his date Cimmanin's shoulder. His hair was mussy, his tie askew, and his shirt only half-tucked into his pants. Cimmanin was in similar disarray. Her gold sequin micro minidress sported a broken spaghetti strap. A couple of leaves dangled from her streaked blond extensions.

"Hey," Donny casually greeted Mia and Shane. "Sorry we missed the ceremony. Traffic on the expressway was terrible."

Mia planted her fists on her hips and glared at the Boldano spawn. "Did you pull over to have sex?"

"Yeah," Donny said, unfazed. "But the traffic was still terrible."

Shane mimicked Mia's glare. "You missed the birth of your niece."

"She got born already? I thought that was gonna happen next week, or whenever. But cool." Donny Junior scratched his head, confused but happy.

"You're an uncle, baby." Cimmanin tickled him and he tickled her back. "Stop," she giggled, not meaning it.

"So," Donny said, "what's my niece's name?"

"Donna Aurora," Mia said, battling an urge to blow.

"Donna? She's named after me?" Donny Junior flashed a wide, self-satisfied grin. "Awesome."

Mia lost her battle. *"She's not named after you, you selfish, rock-stupid idiot! She's named after your father and mother!"* She screamed this at Donny and began pummeling him with her fists. Shane grabbed her by the waist, lifting her off the ground. Mia's mother and father rushed over. Curious guests tore themselves away from the bar and watched the altercation with fascination and drinks in hand. "*It's supposed to be my wedding day and it's an effing disaster! Our officiant's gone, we can't find another one, our guests are drinking so much we're running out of liquor, and you're giving it to your girlfriend on the side of the road?! Argh! I'll kill you!*"

Gia and Ravello tried calming Mia down. Shane did his best to hold her off, but Mia continued to thrash in his arms and aim punches at Donny Junior.

"Do you think this is one of the homeowner's art installations?" one guest asked another.

"I'm not sure," the second guest said.

"Hold up," Donny Junior said, dodging Mia's punches. "You need someone to marry you? I can do it."

Mia stopped flailing. She dropped her arms. "What?" She panted, huffing and puffing like a prizefighter taking a break from the ring. Her veil, now lopsided, hung off what was left of her chignon. A false eyelash had landed on her cheek. One of her sleeves dangled by a thread.

"You can officiate a wedding?" Shane couldn't have expressed more shock if Donny Junior had sprouted wings and started flying around the estate.

"Truth. I got the idea from my bro. It's a good side hustle in case anyone who hooks up at Singles decides to take their relationship to the next level. I got my license from marry-people-and-make-extra-cash-dot-com. I won't charge you two, of course."

"It's legit?" Shane said, doubtful.

"Totes. I had my lawyer check. Last thing I need is another lawsuit. I swear, I only winged the delivery guy on the bike. People are so . . . what's the word?"

"*Litigious*," Cimmanin offered helpfully, begging the question of how she knew the word.

"Yeah. That." Donny tucked in his shirt and smoothed down his hair. "So, let's do this thing."

"Colin! Colin!" Mia yelled.

The event planner came running, clutching a bottle of wine to his chest. "Sorry for disappearing. I want to break up with my partner and date that wine cellar. I am in love."

Mia patted down her wedding gown skirt in an attempt to regain her dignity. "The ceremony is a go."

Gia futzed with Mia's veil. "Bella, maybe you take a few minutes to—"

"No!" Mia barked this. "No minutes. We can't risk anything else interrupting our vows. Places, people!"

Guests ran to their chairs. The bridal party positioned themselves at the head of the aisle and then jogged down it. Elisabetta and Philip hurried after them, followed by the bride and her parents, who racewalked until they reached the bower, where Gia and Ravello quickly deposited Mia by Shane's side. Donny Junior straightened his tie. After a dramatic clearing of his throat, he launched into his wedding spiel. "'Dearly beloved, we are gathered together tonight—'"

Mia spun her hands in the universal sign of *speed it up*. "Get to the vows. Skip the ones we read to each other. No time. Go straight to the *I dos*."

"Fine. Do you, Mia—"

"Yes."

Donny reacted, taken aback. "Yikes, you really do wanna move this along. All righty. Do you, Shane, take—"

"Yes, a bazillion times, yes."

"Then by the power invested in me by marry-people-and-earn-extra-cash-dot-com, I now pronounce you husband and wife. You may now make out with each other."

Shane wrapped his arms around Mia. He dipped her and they enjoyed a well-earned kiss. The guests roared and gave the couple a standing ovation. Yo-Yo Ma launched into a triumphant recessional march and the newlyweds headed down the aisle hand in hand, relief and delirious happiness on both their faces.

"Wait!" Cammie called out. The newlyweds halted their march. Yo-Yo Ma stopped playing. Cammie clutched Pete's arm. "I don't want another minute to go by without remarrying this baby-delivering, big-spending mook. Pete, if you're up for it—"

"I am, I am," he said, not believing his good luck. He took Cammie's hand and led her to the bower.

"Do you—" Donny Junior began.

"I do," Cammie said, cutting him off.

"And do you—"

"Yes!" Pete eagerly replied.

"I now pronounce you rehusband and wife."

Cammie and Pete kissed to more cheers from the guests. Yo-Yo Ma took his bow to his cello.

"Wait!" This time, Larkin yelled it out.

Donny pursed his lips and fixed a stare on her. "You too?"

Larkin approached Posi. She clasped his hands in hers. "I don't want another second to go by without knowing we'll be in each other's lives forever. I've never felt the love I feel for you, Posi—that's your name, right?"

Posi nodded. "It's short for Positano."

"It is? Talk about a coincidence. I own a villa there."

Posi fought to contain his emotions. "This is the happiest night of my life," he said, his voice quavering.

"That's supposed to be my line," Mia remarked dryly.

Posi addressed Donny Junior. "Bro, will you marry us?"

"Yes, but *you* I'm sending a bill. 'Dearly beloved—'" Donny Junior stopped. "What's that noise?"

Posi pointed to his ankle. "My monitor. It needs a charge, so chop-chop."

Donny Junior pointed at him. "You?"

"Yes."

He pointed at Larkin. "You?"

"Yes!"

"You're husband and wife." Running out of steam, the ersatz officiant skipped the niceties. "That beeping's annoying. Go charge the thing."

Yo-Yo Ma took a tentative bow to his cello. Before he could get a note out—

"Wait!" Teri called out.

"Oh, come on," Yo-Yo Ma said, exasperated.

Teri faced Evans. "Evans, my love, my life, my soul, my everything, will you—"

"Hell no," Evans said, cutting her off. "But . . . you can leave a toothbrush at my place."

Teri fist-pumped. "*Yes.* Calling it a win."

Yo-Yo Ma held up his bow. "*Now* can I play?"

"Go for it," Mia said.

Propelled by the pregaming due to the vows delay, the reception was a boisterous, over-the-top affair, culminating with a fantastic fireworks display over the Sound courtesy of the elder Boldanos. The couple also distributed chocolate cigars with pink bands to celebrate the birth of their granddaughter.

Mia was saying goodbye to a few guests when Donny Senior pulled her aside. "We need to talk. Don't be nervous. It's all good."

"You know me so well, Mr. B.," Mia said.

He led Mia to an empty table. Shane was already there. The three sat down. "I made a decision about my retirement," Boldano said. "It's happening. I want more time with my granddaughter now that she's here. I met with my accountant this morning and went over my businesses for the first time in a long time. I discovered that at this point, ninety percent of them are legit, thanks to you and your mother pushing me in that direction. I pulled the plug on the other ten percent and set up your mother to run my operations in Italy. She wants to stay there, and I support her choice. Which left me with the question, who should run what is now Boldano General Enterprises here in New York? It's what you kids call a no-brainer. I want you to take over the business here."

Mia stared at him dumbfounded. "Me? The person who just wailed on your son?"

"Am I a bad father if I say that was kinda fun to watch?" Boldano delivered this with a guilty grin.

Mia searched for words. In her wildest dreams, she'd never envisioned this moment. "Shane and I need to talk. I could never make a decision like this without him."

"I already ran the idea by him," Boldano said. "Don't be insulted. I'm old school like that."

"He swore me to secrecy," Shane said in a soft voice. "I told him it's your call and I support whatever choice you make. All I ever wanted to do was run an event facility where I get to plan the best events of peoples' lives. I get to do that at Belle View. So, if you want to be the CEO of BGE—"

"What our initials would be if we went public," Boldano said with pride.

"I'm good," Shane finished.

Mia gazed out at the water. Lights flickered from across the Sound. The view didn't include Belle View Banquet Manor, tucked away on Flushing Bay. But Mia got endless pleasure from knowing the beloved venue was out there, with its past, present, and future of helping clients honor the most important events of their lives.

"What about Donny Junior and Jamie?" she asked. "They're like my second and third brothers. I would never do anything to hurt them."

"Neither would I. I ran this by them and they're on board. Jamie has no interest in the family business and Donny Junior's never been happier than working at Singles. He wants to discuss funding a chain of them. He thinks it would be a good investment for BGE."

Mia found herself mulling over the idea. "I

need to sit down with your accountant, too. I want
to confirm every single business left under the
Boldano umbrella is legit. If they are and my husband—ooh, I love the sound of that word—if my
husband is okay with it . . ." She looked at Shane.
He gave her a slight nod. "I'm in."

"*Va bene,*" Boldano said. He hugged Mia and
clapped Shane on the back. "I'm gonna go tell the
missus. It was her idea to begin with."

Mia glanced over at Aurora Boldano. The *capo
di tutti capo*'s wife winked at her and mouthed,
"Girl power."

Boldano left. Shane replaced him in the seat
next to Mia. He pulled his wife onto his lap. She
rested her head on his shoulder. He stroked her
hair. "What are you thinking?" he asked.

"How lucky I am." It was a simple response but
seemed to perfectly sum up everything.

Elisabetta strolled over. She'd shed her gown for
a purple velour tracksuit with *Grandmama of the Bride*
emblazoned in crystals on the back of the hoodie.
"*Bellissima.*" She kissed Mia on both cheeks. "*Bello,*"
she said to Shane, then did the same with him. She
held up her espresso demitasse cup. "A toast. To a
beautiful couple. And a granddaughter who fills
me with love and pride every day of my life."

"Aww, Nonna." Moved, Mia wiped a tear from
her eye.

"Now," Elisabetta used her cup to gesture toward the estate drive, "get outta here and go make
me some great-grandbabies. Pronto!"

Recipes

Gnocchi Alla Sorrentina

Brava for this simple, delicious dish! Serve it with a side salad and warm Italian bread to sop up the sauce.

Ingredients:
   garlic cloves
   2 Tablespoons olive oil
   1 28 oz. can cherry tomatoes in sauce
      (*Pomodorini*)
   1 lb. gnocchi
   ½ lb. whole milk mozzarella, divided by half
      cut into cubes and half into slices
   A handful of fresh basil, torn into smallish
      pieces
   2 Tablespoons grated Parmesan-Reggiano
      cheese
   A pinch of salt

Instructions:
   Preheat the oven to 350 degrees.
   Mash the garlic with the back of a knife. In a large oven-safe skillet or pot (I use a cast-iron skillet), heat the olive oil. Add the garlic and cook until it's fragrant.

Add the can of tomatoes to the garlic, along with the salt. Simmer the sauce for ten minutes, using the back of a heavy spoon to stir and break open at least some of the tomatoes.

While the sauce simmers, cook the gnocchi in a large pot of water according to its instructions. The gnocchi will be done when it floats to the water's surface.

Remove the gnocchi from the water with a slotted spoon and add it to the sauce. Add the basil and cubed mozzarella and stir gently to combine.

Place the mozzarella slices on top of the gnocchi-sauce mixture and sprinkle the Parmesan-Reggiano over the whole dish.

Bake for ten to fifteen minutes, or until the mozzarella is bubbly and golden.

Serves approximately 4–6.

Ricotta Sugar Cookies

Ricotta cheese makes these Italian sugar cookies dense and rich, with the tiniest bit of a tang.

Ingredients:
    2 cups all-purpose flour
    1 Tablespoon baking powder
    ½ teaspoon salt
    ½ cup butter
    1 cup granulated sugar (I'm a fan of finely ground baking sugar)
    1 large egg
    1 cup whole milk ricotta
    1 teaspoon vanilla extract (you can also substitute almond or rum extract)

Glazed Icing Ingredients:
    1½ cups confectioners' sugar
    3 Tablespoons milk (more if needed to thin the glaze)
    ½ teaspoon vanilla

Optional:
    Decorative sprinkles

Instructions:
    Preheat oven to 350 degrees.
    With a fork, mix together the flour, baking powder, and salt. Set aside.
    In a separate bowl, cream the butter and sugar together. Use a low-speed blender to combine the ingredients first, then increase the speed and beat the butter and sugar until they're fluffy.
    Using the medium speed on your blender, beat

in the egg, ricotta, and vanilla (or flavoring of your choice.) On a low speed, slowly add the flour mixture and beat until a dough forms.

Chill the dough for at least several hours.

When ready to bake, either drop the dough by tablespoonfuls or form balls and place them on a parchment-lined cookie sheet. (You'll need two sheets or to use the one sheet twice.)

Bake 12–15 minutes, until lightly golden along the bottom. Remove from oven and let the cookies cool completely.

While the cookies are cooling, mix the powdered sugar, vanilla, and milk together to form the icing glaze. Add more milk if needed to achieve a medium-thin consistency.

Dip each cookie in the glaze so either the top or whole cookie is covered. If you're decorating the cookies with sprinkles, do it now, before the glaze hardens.

Makes approx. 2 dozen cookies, depending on size.

Breakfast Pasta

I call this "breakfast pasta," but it makes for a delicious meal any time of day. And feel free to serve it with a side of tomato gravy (that's what my family called tomato sauce).

Ingredients:

8 oz. cooked pasta, your choice of pasta (I like to use fusilli)
2 Tablespoons olive oil, divided
6 whole eggs
2 egg whites
½ teaspoon Italian seasoning, plus ¼–½ teaspoon to sprinkle on top
1 Tablespoon milk
¼ tsp. salt
Pepper to taste
1–2 cloves garlic
¼ cup chopped onion
½ cup cooked peas
½ cup cooked sliced mushrooms
4 oz cooked crumbled bacon, turkey bacon, pancetta, or Italian sausage, your choice
½ cup ricotta
2 large Tablespoons grated Parmesan-Reggiano cheese
4 oz. mozzarella, thinly sliced

Instructions:

Preheat oven to 350 degrees.

Cook the pasta in a large pot according to package instructions. Drain and return to pot. Add a tablespoon of oil to keep the pasta from sticking together.

Beat eggs, egg whites, Italian seasoning, milk, pepper, and salt together.

Heat a large skillet on medium. Add a tablespoon of oil, and then garlic. Cook briefly, then add the onion, peas, mushrooms, and meat choice. Cook for a few minutes, until the onion is wilted. Add the eggs and scramble them.

Turn off the heat and add the egg mixture to the pasta, along with the ricotta and grated cheese. Gently mix to incorporate.

Transfer the mixture to a greased 9"x13" baking pan, spreading the mixture evenly in the pan. Top with mozzarella and sprinkle with the remaining Italian seasoning.

Bake for approximately ten to fifteen minutes, until the mozzarella is melted.

Serve immediately.

Servings: 6–8.

Italian Wedding Cake

Oh, how I love this sweet Italian treat. I wanna marry it! Wink, wink.

Ingredients for the cake:
1 box white cake mix
1 stick (½ cup) softened butter
1¼ cup whole milk
1 Tablespoon white table vinegar
3 egg whites
¼ teaspoon almond extract
1 Tablespoon vanilla extract
1 8 oz. can crushed pineapple, drained
½ cup sweetened shredded coconut
1 cup chopped pecans

Ingredients for frosting:
16 oz. cream cheese
1 stick (½ cup) butter, softened
3½ cups powdered sugar
1 teaspoon vanilla
1 cup chopped pecans

Instructions for the cake:
Lightly spray two 8" cake pans with cooking spray and set aside.

Combine cake mix, butter, milk, vinegar, egg white, almond and vanilla extract in a large bowl. Beat on a low speed to combine, then beat on medium speed for about two minutes, until the batter is silky smooth. Gently fold in the pineapple, coconut, and one cup of pecans.

Pour batter into the two cake pans and bake for 25–30 minutes, until the top springs back upon touching or a toothpick inserted in the middle of the cake comes out clean.

Remove the pans from the oven and allow them to cool completely.

Instructions for the frosting:

Cream the cream cheese and the butter together until well-combined, preferably in an electric mixer. Slowly add the powdered sugar, blending after each addition until all the sugar is combined. Add the vanilla and blend the frosting until fluffy, then gently fold in the cup of chopped pecans.

Place one cake layer on a plate and frost it. Top with the second layer and frost the rest of the cake.

Servings: 12.

ACKNOWLEDGMENTS

This series is an homage to my fabulous Italian family, and it's been an absolute joy to write. I'm eternally grateful to Kensington Publishing for its support and to my terrific agent, Doug Grad, who knew it would be the perfect home for the series. Profuse thanks to perfect editor John Scognamilio, as well as Larissa Ackerman, Lou Malcangi, Lauren Jernigan, and everyone at Kensington. You are all absolutely wonderful to work with, offering energy and enthusiasm that inspire me.

A shout-out to my fabulous partners in crime (writing) at chicksonthecase.com: Lisa Q. Mathews, Leslie Karst, Vickie Fee, Cynthia Kuhn, Becky Clark, Kathy Valenti, and Jennifer Chow. Vickie gets a special shout-out for fact-checking my Catholicism! Can't thank you enough, Vickie. More love to my fellow eleven members of Cozy Mystery Crew. And even more love to the bloggers and reviewers who toil away to support us, their only payment being our undying gratitude. I'm talking to you, Dru Ann Love, Mark Baker, Lesa Holstine, Lisa Kelly, Sandra Murphy, Lorie Hamm, Kristopher Zgorski, Kathy Kaminski, Kathy Boone Reel, and Debra Jo Burnette—profuse apologies but much love to anyone I missed. Not only have you rewarded me with kind words, some of you have also rewarded me with treasured friendships.

And in addition to thanking all readers everywhere, I owe special thanks to my reader support groups: the Gator Gals (Cajun Country Dirty Rice Dozen), the Gator Keepers (thank you for running the show, Marci Konecny and Nicole Vickers!), my newsletter subscribers, and my Bookmark Brigade, with particular gratitude for the inspiration behind it, Emily Goehner. And thanks to Ruth Behling for her generous silent auction bid and wonderful friendship.

As always, I have to thank husband Jer and daughter Eliza for their endless patience. And, as always, profuse thanks to my mama, Elisabetta DiVirgilio Seideman—and my brothers Tony and David, who get extra thanks for taking such good care of Mom during multiple tough times. Love you ALL!